WASTED

by
DAVID DARRACOTT

D1522700

Lightning Rod Books

Atlanta, Georgia

LIGHTNING
ROD
BOOKS

Lightning Rod Books
Atlanta, Georgia

First Edition, May 2014
ISBN-13: 978-1492109433, ISBN-10: 1492109436
Library of Congress Control Number: 2014909716
Author Photo by Michael Mollick
Cover and Interior Design by Cyrus Wraith Walker

For All My Family

Acknowledgments

Typically, many people contribute in bringing a book to life and that is certainly the case here. This novel was a long time in the making, and many readers along the way added focus to the characters, the story, and the final version. A complete list would be impossible, but chief among them, are my most frequent and excellent readers: Francis Clark, Larry Kahn, and Michael Mollick, who provided insightful suggestions that made the book better. To all others who also contributed, I am indebted as well.

The fault, dear Brutus, is not in our stars, But in ourselves …

Julius Caesar, Shakespeare

JULY 1985

Chapter 1

To Player's eye, Fort Lauderdale hadn't changed much in the older areas near the ocean. He hadn't been down here in ten years, but as he drove the white-baked streets and bounced over the arched bridges, he could see that it was still a city of water, built for boats rather than cars. With its grid of canals crisscrossing the landscape, it was a city composed of small square islands covered with emerald green foliage and houses with tile roofs.

The look of it didn't change much until he drove farther inland where there had been no city at all just a few years before. There it became a typical Florida suburb of dense subdivisions and straight, flat highways shimmering in the sun. There, it was the Florida created by land developers who kept marching inland and pushing their projects up against the Everglades, always paving to accommodate the great migration from the north.

But he wasn't here to see the sights. They had a job to do and he could feel the tension starting to grow in his stomach. To settle himself down, he drove for another hour just to weigh the changes in the landscape and to see how much his eye had changed in a decade. Ten years earlier, he would have focused on the nightspots and hangouts, places where he could find good-looking women and late hours, places with hot bands and cold drinks. The tanned young people were still packed into the motels, looking to party for a week or two in the sun, but the scene didn't have the same appeal for him it once had.

Finally he decided he'd changed more than the city had.

Eventually he drove to the Holiday Inn on Federal Highway

where he was supposed to meet Jaye and Sharpe. It was late morning when he arrived, but they weren't in their room, so he went back out and drove around the city most of the afternoon. That night he still couldn't find them anywhere in the motel so he ate dinner alone and finally went to bed. It was after eleven when Sharpe called his room, but Player was almost asleep so they agreed to wait until morning to talk. At breakfast he felt rested and eager to get on with it. He ate eggs and bacon and drank half a pot of coffee while Sharpe filled him in on what they'd accomplished while Player had been up the coast in Georgia. Everything was unfolding according to plan, Sharpe told him. He and Raoul had met several times that week and worked out the details, so everything was set. They were all supposed to meet again that afternoon with Carlos to complete the deal.

"Wait a minute," Player interrupted. "Who's Carlos?" Sharpe had not mentioned him before.

"He's Raoul's father, sort of oversees the family business."

"What family business? I thought we were dealing with Raoul on this thing."

"With the amount of money involved, even Raoul has to have a deal approved by his old man. Apparently Carlos puts great stock in his personal appraisal of people, so he insists on meeting all three of us."

Player could see that, but he didn't like the intrusion of a new element into the plan."The only thing that's not settled is the drop site," Sharpe said. "We had to wait on you to let us know if the place will work."

"It's perfect. A deep water creek in an empty marsh, just like I remembered." Player lit a cigarette with his Zippo and wondered out loud, "You think they'll balk at having the drop site up in Georgia instead of here on their home turf?"

"They've already agreed to it in principle. In fact, Raoul liked the idea. He said it showed our savvy to choose a fresh site."

Overall, Player was pleased. It sounded as though Sharpe had handled things pretty well on his end. They talked for another half hour, with Sharpe explaining when and where Raoul wanted them to pick up the money and supplies and how they were supposed to coordinate the drop-off.

At ten o'clock Jaye still hadn't come down to the dining room and Player asked where she was. Sharpe told him she had gone to her family's house to talk to her father again about the boat. "Is she having trouble getting it?" Player asked.

"I don't think so. At least she's not saying, if she is. Every time I ask, she tells me to be patient."

"That's not much of an answer."

"I think it's been tough asking them for it, so go easy on her."

"Has she got a problem with her family?"

Sharpe shrugged.

"Is there something wrong with the boat?"

Sharpe shrugged again.

"Is there something you're not telling me?"

Sharpe looked annoyed. "When are you going to learn to trust me, old Buddy? Just relax and leave it to her."

Chapter 2

That afternoon they went down to the big waterway for the meeting with Carlos and Raoul. The intracoastal reminded Player of a city highway, because it served as the main avenue for boats in a city of boats, with the smaller canals feeding into it like residential streets. They cruised the dark water slowly in a rented twenty-two footer, a small boat by local standards, and the huge waterway was crowded with sailing yachts flaunting registries from all over the world. Player watched hundreds of the big white boats go by and he shook his head in amazement. How could there be so much money to go around? Only the very rich could afford boats like these.

Sharpe seemed to read his mind. "There's more cash in south Florida than anywhere in the country and most of it is drug money. Boxes of it. Grocery sacks. Suitcases full of it. Cash pours into here from everywhere."

"And the wholesalers here have to spend that cash on something."

"That's right," Sharpe said. "Why not yachts? There's an entire subterranean economy here based on cash that flows unrecorded through banks, car dealerships, you name it. I've even heard of real estate agents who specialize in cash purchase condos."

"To launder the cash for a percentage, of course."

"Of course."

Player glanced back at Jaye. She avoided his eyes and appeared curiously disinterested. Sitting in the back, she had said little and ignored their conversation. He was about to ask her if something was wrong when their voices were suddenly drowned out by a deafening sound that came on them very quickly, an engine roar that overwhelmed the sound of every other boat on the canal.

They looked to their left and a long boat appeared out of nowhere, moving fast, pushing that grinding sound ahead of it. The boat was dark blue, wedge-shaped, and sat low to the water with a sharp nose that rode up at an aggressive angle. Toward the rear, a man's head was visible in the cockpit, slightly breaking the straight profile of the hull. As the boat got closer, he realized it was much larger than it seemed at a distance because its lines were so lean. It was at least forty feet, built purely for speed.

"I think that's a Donzi," Sharpe yelled in his ear.

The black wedge shape cut by them at such speed, every boat on the waterway seemed to hang motionless for a second. Thirty foot wings of spray stood out from the hull, and Player felt a drum-like vibration deep in his chest as the roar swept past them. Then, just as suddenly as it had appeared, the boat and its supernatural sound were gone. Their twenty-two footer sat rocking in the heavy chop the big boat left behind, and they had to hold on as the wake kicked off the concrete walls of the canal and passed under them again. The boats nearby went back to their plodding pace, and a thousand pairs of eyes returned to their books or instruments or hiding behind shades. Player squinted into the glare ahead where the boat had disappeared.

"You don't see many of those at Hilton Head."

"Must have been doing fifty and not even straining."

"In a No Wake Zone, at that."

"It was a Cigarette, not a Donzi," Jaye said, from behind them. "And they do pretty much what they want around here."

Player turned again and glanced at her, because it was the first thing she'd said in the past half hour. Quiet all day, she sat in the rear seat beyond the shade of the awning where her long limbs gleamed in the sunlight. He watched her squirt tanning oil from a plastic bottle into her palm, then she extended a leg straight out to examine it as she worked the oil into her skin. Her legs were beautiful, a rich smooth color that seemed so unlikely with her light eyes.

Player turned back to the wheel and tried to focus on the traffic ahead. He had to be careful around her. Now, more than ever in his life, he needed to concentrate on the job at hand, yet there she was, constantly tugging at his thoughts, with her simplest movements catching his eye. That was really why he hadn't wanted her along on the job. She was too much of a distraction.

He wondered how awkward, or intimate, things had become between those two since they'd been down here, because she avoided looking him in the eye. When he'd first seen her at the rental dock, he was glad, and almost threw an arm around her shoulder to kiss her, but he caught himself in time, and it was just as well, because she was acting very cool toward him. Maybe she was still angry because he'd wanted to exclude her from the venture, or maybe she and Sharpe were closer after their days down here together. After all, they were sharing the same room now. But he couldn't be sure. Part of her beauty was that despite the usual open smile she was so hard to read; so much of her remained closed off.

Again, her voice beckoned from behind, but she seemed to be addressing neither of them in particular. "They use those big Cigarettes to make quick runs out to the islands or to mother ships in international water," she said. "They take on a couple of crates of cola, whatever, then they scorch the water slipping back into here or Biscayne. Quick. Neat. Nothing on the water can catch them."

"Why don't the cops just search them every time they come in?" Sharpe asked.

"That was their main method a couple of years ago," she said. "But somebody always dreams up a new wrinkle. Drop it to a diver. Switch it from boat to boat. It's a cat and mouse game that ties up too much manpower for the cops to win."

"But still, the runners get caught sometimes," Player said.

"Yeah, sometimes."

After another mile, Player followed Sharpe's directions and made a right turn onto a smaller canal. They followed it for ten minutes and the traffic grew lighter, then disappeared. The houses got larger and the grounds more elaborately landscaped the farther they went up the canal until eventually everything in sight was an estate with a private dock.

Sharpe touched Player's sleeve and pointed at a white stucco mansion a few hundred yards ahead and Player cut the engine to take a look. The mansion was very bright in the sunlight, so white it was difficult to look at it directly. Coconut palms and banana trees surrounded the ground floor, and a line of oleanders formed a barrier around the outside perimeter of the grounds, perhaps concealing a wall. That barrier is a defensive perimeter, Player thought, as he studied the thick oleander. Almost immediately he wondered why those exact words had popped into his mind. He hadn't heard the term defensive perimeter since he was in the Reserves in his early twenties. He picked up a pair of binoculars and focused them on the grounds then realized his mind had made the association because the mansion bore a definite resemblance to a military compound.

He panned the glasses slowly, watching a couple of guards as they crossed the lawn. They wore loud sport shirts and had dark greasy hair. Submachine guns were slung on their shoulders. Player moved the glasses again and saw a pair of Dobermans trotting along a path inside the perimeter wall. He watched the muscles flash beneath their sleek black coats, their heads swiveling from side to side, and to Player, the dogs looked dangerously strong and stupid.

He shifted the glasses to examine the guards again. He could easily imagine those bored and violent-looking men reveling at any chance to use their submachine guns on an intruder. He imagined the vicious grins they would wear as they sprayed bullets into the banana trees, shredding foliage and ripping the air apart with gunfire.

He stopped his thoughts before they went too far, knew he was getting too apprehensive about meeting this man. Yet only a very dangerous man needed armed guards and dogs and lived in a house that looked like a Spanish fort.

He kept moving the glasses across the grounds, looking for surprises or hidden dangers, seeking any edge of knowledge he could get.

"So you've got it all worked out with this guy?" he asked Sharpe.

"I met with Raoul twice and he likes the plan. The deal is set."

"Not Raoul. I mean this guy. Carlos."

"This is just a formality. The deal's set."

Player lowered the glasses and turned to face Sharpe. "A formality? There's no such thing as formality with a guy like this. You don't just walk into a gangster's house and ask for his blessing and his money. You're sure this is under control?"

Sharpe stared back with a peeved look on his face. "The deal is set," he said. "Under control. When are you gonna learn to trust me, man?"

Player held his friend's eyes for a moment and nodded silently, then took the wheel and started the engine. He pointed the boat toward Alvarez's mansion, thinking, wondering really, just what he was going to do if Sharpe didn't have the deal under control.

So much had happened so quickly it all seemed unreal to be here, doing this. He thought back to that party when he had first met Raoul at his ostentatious house in Atlanta. Hard to believe it was only a week ago, but that was the night everything changed.

In just that one weekend he had gone from a working clod, mainly concerned about his boss cheating him, to a man who had to worry about guard dogs and guns.

Chapter 3

The week before the Fort Lauderdale trip, on Friday night, Jaye stood at the corner of the bar, waiting for Player to come out of the back room. When he appeared through the swinging door she smiled and waved him over. Still wearing his work khakis and running shoes, he had a gray tweed sport coat slung over his shoulder, and she watched as he spotted her and came over.

When Mitch handed her a drink in a plastic cup, she read the mild surprise on Player's face.

"So, you two have met already," Player said. "I should have figured."

"Yeah, we're getting drinks to go," she said. "Your friend here, Mitch, asked me to go to a party with you two, if it's okay."

"Sure," Player said. "I love crowds."

Jaye could see he was being sarcastic, but hell, it was a chance to get to know him better. She'd wanted to spend time with the renown Jack Player since the first day she started to work here, but he was slow to make a move, cautious around her. Jack was famous in the bar as the guy you had to know, and besides, his lawyer friend was awfully cute and persuasive, so why not both of them? Jack Player and Mitchell Sharpe, the pair everybody here in Les' Place talked about.

Sharpe turned around from the bar with a drink in each hand and she noticed that Jack really gave him the eye; not angry exactly, more of a knowing look. She was glad for the chance to go out with them, but she still wasn't sure how this evening would work with the two of them. Mitch had managed to single her out and set things up so quickly, apparently assuming that she would want to go out with both of them. Jack might not like that, even if the guy was his friend.

"Okay, compadres," Sharpe said with his cup raised. "Let's rock and roll."

It felt good to be leaving work after a long day. She'd been on since four o'clock and every minute worked during Happy Hour felt like two. They carried their drinks to the front door and had almost made it outside when Les caught up with them. He circled around them to block their way out.

"Trying to cut out on me again, Player?" Les demanded. "Huh?" He hitched his pants and glared at them, but they simply walked past him and out the door. Les followed them outside and blocked Player's path on the sidewalk, put his veiny hands on his hips. Les's face looked as if he lived in a steam bath, florid and teeming with blood vessels.

"I got customers waiting in there, Jack," Les said. "Are you on my team or not?" Then he got right up in Player's face. "You playing for me or against me?"

Player shrugged, obviously didn't want to stop and argue, but Les threw out his chest and it seemed to Jaye that Player had no way to avoid him. Les wanted a confrontation, not indifference.

"Huh, big fellow?" Les said. "Talk to me."

Sharpe did a little tap dance and started to say something, but Les snapped his fingers inches from Sharpe's face, "I don't want to hear any of your lawyer crap."

Then Les turned back to Player, his voice growling. "I told you before and I'll tell you again." His thumb jutted toward Sharpe. "This guy, he's nothing but trouble." He was on a roll now, and he took a step closer to Player, shoved out his chin. "You want to stay on my team, you give one hundred percent. Losers cut out early. You want to be a winner, you play my way."

Les's hostility dumbfounded her. New to the job, she had not yet seen this side of him and she stepped forward to intercede, but Les cut her off too before she could say anything.

"You're new here, young lady, so I'm giving you fair warning and you better listen. You run with these two and you'll come to no good. Player's not too bad on his own, but you mix him in with smart mouth here," again the thumb stabbed at Sharpe, "And they're both nothing but trouble. Mark my words."

She could see that Player had finally had enough. He reached out and put the palm of his hand on Les's chest and eased him away. It wasn't really a push, just a firm pressure, but Les took it as a challenge to his manhood. The tiny broken veins on Les's cheeks and nose turned scarlet and he started to cock his fist, but Player cut him off with another forward move of his hand. This time it was a definite push that sent Les a full step backward.

"Don't even think about it," Player said, as he stared Les down.

"I think you'd better shut up, Les." Sharpe said maliciously. "And that's sound legal advice."

They stared at each other for a moment until Les got control of himself and backed off then stomped inside without saying any more. They stood for a moment and looked at each other, astounded by the mindless rage Les had thrown at them. If Les had not been so insulting to Jack, she thought, it would be funny. The scrawny old guy trying to pick a fight with Jack, who now looked angry enough to go after him and settle it, but she touched his sleeve and shook her head as if to say, it's not worth it.

"What a bunch of shit!" Player exploded.

"You're right, old buddy," Sharpe said. "He's a jerk. Now just forget him, and let's go have a good time."

"He's right, Jack," she said. "Let it go."

Jaye took Player's sleeve and led him away from the entrance, and the three of them started across the parking lot toward Sharpe's car, which was parked directly beneath a street light far away from the other cars in the lot. Sitting beneath the dome of blue fluorescence, the Porsche looked like a shrine to excess; its stance low and wide, straddling two parking spaces to protect the fenders, its mirror finish gleaming expensively in the blue atmosphere.

Sharpe tossed the keys to Player and took the passenger seat, motioning her to climb onto his lap. Everything happened so fast, she didn't try to object. Player was silent and tense as he put the top down so she decided to keep quiet too. She squeezed into the passenger seat with Mitch and tried to keep her dress in place.

She watched Player as he took the wheel and pulled out into the traffic and turned left on Peachtree. To her, he seemed almost in a daze, not sure what he was doing. He hadn't even asked if she wanted to sit with him instead of Mitch, but things were still so tense she wasn't going to make things worse. He drove at the speed limit in the right lane and didn't try to beat any yellow lights which relieved her a bit. She supposed he was still boiling inside and she hoped he wasn't one of those guys who let out his anger behind the wheel of a car, especially a car like this one, but he drove quietly, brooding, carefully working the car through the traffic as it crawled north toward Buckhead.

"You know," Player said finally, "I really don't have to take that kinda crap off Les."

Sharpe sighed and made a wide gesture with his hands, then threw back his head and spoke to the open sky. "It's a nice summer night. The top's down and we've got big drinks in our hands and a beautiful woman with us. Just enjoy it, old buddy."

Sharpe rolled his eyes at Jaye and tilted his head toward the radio so she turned it on and searched for a station.

"In fact, I don't have to take that kind of crap off anybody," Player continued.

Sharpe made a disgusted snorting sound as if he'd heard all this before and he was tired of going through it, as if he had no choice but to get it out in the air.

"Yeah, you do," Sharpe said finally.

Jaye squirmed as she kept dialing the radio, but commercials seemed be the only thing she could find, and the whacky voices and jingles seemed to make the tension in the car worse until Player reached over and pushed her hand away from the tuner and snapped the radio off.

Sharpe's voice changed from the old friend tone to matter of fact. "You have to put up with his crap just as long as you stay in that bar," he said. "You'll take anything Les dishes out."

"Nope," Player insisted. "I'm getting out."

"Oh yeah? When?"

"Soon."

"Oh yeah? What are you going to do?"

"I don't know," Player mumbled. "Something."

"Now we hear Jack Player's master plan," Sharpe mocked. "He's going to do what? Something! When? Soon!"

Player's face turned a violent red. "Just shut the hell up, would you?"

Sharpe did, and they rode in silence as the traffic grew heavier near Peachtree Battle then slowed until it was barely moving at the bridge over the creek. They stopped for a red light and Jaye took a swallow of her rum and coke. The sound of engines thrummed on the pavement as first one car, then another, then several more pulled up to the intersection, each adding its own note to the undercurrent of combustion and music.

She looked around at the cars and it occurred to her that it was Friday night; everybody was out on the streets with their windows down and radios on. She listened to the jumble of noise around them; the guitars wailing, the sound of teenage laughter, and the feeling of those years came back to her in a nostalgic rush. Not so long ago she would have been one of those girls having a great time, but things were very different since she'd left home and she wondered if she would ever feel that carefree again.

A white Mercedes pulled alongside them in the lane to Player's left, and it stopped close to the Porsche. The driver an older blonde woman with her hair pulled back and tied with a silk scarf. Jaye watched her eyes as they ran over the fluid lines of the hood, then back to the passenger compartment where they stopped on Player. She gave him a once over, much like the one she had just given the Porsche, a kind of appraisal, and apparently he met her standards. She smiled and gold flashed at her throat, then the light changed and the Mercedes pulled away and was soon lost in traffic.

Sharpe squeezed her knee, a sort of signal. "The world looks different behind the wheel of a Porsche, old buddy."

"It's the man that counts," Player said. "Not the toys."

"Then pull up beside her in your old junker and see if she gives you the same look."Player snapped the Porsche into second. "You really think money is absolutely everything, don't you?"

"Damn near," Sharpe said.

Jaye sat up to watch them, wondering if Player's mood was going to rupture again. She wondered what was going on with these two. Were they always like this? It was almost as if Mitch wanted to set him off now, saying such insulting things in front of her. Jack didn't have any money, so what? Neither did she, not anymore.

"Player, ten minutes ago you were furious about taking that crap off Les," Sharpe said. "Tomorrow, you'll have to take another day of it and the whole thing will start over again. And it all gets down to money."She saw Player's jaw stiffen as a tinge of color started to rise up his neck.

"Old Buddy, you're a bartender," Sharpe said. "Maybe the best bartender in Atlanta, but still a bartender. You've got no power to run your own life, so you'll take shit from Les until you do something to change it."

Jaye felt an awful quiet fall on them for a moment as she wondered how Player was going to react. He answered her thoughts by twisting the steering wheel violently to the left. She heard the tires scream beneath them as the Porsche jumped through a tiny gap in the oncoming traffic. They shot onto a side street that was dark and lined with trees, but he kicked the car through second and third and before she knew it they were doing eighty. The yards became a green blur as the Porsche blasted down the street, throwing its high-pitched screaming sound outward, and each tree they passed seemed to snatch the sound away and change its pitch, making the engine's whine rise and fall in the darkness.

She felt relieved for a second when she saw the twin red tail lights of another car far ahead, knowing that Player would have to slow down, but then unbelievably, they were on the tail lights so fast that she stopped breathing for a moment when she saw he wasn't slowing down at all. He was going even faster and swung the Porsche out and passed the tail lights of a long gray car as if it wasn't even there, and then they were going faster still, accelerating through a curve on the straining tires, through thicker trees now and beneath a canopy of leaves until it seemed as if the Porsche had become a streak of light shooting through a green tunnel. Then they started down a hill and to her it felt as if she was on a roller coaster as the air roared overhead and tore at her hair, captured the strands and stretched them out above the car, turning them into a dark flag that snapped wildly in the slipstream.

She tried to relent and get into the speed but she couldn't. Her heart was running wild, so crazy wild she tried to escape by settling back into the soft, scratchy warmth of Sharpe's vest. She pressed her face against the silk of his tie as she strained to breathe, and when she opened her eyes, all she saw was tree trunks and bushes off to her right that had become a streaking wall of green.

Sharpe's hand moved up her arm and caressed her face and she felt his other hand reach over toward Player. He must have touched Player's forearm near the steering wheel, because something caused him to slow down. The whine of the engine eased back to a purr. Things outside the window began to return to normal, stopped bending and flowing, and gradually the mailboxes and azaleas and driveway markers appeared again, and then finally it felt safe to sit up.

She reached for the top of the windshield and pulled herself upright. Her eyes were wet and she felt flushed. She looked at Mitch and even though he appeared calm, Jaye noticed some creases just above the gap between his eyebrows that weren't there before. He stared at Player intently.

"Did it help?" Sharpe asked him.

Player was almost subdued now as his fingers relaxed on the wheel. "Sometimes you have to kill one emotion with a stronger emotion."

She looked over at Player and wondered if this was really the same guy she knew back in the bar. Right now all she wanted was to calm the jitters he'd given her, and she reached for her purse and fumbled around inside it.

"There's another choice," Jaye said. She came up with a joint and held it aloft as she pushed in the cigarette lighter. When it popped out she fired up the joint and took a long pull to relieve her tension. She passed the joint off as she exhaled slowly, feeling better immediately.

"You guys need to lighten up," she said, glancing at Player. He seemed calm now and looked over at her with a slightly embarrassed grin. She patted his thigh and gave him a reassuring squeeze. "After all, Jack, it's party time."

Sharpe blew out a stream of smoke and rapped a little rhythm on the dashboard with his fingers. "I knew it. This lady likes her thrills."

Chapter 4

Twenty minutes later the Porsche got off I-285 and took to the green hills of Riverside Drive, a dark snake of a street that twisted and dipped through the trees, funneling them ever deeper into the steep woods beside the river. Even though neighborhoods lay all along the road, the houses were rarely visible because most of them sat far back from the street, shielded by thick woods. Often, driveway markers or gates were the only evidence of the people rich enough to live back in those green depths.

The area seemed mysterious and beautiful to Player, because after years of living in apartments, he never saw enough trees or open spaces along the crowded streets of the city where he spent most of his time. For him, a drive home usually entailed a stop and go ordeal through miles of traffic lights, past hamburger stands and coin laundries, only to arrive at a crowded apartment complex that consisted mainly of parking lots and cars.

He stuck his head out the window and took a deep breath of the air that smelled so clean here, so different, somehow so rich. He looked at the thick green woods and felt a longing for an easier life, a life more like the one that was lived here. This was the part of town where you could sunbathe beside the pool and no one would ever see you; this was where people sent their kids to private school so they grew up playing soccer instead of football; this was the part of town where people didn't have to worry about eight hundred dollars for a new transmission. In this world, money was not a constant, depressing problem.

And it appeared all the more beautiful now because the three of them were stoned and feeling ripe, and nothing in the world could possibly be wrong as the night rolled past them, warm as liquid. A jazz guitarist played on the stereo, Benson doing "Masquerade," and they laughed as the green woods went on and on, peeling apart before the Porsche's headlights. Player drove with one hand on the wheel and listened to the music while Sharpe tried to find the house.

He said he couldn't remember if the number ended in ninety-six or sixty-nine, so he was trying to locate it by recognizing the entrance. Finally, Sharpe seemed to make up his mind as they passed a gate with black metal bars, the doors standing open.

"Back there. That's it."

Player put the car in reverse and backed up to the gate, but there was no identification on it except the street number, which ended in neither ninety-six or sixty-nine.

"You sure this time?" Player asked.

"This is it, man. This is it."

The stone uprights were a good ten feet high, and the black iron bars of the gate were topped with spikes. Player drove in and the woods on each side of the driveway grew darker immediately. It looked as though civilization itself might vanish back in that dense vegetation, yet the headlights revealed a driveway that twisted off and disappeared into the trees. Green branches raked the fenders of the car as Player drove up a short hill, then over it, and then down as the driveway dropped away steeply. He knew they must be winding down the face of a bluff toward the river, but it had to be far below them still.

They went another two hundred yards before they got their first glimpse of the house. It appeared briefly, disappeared, then reappeared through an opening in the foliage, festive and inviting in the distance, an island of light in a sea of green. The house looked large as it materialized off in the trees, then it kept growing improbably larger as they got closer, built of weathered wood, steel and glass. They descended the driveway and pulled off onto a grassy parking area and climbed out of the car. The number of cars parked on the lawn surprised Player, a hundred at least, and two out of every three seemed to be a Mercedes.

Player took in the scene and whistled. "Are you sure we're at the right place?"

Sharpe gave him one of those grins, checking his reflection in the side view mirror.

"Old buddy, when are you going to learn to trust me?" He did his best big-shot routine, running his tie tight and straightening it with a flourish then moving his fingers back through his hair. "Just stick with me, and I'll take you places you never even thought of going."

"Who owns this place?"

"A guy I want you to meet, name of Raoul Alvarez."

Inside the house, the party seemed to be one of those gatherings you hear about but never expect to see. It was noisy and crowded with guests who dressed as if the event was a major opportunity to be seen; he guessed there were three or four hundred people scattered among several rooms on the main floor. Most of the women seemed to be wearing silk dresses and a lot of jewelry, and many of them had year-round tans, showing as much bare skin as an evening dress could show.

They found a bar at the back of the main room, and while Sharpe ordered drinks, Player took a look around. The room had one long wall made of glass that faced onto old growth forest behind the house where the trees were rigged with spotlights that made everything look bright and artificial. White lights on the ground pointed up the trunks, and smaller lights were angled artfully through the leaves so the shadows and colors looked dramatic, turning the trees into a huge painting. Beyond the trees, Player caught a glimpse of tennis courts and some low buildings.

They ran into some of Sharpe's friends at the bar who greeted him with a lot of loud laughter and back slapping. Player turned away and studied the crowd. He didn't want to meet Sharpe's friends and go through the rounds of introductions; he preferred to watch and listen to the tenor of a party by floating around its edges.

They got their drinks and Player gave his rum and tonic a

professional appraisal, swirling it around in his mouth. It was just right. He took a second sip and looked around the room again. You had to give the host credit, whoever he was, he knew how to spend money: the furnishings, the artwork, the drinks, everything was tasteful and expensive.

Player put an arm around Jaye's waist and guided them away from Sharpe's rowdy friends toward the sound of jazz in an adjoining room. They went through a doorway and saw a crowd collected around a trio. They moved closer and found a good place to stand and watch as the trio rounded out "Satin Doll" then moved into a more bluesy sound.

The singer eased into a Billie Holliday song and applause rippled through the crowd. He guessed she was a club act at one of the big hotel lounges, one of those throaty, smoky-room shows that got better with every song while the patrons got sweatier and looser, and then when midnight came, they would stumble out into the bright lights of the lobby and wonder how they had become so wrapped up in the bittersweet pain of her voice.

She was doing the same trick on the crowd around the dance floor. They grew silent and listened as she milked the lyrics, and when the song ended, she stepped away from the mike and bowed and the crowd gave her strong applause.

As the crowd started moving again, Sharpe put a hand on Player's shoulder. He'd caught up with them, killing Player's hopes of having Jaye alone for a while. Sharpe steered them across the dance floor, nodding hello and winking at people. They went through a doorway into a game room where they saw a bar in one corner with a mirror behind it.

As they moved to the bar for a refill and walked past a group of people bent over a table with a Go grid carved into its surface, but no one was playing the game. Instead, their attention was focused on a silver cigarette case lying open on the table which held a good quarter inch of white powder. Three couples laughed as they passed a tiny silver spoon among themselves.

One young guy with reddish hair and a turbulent complexion dipped the spoon twice into the cigarette case and inhaled as much powder as the spoon would hold. His nose was already flushed and it became inflamed as he pulled hard on the spoon, drawing the cocaine deep into his sinuses. His date giggled and thumped his red nose with her fingernail. They all laughed, then took turns sniffing from the spoon themselves.

Player sipped his drink in silence as he thought about what Sharpe had said earlier in the car. Sharpe often overstated things, but he did have a point, though Player would never admit it to him. Money on this scale made a difference. Just being near it tonight—the expensive clothes, the cars, this house—it worked on you. Maybe Sharpe was half right, maybe most people would do anything for money under the right circumstances. When you got down to it, maybe drugs and the money that followed them were just too powerful for anybody to resist for long.

Player swirled his drink and took another look around the room. "You're rubbing some rich elbows these days, my friend."

"No question about it," Sharpe grinned. "And it feels good."

They laughed mildly together then leaned against the bar to watch the crowd. Sharpe nudged Player and pointed out Jaye as she walked across the room toward them.

"I'm glad we brought her," Sharpe said.

She'd left them a few minutes earlier to search for a bathroom, and now, returning, her height and long dark hair stood out in the crowd so prominently it reminded Player how beautiful she could be. At a glance, he saw her ease among this crowd and it occurred to him again that she must be rich, or at least she came from a rich family.

"You mean, you're glad I brought her," Player said.

"I invited her," Sharpe insisted. "Not you."

"You just jumped in front of me, that's all. She wouldn't have come along without me."

Sharpe gave him an elbow to the ribs. "In your dreams."

She joined them smiling, her makeup fresh and her eyes electric, and Player detected a slight, erotic aura of perfume as her cheek brushed against his shoulder. She touched his forearm with her fingertips and looked at him with that bold gaze. She tugged on his hand, gathering him toward her and he let himself respond and lean into her body, but Sharpe's arm was around her waist and he could feel the elbow between them. Player looked at her upturned face; her mouth was slightly open to him. He bent his head down and leaned closer, but she looked away and turned both of them simultaneously toward the sound of the music, toward the party.

"Let's go in there and get crazy, boys."

Chapter 5

Player sat in the night air on a large wooden deck which extended from the upper story of the house. Suspended there in the darkness, overlooking the woods with nothing but trees all around, the party seemed far away. Even though music still pounded through the walls and up the stairways, by the time it got to the isolated deck, the noise sounded comfortably dim. Feeling a bit numb and supremely relaxed from intoxicants, it felt good to be sitting outside in the dark, listening to birds and crickets, watching leaves flicker in the spotlights.

Alvarez's house was built on the face of a bluff overlooking the river, and the woods plunged steeply toward the dark water that swirled somewhere below. He could just make out a vague layer of mist hovering over the Chattahoochee. Houselights of the rich glimmered on the bluffs beyond.

He had to admit, it was a primo life the owner enjoyed in this private palace. Player could only imagine what it would be like to live such a rich and carefree existence. Here, money flowed as freely as beer back at Les's Place.

Some have too much, he thought, and many not enough.

He finished off his drink and lit another cigarette with his trusty Zippo, one of the few things he'd managed to hang onto over the years. One thing that was always there, always worked.

He'd been waiting more than twenty minutes to meet the host of the party. Sharpe had directed him up to the deck to join Alvarez, but now that Player knew how nice it was to sit out here in this peaceful darkness, he didn't care if the host showed up or not. It was so pleasant, he could go to sleep right here and now in the teak chair.

Perhaps he did go to sleep; he wasn't sure.

But something shocked him out of his tranquil state. He heard a sound behind his head that yanked him into hyper-alertness in less than a second. Chemicals gushed through his bloodstream and brain. All that in less than a second, all because of a metallic sound.

A soft *tiiiiiiiiiick*, followed by a louder, distinct *Sssssnaaaappppp*! The sound of machined parts, somewhat like a door lock clicking into place, but heavier and more precise.

Only one thing in the world made that sound.

Though he could not see it, inches from his head behind the right ear, the hammer of a gun had been thumbed back, followed by the trigger locking forward into the cocked position, ready to fire.

Somebody was about to kill him. Then, dead silence.

"Why?" he stammered.

No answer. Fighting the impulse to lurch upright, he somehow managed to keep his seat.

"Why?" he asked again.

Seconds later, another sound followed—a snicker—then a sputter of breath.

"What the—"

Player sprang upward and whirled around, his hand lifting the chair to use it as a weapon.

It was Sharpe, grinning, with a pistol in his hand. His wild laughter broke loose in an uncontrolled tremor.

"You crazy bastard!"

Sharpe cackled again and danced in place, raised his hands in the air, the pistol dangling from an index finger. He spun the weapon by the trigger guard as if it were a toy, all the time laughing like an insane man, hooting, doubled up at the waist, laughing and dancing from foot to foot.

"You maniac!" Player came within a half-tick of smashing his head with the deck chair. "What in hell are you doing?"

Sharpe couldn't stop laughing long enough to answer. He

collapsed into a chair and held his head, howling uncontrollably. His contorted face tilted back, twisted with manic laughter that kept pouring from him like a weird song that wouldn't end. Player took a step toward him, vibrating with anger.

He snatched the revolver from Sharpe, slid the release forward and pushed out the cylinder. Empty. At least the chambers hadn't been loaded. The relief he felt was immense, but his body needed time to catch up; his legs had turned to liquid; his heart slammed against the inside of his sternum.

Sharpe's laughter settled into a steady intoxicated giggle as he shook his head from side to side, tears glistening on the bones of his cheeks. Snot ran from his nose as he kicked his feet up and squirmed in the chair, making horror movie faces at Player, still rubbing it in.

"Wh-wh-wh-wh-wh-wh-whyyy?"

Player collapsed into his own chair. With rubbery muscles, all he could manage as retaliation was to throw the overflowing ashtray onto Sharpe's lap.

Then he slouched, his inert arms dangling over the sides of the chair. Helplessly limp, his breathing moderated a bit as he looked across at his oldest friend in the world.

Some friend, he thought. Nobody in the world could do that without getting his ass kicked—nobody except Sharpe.

"You're a lunatic," he said. "Where'd you get that thing?"

"It's Raoul's. I couldn't resist."

Player sat up, gradually got his equilibrium back. More minutes passed and finally he managed to grin, but he wasn't sure if it was actually a grin or a grimace, and he didn't care how Sharpe read it.

Even among the best of friends, Sharpe's impulse was always to go too far. Player wouldn't forget that stunt, ever. Payback would come eventually.

A half hour later, with Sharpe gone off to search for Jaye, Player was still sitting on the deck, thinking about the sound of the gun and the flashes of finality it had set loose in his brain. He tried to shake it from his thoughts and turn his attention to the man across from him; at last Raoul Alvarez had arrived.

A low patio table sat between them, their faces three feet apart. The swarthy host shifted his weight to the front of his chair and leaned over the table, flashing a too white smile. A bleached blonde sat next to him, blank and thin.

"Mitch has told me about you," Alvarez said. "He says you are an able man, but you have no ambition."

The remark irritated Player. "Maybe what Mitch should have said is that I'm just not as greedy as he is."

Alvarez let out a deep laugh that set several gold chains in motion beneath his unbuttoned shirt. The white ruffles of the shirt stood out against his black tuxedo and the thick hair of his chest. Player watched the chains settle back into place and wondered why a man with so much money felt the need to be so showy. The ivory teeth, that deep tan, all that gold made Alvarez appear to be a criminal, which of course he probably was. The thought was slightly amusing, but also unsettling. Why would this guy want to meet him anyway?

Alvarez put his drink down on the glass tabletop. "Ambition is my word, not your friend's. And all men are greedy, right?"

Player didn't answer as Alvarez pulled a gold case the size of a checkbook from his inside coat pocket. The girl leaned close to him and began to knead his thigh. She was very silent and the appearance of the case was the first thing to produce any sign of life in her.

"Everybody wants to be rich," Alvarez said, "But most men don't believe it's possible. Or they won't pay the necessary price."

Alvarez lowered the case and raked a small pile of white powder out onto the table. It was lumpy as damp sugar. He removed a gold razor blade from the case and used it to chop the powder until it was fine and loose. Then he divided it into six neat lines that sat like a row of white matchsticks on the glass.

"Greedy men, on the other hand, are willing to assume risks," Alvarez continued, "Because for them, the act of taking is almost as important as the acquisition itself."

The girl reached past him and rubbed a finger through one of the lines. She opened her mouth and daubed the powder on her gum beneath the upper lip. Alvarez elbowed her away roughly.

"This damn girl's got no manners anymore. All she cares about is the dust."

She sprawled back in her seat and pouted. With that thin skirt riding up her thighs and her lips puffed out, Player could see the attraction, but he guessed it would be short lived because Raoul would be a man with interchangeable women.

"So when I say to you that you have no ambition, I simply assume you are satisfied with your life. What are you, Jack Player? Does gain have no interest for you?"

Player considered the question for a moment while Alvarez removed a money clip from his pants pocket. He peeled a hundred dollar bill from the clip and diamonds flashed on his fingers as he rolled it into a tight cylinder.

Player looked at the money clip Alvarez had casually dropped onto the table and he realized it contained thousands of dollars. Alvarez carried more money in his pocket than Player could raise in a week. How could you admit to a man like this that your life was a never ending fight to get from one paycheck to the next?

Alvarez handed the rolled-up bill to Player and offered him the lines on the table with an upturned palm. Player rarely did cocaine but he decided this was no time to decline so he bent over the table and held the cylinder to one nostril. He pressed his other nostril closed with his free index finger and inhaled sharply, vacuuming one line through the cylinder. Then he straightened up and sniffed to pull the dust into his head. He switched the rolled bill to the other nostril and did a second line.

The girl twisted on the edge of her seat, watching Player. When he finished, he handed the rolled bill to her and she plunged into the cocaine with unstylish zeal. Alvarez looked at her with disgust and shook his head to show his disapproval. Looking much relieved, the girl didn't seem to care. She melted into the cushion and began to massage her scalp with her fingertips.

Alvarez did one line in a businesslike manner and leaned back with his drink. "You never answered my question."

Player shrugged and asked his own question. "Which are you, Raoul, ambitious or greedy?"

The man's teeth flashed. "I used to be greedy. Now I can afford to sit back and be safely ambitious." He threw his arms wide in an expansive gesture and they shared a laugh.

"How did you make so much money?" Player asked.

For the first time, he looked at Player with a trace of condescension. What a silly question, his expression seemed to say. He kicked the underside of the table and the gold case jumped, scattering white powder across the glass, giving Player his answer.

"You gracefully declined to answer my questions about the state of your life, Jack Player. Allow me to decline yours now."

Player nodded in compliance, and Alvarez smiled at their little pact as he chopped more cocaine. They did two more lines each, the girl four.

A few minutes later Player looked out at the darkness and the night was alive with moonlight and swaying trees. With the assurance of the drug surging through him, Player felt better than he had all week. His problems seemed insignificant and he banished them from his mind with ease. It was nice to be rich for an evening.

Alvarez examined him closely. "Life does not have to be so difficult," he said to Player. "There are many ways for hungry men to move up. Permit me to help, if I may."

Alvarez had sensed his desperation so easily, penetrated his deepest thoughts, and Player was annoyed with himself for almost giving in to the seductiveness of the scene around him. Music and drugs, big houses and cars; they had a way of tearing at your head and distorting your perception, but this was Raoul's world, not his. Reality was waiting for him on the other side of town. He felt clear-headed suddenly as he got up out of his chair to leave.

"But those men are greedy, like you say, and they're willing to take risks," Player said. "Apparently, I'm not."

Alvarez shrugged indifferently and there was a Latin fatalism in the gesture. "Life is nothing but a toss of dice. No?"

By three-thirty the crowd had grown very rowdy and Player found himself wandering past the dance floor, his head pleasantly numb. Most of the remaining guests had gravitated to the music and the room was crowded with delirious late-nighters who would stay as long as it played.

Player hadn't seen Jaye or Sharpe for a long time and he was making a lazy search for them when he felt a hand on his arm. A busty girl he had never seen before pulled him toward the dance floor. His first impulse was to resist her, because he didn't want to squeeze in with all those sweaty, flailing people. He wasn't in a communal mood. But when the girl turned him toward the dance floor, he caught a glimpse of Jaye, and almost as soon as he saw her, she disappeared among the confusion of heads and arms, so he let the girl pull him into the crowd where she started dancing frantically, her shoulders and hair jerking to the music.

Player faced the girl and made an uninspired attempt to dance, but he didn't want to lose Jaye, so he kept at it and worked his feet in the direction he'd seen her. The dancing bodies packed around him smelled of sweat and alcohol, and every time one of them bumped against him a damp splotch was left on his shirt, but he kept moving deeper into the crowd. It took a few minutes to maneuver into the most crowded part of the dance floor where he found them.

Their arms were thrown over the shoulders of another couple and the four of them faced inward and formed a sort of football huddle with their heads bent close together and arms interlocked. The huddle revolved slowly among the jostling bodies, their backs turned outward to fend off the dancers. Player saw a hand moving inside the huddle and he watched it pass from nose to nose, pausing long enough for each of them to take a hit from a small cocaine bong. Player guessed it had gone around several times because Sharpe had a whitish tinge on his mustache and a wild look on his face.

Jaye's head leaned toward the glass vial and as she inhaled the powder her shoulders convulsed, then she threw her head back and screamed in total abandonment. Her open-mouthed profile stood out for a second against a blaze of backlight and Player saw a startling look of rapture on her face. At that moment, with the image crisp on his retina, he sensed the failings within that blinding silhouette of beauty.

Much later, he would recall that image when he had to admit that she was, after all, human.

Chapter 6

When they left Alvarez's house, the Porsche had a fine coating of dew on it that dulled the finish and made it look almost ordinary. It sat among the twenty or so cars still parked on the grass outside even though it was nearly morning. As Player drove back down Riverside to the Perimeter and made it around to I-75, the tiredness set in. It had been a long day, and even with the effects of the cocaine still crackling in his head, his shoulders began to slump and he drove with one hand at the bottom of the wheel, cruising down the empty expressway to the West Paces Ferry exit.

It was close to five and all he wanted was to get in bed before the sun came up, maybe get a few hours of sleep before he had to go to work again and withstand the Saturday grind one more time. He turned off Northside and headed back across the sleeping side streets toward Peachtree.

Sharpe hadn't said a word on the drive home, simply sat and watched the dark houses glide by while he kept his hangover at bay with a beer, Jaye asleep on his lap. Somewhere in the leafy neighborhoods between Northside and Peachtree, he finally spoke up, "So what'd you think about my Latino friend?"

"Some friend. Kinda like you."

"You've got to admit, he's a fascinating dude."

"In a sleazy sort of way, yeah."

"Don't talk about my high society clients like that," Sharpe joked.

"Is he really a client?"

"Naw. A lot of my clients would love to be at his level,

though." Sharpe lit a cigarette. "Your thoughts?"

"What do you want me to say? He's loaded with drug money. Is that supposed to make him likable and romantic?"

"Loaded, I think, is the key word there."

"Man, this money thing of yours is getting worse all the time. You're gonna start running a fever."

"Are you about to tell me once again, even after tonight, how money doesn't matter?" Sharpe said, his voice rising a notch. "But before you do, tell me how you're going to feel when you wake up in that dingy apartment of yours in the morning. Then tell me how you'll feel after eight or ten hours of working in that damn bar again tomorrow. And the next day. And the next."

Sharpe's voice had been nasty and Player felt deflated. His fingers seemed to have no strength in them, so heavy he could barely keep them on the steering wheel. He had no energy left to fend off the mean truth Sharpe had thrown at him.

Sharpe turned off the radio, turned to him again. "What are you going to do with yourself, man?"

Player's voice came out barely audible. "I don't know. I honest-to-God don't know."

"Listen, one year at Les' Place was okay, even a couple of years. You were young and frisky, wanted to chase some skirt and have a big time. That's understandable. But eleven years? What's happened to you, man? We ran neck and neck in school, then we got out and you quit moving forward."

Player felt so empty he could barely drive. He lit a cigarette and had trouble holding the Zippo steady, but as he blew out a ragged stream of smoke something released inside him, a need to confess what he'd held tight inside for a long time. It broke loose and flared, allowing him to say something he could only say to Sharpe, only in catharsis.

"Okay, so I'm a failure."

Sharpe sat back, looking smug and satisfied to hear him admit it finally. Jaye stirred but remained asleep on Sharpe's lap, and he stroked her hair to keep her still.

Player pulled on the cigarette and felt exhausted deep in

his guts. He had been born with the ability to do something worthwhile, yet he'd never stretched himself. And having voiced it finally, admitting that he'd lived a life of wasted promise, he was now free to feel his self disgust and found it to be a potent emotion.

"I'm sick of my life, Sharpe. Sick of being broke. Sick of being nobody."

Player threw his cigarette out the open top of the car and watched it in the rear view mirror. It trailed a few orange streaks in the wind then hit the street in a burst of sparks. The flash of fire was over almost as soon as it happened and the mirror became a dark rectangle again, but the moment wasn't lost on Player. He hadn't felt even momentary fire in a long time, and it had been so long, he had no idea how to ignite his life again.

They were silent now as he turned left on Peachtree Battle, working his way back toward Les' Place, south of Buckhead. As tired as he was, he almost didn't want the night to end now that Sharpe had opened him up. Tired as he was, he didn't want to go back to his apartment, with nothing but raw thoughts waiting there.

At last, Sharpe broke the silence. Again, his voice had shifted a notch, bore an urgency that Player could not ignore. "Are you finally, truly sick enough of your life to do something about it?"

The question made Player's scalp tingle. He didn't know what Sharpe wanted, but he knew there was something new and strange behind the question. That strangeness in Sharpe's voice told him that somehow his friend had looked deep into Player's rattled soul and found something wanting, something dark and pliable, and now he was about to exploit it. Player didn't like the feeling, but at that moment he was emotionally stripped, so defenseless he had nothing left to fend off this probe.

"What are you after, Sharpe?"

He exhaled slowly before he answered. "I want to remake our lives, and I want to know if you're up to it."

"What are you talking about?"

"You saw that party tonight. Lawyers. Bankers. Politicians.

They all have one thing in common. They want dope and somebody's getting rich off it. Why not us?"

"Oh, man," Player sighed.

"I'm saying, let's take the biggest step we've ever taken."

"Like what, exactly?"

"Let's go to Colombia and bring back a load of dope."

Player's head jerked sideways. He had to see Sharpe's face, to make sure this was one of his stupid jokes. Even in his wildest moments, Sharpe had never suggested anything so outrageous.

"One run is all it'd take, and we'd be rich for the rest of our lives."

Player felt lightheaded as he realized Sharpe was probably serious, and it left him reeling. A major axis of his life had shifted.

The right front tire of the Porsche grated against a curb and Player snapped his eyes back to the street just in time to see a telephone pole flick past the front bumper. He yanked the wheel to the left, got the car back on the road and slowed down.

"Have you literally gone crazy?" he said.

"We can make a million apiece, easy."

Player shook his head in disbelief. "Think about what you're saying. You're talking about committing a major crime. We could go to prison."

"It's worth the risk."

"Nothing is worth prison," Player said. "I won't go to jail for anybody or anything in this world."

Excited now, Sharpe grabbed him by the arm. "Listen, you're dying inside because you're a failure. There's only one cure for it and that's money."

Sharpe's voice had grown loud and he had Player by the sleeve, shaking it so hard Jaye began to wake up. She twisted in Sharpe's lap, seeking stillness.

Player jerked his arm free. "This is no joke. You're talking about crime and I don't want any part of it."

Back on Peachtree, he drove fast to Les' Place and whipped the Porsche into the parking lot, a deserted slab at this hour except for Player's rusty MG. He pulled the Porsche alongside his car and jumped out, slamming the door behind him.

"Player, listen."

"No, damn it."

As he fumbled for his keys, he saw Sharpe work Jaye off his lap, get out and come around to the driver's side. There, Sharpe spread his feet apart and took a stand in front of Player, blocking the door of the MG. Player tried to reach around him for the door handle, but Sharpe took a side step and blocked the way again, seized Player by the lapels.

"I've listened for ten years how you're gonna do something big, one day," Sharpe said. "Well, you're ten years older and still a bartender, and you're gonna stay one. You know why? Cause it's easy. Easy to be complacent and pick up that steady, shitty little paycheck."

"Move, damn it!"

Sharpe did not budge. Player refused to listen to any more and he elbowed past Sharpe to put his key in the door. Sharpe grabbed his arm and twisted him around.

Player felt his eyes water with hurt.

Sharpe pulled his face close. "I'm giving you a chance to start over, man. Now, if you want to go back into that bar tomorrow and take things easy a few more years, go ahead. But one day you'll wake up and you'll be fifty and you'll still be a bartender."

Player pushed him away from the car and got his key into the lock and turned it, but the door was stuck. He yanked on the handle, tried it again, but it wouldn't open. Furious, he kicked the side of the car and his foot tore through the rusty metal, gouging a hole at the bottom of the door.

"Damn it!"

Player jammed his fist through the canvas roof above the window and shoved his arm down through the torn fabric all the way to his bicep until his fingers reached the door latch inside and snapped it free.

He got into the MG and cranked it up, but the engine quickly died, so he kicked it to life again, tromping on the accelerator until it ran well enough to get the car moving. In his rear view mirror, he saw Sharpe leaning against the Porsche, watching the rusty little car sputter across the parking lot, a trail of blue smoke wafting behind it.

He braked at the sidewalk, then lurched onto Peachtree and raced the engine to keep it from going dead again. He shifted into third and the transmission groaned bitterly. It occurred to him how perfectly the MG matched him at this moment, strained and barely making it, with no prospects ahead.

Chapter 7

The next night, Jaye could tell she'd really messed things up with Player. Between orders, she made several tries to get his attention so they could talk, but every time she got near him, work seemed to carry him the other way. She watched as he bent over the washing sink and noticed that his blond hair was gummy and barely combed. Now that she thought about it, he looked awful, like he hadn't slept at all last night, maybe hadn't even taken a shower.

Finally she decided to confront him while he was rinsing wine glasses.

She walked over to his station quickly and had her elbows on the bar before he saw her. He glanced up, didn't say anything, then lowered his head again. She had never seen him look so rough; he hadn't even shaved.

"Is my bartender feeling so bad he can't even talk tonight?"

He looked up then and she was startled by the coldness on his face. She put on her most sympathetic smile but it had no effect. He straightened up and stood there with soap dripping off his hands, staring as if he expected her to say something.

"I had a great time last night, Jack."

"I bet you did." He wiped his hands on his apron. "I bet Sharpe did, too."

So that was it. She put down her serving tray and lit a cigarette. "Jack, if you'd let me explain."

"I don't want to hear it."

"When I get dust in my head, I'm not very sane."

"I don't care. Forget it."

She pulled her hair back from her face and draped it behind her left shoulder. Suddenly she felt a decade older, tougher, wanted to show Player that she could be hard too. "It's your fault, you know. You should have made a move when you had the opportunity."

She'd hit the truth and they both knew it. She could see it on his face. Player tried to cover it up with a disinterested wave of his hand, then he bent back over the sink and went to work on the glasses again, but she wasn't going to let him off that easy.

"I guess it doesn't matter anyway," she said. "You had your chance and didn't do anything about it. Now it's gone."

She tossed her cigarette in the rinsing sink where it hissed briefly, inches from his hands. She walked away, that gliding ease of her hips unchanged; that, a mockery in itself, was sure to sting.

Chapter 8

She was right, of course, he admitted. Her attitude now was a far thing from the first time he'd exchanged those looks with her. It was during Happy Hour the day before and he remembered the thrill he had felt when they first connected. He had been tending bar since ten that morning and he was getting ready for the rush hour when it happened.

Everybody in Atlanta knew Les's Place was a good Friday night bar, a place to meet women fresh out of college, a place where the young men were still on their way up. There was a kind of expensive trendiness about the bar that made it popular with the well dressed set who came down out of the office towers at five. Most of them dropped into the bar in their business suits to have a few drinks while the streets cleared, and perhaps with luck, to meet someone new.

Player looked up from his work, drying highball glasses, and saw that the tables were filling up fast. He knew exactly how it would happen because he had seen it all before, countless times. The paralegals, account execs, and software crowd would come in from their offices looking tired but hopeful.

The young women would let their eyes stray to the men lined up at the bar, but they would be careful to limit eye contact since they didn't want to look too available. The men would laugh at their own jokes and drink imported beers, and when they saw the women come in, they would straighten their ties and smooth their hair.

He went to the cash register to ring up an order and almost smiled because he knew exactly how it would happen; the old mating ritual he'd seen so many times before. He took another glance around the high-ceiling of the main room, with its big plants and oak paneling, the polished brass bar railings and old brick, jammed and noisy with the Happy Hour crowd. It remained the same every year. Only the faces were new. More of the women wore business suits now, and club ties were the thing again for men. White shirts were back, too. Years before, he had enjoyed the scene, but now it was just work.

When he saw her across the room, his mood lifted instantly. She was a new waitress, Jaye Randall, and he felt his insides tic for just a moment at the sight of her. It had been a long time since his wife left and no woman had interested him since then, but Jaye might be the one who changed things. She'd only been working there three weeks, and every day Player found himself watching her more.

There among the bland business people, she worked her way between the crowded tables, twisting and bending past the elbows and chair backs, moving inside her black cocktail dress. The dress was long and had a slit up the side that parted along her right leg, exposing the tanned skin halfway up her thigh. The waitresses hated those inviting dresses but Les insisted they wear them because it was good for business.

Player studied her leg for a moment and wondered if his first impression of her had been accurate. When she started working there she seemed a bit cool, but it didn't seem to be an act. He had watched her since then because there was definitely something different and appealing about her, but he forced himself not to get his hopes up too much. Women had burned him too many times. Oh, had they burned him. Besides, he'd found over the years that beautiful women rarely fulfilled their promise, and Jaye was way beyond beautiful.

It wasn't just that her leg was lean and near perfect and her body just the right mix of softness and muscle. It was the movement of it all beneath the thin black material. He watched her serve a round of drafts, and as she leaned over and placed each glass on the table, her thigh peeked in and out of the slit skirt with an unhurried motion that was different from any woman he could remember. Plenty of women were capable of posing motionless in front of a camera, he thought, but few had the beauty of movement this woman had. She moved with an educated ease, as though nothing on earth was worth a hurry, and it made him curious about her background. She almost certainly came from money, he guessed, the sort of money that removed rough edges.

She finished serving the drafts, straightened up and turned toward the bar with the empty serving tray resting on her upturned forearm then she happened to look in his direction and her eyes widened when she caught him staring at her. Player felt boyish and started to look away but then wondered what would happen if he just kept staring. Would she be predictable and throw an annoyed look back at him or ignore him as most women would? Please surprise me, he thought. Don't turn out to be another disappointment. Astonish me with an original response. Show me that you're something special.

To his amazement, she did exactly that, as if she'd read his mind. She looked straight at him, raised her chin and smiled so openly that an unmistakable current passed between them, and he felt a wobbly sensation in his knees. She had surprised him all right; he hadn't seen a smile that genuine in years. It seemed to say, Okay, I caught you looking and I'm pleased that I did, and what's more I won't act indifferent the way most women would, because I don't play the game the way most women play it.

She moved off to another table and there was no trace of exaggeration in her walk, no affected sexiness even though she knew he would still be looking. She disappeared in the crowd and he shook his head with a grin, wondering if he'd just made contact with someone who could change his life.

But that was then, before the party.

SEPTEMBER 1976

Chapter 9

Player's old Triumph rattled up the driveway and shuddered to a stop in front of the plain, red brick house that was typical in the eastern part of Atlanta, near Decatur. A two bedroom ranch built in the fifties, it had a flat profile and a picture window in front that was mostly obscured by overgrown shrubbery. The branches of aging pine trees extended over the yard, and an inch of brown needles covered the roof and the cracked concrete driveway.

The house was rented, of course, because he'd never owned property in his life. Even the title to his old Triumph remained in a bank file with a lien attached.

The engine coughed a couple of times then died as the driver's door creaked open. The car was low and much too small for Player's bulk, but somehow his left foot emerged from the car and searched for the payment, found it at last, then the door opened wider. Rust on the hinges groaned as Player put his weight on the door to climb out and steady himself on his feet.

"That's right, Marikay," he said. "I'm wasted again."

He laughed, slammed the car door and groped his way to the front steps of the house.

"But tonight I am on time." Don't even think about giving me any shit, he expected to tell her, because I am here. He almost stumbled on the cracked top step but managed to get the key into the door and push his way into the house.

Inside, it was dark and quiet, too quiet. She should still be up, watching television.

"Marikaaayyyy! It's early, and I'mmmm home."

He flipped on a light switch and started across the living room, kicking aside some cardboard boxes scattered across the floor. He glanced around and noticed empty shelves on the bookcase, the remaining items jumbled. The room looked as if it had been hit by a big wind.

"What the hell?"

He headed toward the back of the house, turning on lights as he went. In their bedroom, he looked around, taking in the mess she had left behind. Still, his intoxicated mind had trouble catching up with the obvious. Abandoned clothes littered the bed and dresser drawers hung open, half empty, the remaining contents in disarray.

"What the—"

Inside his head, he replayed the argument they'd had before he went to work. It was the same old argument, but she had been more angry than usual. She was tired of apartments and rented houses, she said, and most of all, just plain tired of him. Her words were sharper, more accusatory than normal, but he hadn't really heard them, didn't want to hear them. Standing at the kitchen sink, putting away the dinner dishes, she'd hardly looked at him.

"You are so stagnant," she said.

"It won't always be like this," he said. "I have plans."

"Plans."

She let out a tense laugh, half crying at the same time. "Jack, if somebody offered you a way to make a million bucks tonight, right now, you'd pass it up." She threw her dishrag in the sink in disgust. "All you do is stay in that damn bar, night after night, year after year, afraid to do anything else. And like an idiot, I just stand by and watch."

"I told you, I'm going to get a piece of the business, soon," he said.

With that, her tears started in earnest, and as usual, he left.

Player went over to the closet and the certainty of her departure began to hit him. Most of her clothes were gone; a few dusty shoes scattered on the floor. He sagged with the reality of it, made his way over to the bed and sat down, dazed. On the night stand he noticed a folded piece of yellow note paper, reached over to pick it up and saw something shiny sitting on top. He leaned over to get a closer look and turned on the lamp.

His wife had left him her wedding ring.

JULY 1985

Chapter 10

Player picked up another dirty glass and turned it in his hands, examining the smudges. It was perhaps the hundred-thousandth glass he had washed in his eleven years at Les' Place. He tried to be philosophical about his monotonous job, but he just couldn't.

All that morning he had lain in bed watching the curtains of his bedroom window as they grew brighter and brighter, searching for a metaphor of optimism in the arrival of daylight, a sign of something, but none came. Finally, by eleven, he realized the bleakness deep in his center was not going to go away and he rose for work.

So here he was, back at Les' Place, up to his elbows in the rinsing sink, washing wine glasses. The years came and went, his sense of failure growing with each one until he felt explosive, and the only way he seemed able to deal with it was to just keep on doing the same thing every day--get up, come to work and wash glasses. The first time in his life that he felt this bleak was when Marikay left him. He was thirty-one then and they'd been married two years. She finally grew tired of his promises to get serious about a career, and maybe she just became too embarrassed about him to let it continue. She was a CPA and it must have been hard for her at times to explain--ah yes, my husband, he's brilliant and full of promise, but right now he's working as a bartender. The problem was that the story never changed and she got tired of making excuses for him month after month, as one year turned into another.

Eventually her friends learned to quit asking about him, but that was almost as embarrassing as trying to answer their polite questions. Finally, she admitted to herself that he wasn't going to change and she walked out.

It didn't ruin him, but it left him with a bleakness that lasted for months. He never again thought of himself as young after the divorce, and because the future seemed empty, his life at the bar became more entrenched. Sharpe was right about that--one reason he stayed was because the life was easy. He fell into the routine of going through the days without ever pushing, and the paycheck was just enough to pay rent and food, keep his car running, buy a few decent clothes, but never enough to get ahead.

Player ran himself a beer and downed it in a few long gulps, a sure sign of the bleakness; he never drank during the day except when that barren feeling was all over him. He knew it would take days to shake it.

A finger stabbed him between the ribs. He turned and Les was giving him the hard eye.

"You look like crap today," Les said. "Out with your smart-ass lawyer friend all night, I bet. Another big party, huh?"

Player groaned inside. This was too much. "Don't mess with me, today."

"Oh, you're giving me orders now." Les rubbed the back of his neck and looked peeved."I'm not kidding, Les. I don't want any hassle."

"Oh, Mr. Tough Guy doesn't want trouble."

Player grabbed Les by the front of his shirt and slammed him against the side of the bar and held him there until Les motioned that he'd back off. Player held him there for another second or two just to make sure the message sank in, then he let go slowly. Les straightened his shirt and sidled away, glaring at Player as he headed for the back room.

Player leaned against the bar and took a slow, deep breath. He reached for a glass to draw himself another beer then put it back down. His hand was shaking too much to hold it steady beneath the tap.

About nine, Sharpe came into the bar and took his regular

seat across from Player's mixing station. He joked with Player as usual and made conversation as if nothing had happened the night before. Player felt very cool toward him, but knew he would forget about it eventually. He concluded that Sharpe went through all that drug smuggling and failure business last night just to knock him off balance, all to make it easier to put the move on Jaye.

Yet again, Sharpe had outdone him.

He glanced over his shoulder and watched as Sharpe talked up some guy Player didn't know. Sharpe stroked his hair, starting at the temple where just a few gray flecks appeared, then over the ear and around to the back of his head, stroking it over and over, not as a nervous gesture, but to draw attention. As much as anything, that abundant head of hair defined Sharpe, always full and dark and groomed in the latest style. Immaculate in his looks and clothes, he stayed up with every trend, always worked every room for contacts, displaying his charm and vanity at every opportunity.

He made friends everywhere he went, friends by the dozen, maybe hundreds, but it seemed to Player they were always people who had something to offer: a sailboat at the lake, Masters tickets, maybe a vacation condo in Florida. Sharpe was stylish and funny and people enjoyed his company, so if somebody had something he wanted, he gave them a certain amount of his time, and his lifestyle revolved around these accommodating friends. While Player spent his hours slogging away behind the bar, Sharpe always had somewhere to go, somebody to see.

Player ran a fresh beer, went over to the spot where Sharpe was sitting and put it down on the polished wood bar between them. The ashtray in front of Sharpe was overflowing with butts so Player emptied it, wiped it out, and replaced it. He buffed the bar clean of spills, helped himself to one of Sharpe's cigarettes and lit it up, took a deep drag.

"At your service," Player said.

"So, what did Les say?"

Player shrugged.

"I can't believe you intend to bind yourself legally to that old jock. Don't you know a business partnership is more demanding than a marriage?"

Player didn't answer. Sharpe had touched yet another raw nerve as only he could.

"The partnership is gonna fly this time, right?" Sharpe asked.

"I don't know."

Player had customers waiting at the register, which gave him an excuse to get away from the questions. "I'll be back in a minute."

Sometimes Player wondered how they had remained such good friends through the years as they'd gone in very different directions. Some things just couldn't be explained. He'd watched Sharpe move up from his first job out of law school as an Assistant District Attorney to the point of now having his own firm. He started out doing small change criminal work but added clients and cases every year until finally he made good money. The surprising thing was that even though he was doing well now, he didn't slow down at all. There seemed to be no end to his making contacts, sniffing out new deals and finding leads to make money, and the more success he had, the more he wanted.

That was a lot different from the old days when they were young and only wanted to make enough money to look good and party most of the time. Though he would never admit it, Player admired Sharpe's success, and furthermore, he bitterly envied it. Despite all that, through all the changes in their respective lives, through Player's divorce and setbacks, through Sharpe's successes and money, they somehow had remained friends for nearly twenty years.

When Player returned, Sharpe wiped a streak of foam from his mustache, waved Player closer and lowered his voice. "So, did you talk to Les or not?"

"Yeah, we talked."

Sharpe waited and when Player said nothing, Sharpe leaned closer. "Well?"

"He said the same old thing."

Sharpe sat back, disgusted. "Oh, shit. Here we go again."

Player sighed. "I told him it's time we got serious about the deal we made. Of course, he gets this look on his face like he doesn't even know what I'm talking about, and I said, 'This is the year, Les. You told me I'd get a piece of the business if I stayed on as manager for another three years.'"

"So, then what?"

"He walked off, scratching his head."

"He did what—"

"So, I blew a gasket and told him off."

"The man's a jerk wad, no doubt about it." Sharpe hung his head and shook it from side to side. "You should have put it on paper, like I told you."

Player frowned and walked off. "Thanks for reminding me, again."

Chapter 11

By eleven, Player realized that Sharpe had only been warming him up—his friend didn't give a damn about the uncertain partnership with Les. Last night had not been some kind of odd dream, after all. As they talked, Sharpe slowly and carefully reintroduced the idea of making a big run that would net them a fortune.

As he listened to him talk about the plan, Player came to realize that Sharpe would never see the hidden dangers of something like this. Even though he was a shrewd lawyer, he had no practical sense, and he'd never understand that you could plan a crime for years and there'd still be a hundred things that could go wrong, because you couldn't eliminate the human factor. In the end, you'd have to rely on people you didn't even know, and that could get you killed. Maybe that was the best way to put it to him.

"Wait a minute," Player interrupted. "Has it ever occurred to you that somewhere along the line you're going to have to deal with some really nasty people? No matter how well you plan this thing, you're still going to have to buy and sell the goods from some greasy characters. They'll kill you for the money on that end or kill you for the load on this end."

"I've worked that out," Sharpe said. "Alvarez has contacts we can trust."

"Oh, I understand now. Alvarez takes care of those minor details and everything will be all right."

"Well, yeah, because he's financing the whole thing and he's got to protect his investment."

Player wasn't expecting that. "You've already talked with Raoul about putting up money for this thing?" He never thought Sharpe had gone that far.

"Hell, yes, why do you think he wanted to meet you last night?"

"Damn," Player whispered to himself. So the party, the introduction; it had all been arranged ahead of time, and he never saw it coming. "Next time you get some lunatic idea, how about asking me before you take me to the audition."

"Right. Let you decide, then maybe we'll do it in about twenty years."

Player lowered his voice and leaned close to Sharpe. "Mitch, why risk everything on a crazy scheme like this? Me, it might make some sense. My life's going down the sink anyway, but you've got something to lose."

"I don't want to wait twenty years to start living."

"What's wrong with the way you live now?"

"I'm tired of working my butt off for a Porsche and a condo. I want more. And I want it now, not when I'm sixty years old."

Player smacked the bar with his open hand.

"Listen, dimwit. You don't know anything about smuggling. Have you even considered where you're gonna get a seaworthy boat? Even if you had a boat, how are you going to get it across the Caribbean? You get lost driving to Dunwoody."

Les looked up and glared at them from the other end of the bar, but Player stared back at him until Les bent to his work again.

Sharpe leaned close to continue his spiel, but Player kept his eyes on the rinse sink and dipped a few more glasses as it dawned on him. Suddenly, he knew what was coming next.

"You know about boats," Sharpe said. "You and Marikay used to run that big boat out of Hilton Head."

Player raised his eyes and watched Sharpe in silence.

"You could get a boat to Colombia and back, couldn't you, old Buddy?"

Even with his growing anger, Player couldn't help but

appreciate Sharpe's guile. Player had made himself stop remembering those days a long time ago; he and his ex-wife and those long afternoons out on the Atlantic, cruising her father's motor yacht up and down the coast. They had gone as far north as Charleston and south all the way to Ft. Lauderdale once. For over a month, three summers in a row, they'd lived the lazy, rich life at her parents' house in Sea Pines and cruised the barrier islands on that yacht. It seemed so long ago, that life so far away, he'd almost forgotten it, or made himself forget it.

But Sharpe had remembered.

"I don't know if you ever made any real deep water trips, but you could handle it in a pinch, couldn't you?"

Player gave him a little joyless smile. Would he ever quit underestimating Sharpe? "You're something, man."

"Got to admit it, the idea intrigues you because you haven't had a real challenge in ten years. This is right up your alley. Macho man covers a thousand miles of ocean, faces danger and hardship to bring back his fortune. Almost too good to be true."

Player shook his head. "That's because it is too good to be true. You've seen a thousand people go down on drug charges, and I'm not going to prison for anything or anybody."

That cooled Sharpe off for the moment. Maybe he thought he'd had Player hooked. He sat back and made a snorting sound, then after a pull on his beer and a few nervous shifts on his barstool, he leaned forward again.

"I know what it is. You're pissed because I put a move on Jaye. That's it, isn't it?""You think this is about her?"

"So, she's not the problem."

"Of course she's not the problem. Your crazy idea is the problem."

"That's good, because she's part of the plan."

"What?"

"She's the way to get a boat."

"Oh, hell." Player carelessly threw a glass into the sink where it shattered. "I'm through arguing with you. Forget it."

"You can forget it, too," Les said from behind him.

Player turned to the sound of the voice and Les was standing there, close to his face. Too close.

"Get out." Les took a step and blurted the words into his face. Player could smell the Marlboros on his breath. "You're fired."

"Fired?" Player's head felt as if it would erupt. Heat flashed along the skin of his neck and up his face. "Fired?"

Sharpe stood up. "Just cool down, would you, Les?"

"You, too." Les threw an arm in Sharpe's direction. "Get out. Both of you."

Player realized then what was happening. "You can't fire me. I've put eleven years in here."

"You're through telling me what I can and can't do in my own place," Les shouted.For the first time in his life, Player felt anger take a truly dangerous form inside him. Fired. What a cheap, cowardly way for Les to weasel out of their deal. Rather than explosive temper that was over in seconds, he felt his anger pouring out in a violent desire to cause Les real harm. He took him by the arm and spun him around, then tightened the arm into a hammerlock. Les stood on his toes and gasped, his facing showing the pain that streaked into his shoulder.

"Now, Les, I won't hurt you unless you get in the way, so shut up and stand back."

Player relaxed the pressure on Les' arm and almost as soon as the pain eased, Les elbowed him in the stomach and started yelling.

"Goddamn you! Player, goddamn—"

Player tightened his grip again and Les screamed. Player held onto the wrist with one hand and took one of Les' fingers in the other and he bent the finger sideways in one quick motion until he felt it give. The bone snapped loudly and Player heard somebody groan.

Les wailed in pain and fell to the floor, holding his broken finger. Player watched the old guy sobbing and felt a twinge of regret, then he sensed everyone's eyes on him and he looked up and saw a semicircle of stunned customers on the other side of the bar, understood what he had done. They stared at him in accusation and fear.

Player saw that he was a condemned man now. No matter what Les had done to deserve it, he was permanently marked as brutal. Eleven years of lies and provocation meant nothing to them. All they saw was an old guy writhing around on the floor, but with this new anger, this hatred burning inside him, Player didn't care what they thought. He'd listened to them moan and groan about their own problems for so long he just didn't care anymore; all he wanted was a release.

"The hell with all of you."

Jaye broke through the crowd and looked at him wildly. "Jack, what are you doing?"Player turned to her, but didn't really see or comprehend anything.

He backed away from the crowd and grabbed a vodka bottle by the neck, then took a swipe at some overhead glasses that hung by the stem from a slotted rack and he smashed a whole row off with one sweep of the bottle. He swung it again and kept swinging it until he smashed every glass off the rack, then he threw the bottle into a shelf of gin. The bottles splintered and spray flew everywhere.

By now, everybody in the bar had drawn around as close as they dared, all trying to get a view. A few voices pleaded with him to stop while others urged him on, shouting and cheering. The noise grew as he yanked more bottles from the carefully arranged shelves and smashed them on the bar and the floor, even flinging them off through the air to crash at the far end of the room.

Les stood and worked up enough courage to challenge him again. "Stop it, Player. Stop, or I'm gonna call the cops." Les grabbed the phone and a couple of patrons joined in and yelled threats, but no one crossed the bar to stop him.

In the midst of the melee someone warned him the police were coming, but Player was only dimly aware of the voices and he kept smashing glasses and bottles until Sharpe jumped over the bar to restrain him, but Player threw him aside easily. Sharpe grabbed him again, this time trying to pin his arms from behind.

Player still resisted until Jaye came behind the bar and put her hands on him.

She touched his face and said gently, "It's over."

That calmed him down and allowed Sharpe to get him moving toward the door.

The crowd stepped aside, hushed, as Jaye and Sharpe took him by the arms and led him to the exit.

A moment later, Les came out of hiding, yelling out to them. "I'm gonna have you locked up!"

As the three of them disappeared outside, Les couldn't resist a last insult. "You're a loser, Player," he shouted. "Nothing but a loser," he shouted again, as the door closed quietly behind them.

Chapter 12

After Player's rampage, they took him to Sharpe's condo off Piedmont and tried to get him to talk about it so he would feel better, but he wouldn't answer their questions. After a few drinks he insisted on going home. They protested because they thought he might go back to fight with Les again, but he said he was okay now, he just wanted to be alone. Finally, they realized there was nothing they could do for him so they drove him home.

Sharpe refused to take him by Les' Place for his car and explained he could pick it up later after things had settled down. On the way to his apartment, Player said he wanted some beer so they stopped by a big liquor store on Buford Highway and bought him three six packs before they dropped him off. Sharpe said it probably wouldn't hurt anything for him to get drunk at home since he didn't have his car and couldn't drive out and get into more trouble.

When they stopped at his apartment, Player got out without saying a word, but then he hadn't said anything all the way home anyway, didn't want to. Sharpe told him to call if the police came to arrest him, even though that was unlikely. They probably wouldn't pick him up on just a disorderly and property damage call, Sharpe said; it really depended on how much Les made out of the broken finger. That was battery, and a serious charge, but Sharpe told him he'd try to cut a deal with Les by Monday morning to drop the whole thing.

"But I don't have any money to pay Les off," Player mumbled.

"That's okay, old Buddy, I'll take care of it."

Jaye offered to stay with him until he felt better, but he waved them both off, turned and slowly climbed the metal steps to his three room apartment. He didn't want to see anybody, even Jaye, while he felt the way he did right now.

That night and all Sunday morning, Player sat inside and drank, but he ran out of beer around noon and had to go to two neighbors to borrow enough to last him through the night. His isolation was interrupted about seven when Sharpe called and told him not to worry, that he'd talked to Les' lawyer and he was pretty sure he could settle everything for damages. Then Jaye called an hour later and tried to soothe him but he hardly spoke to her. After a long silence she gave him her number and told him to call if he needed anything, then she said goodbye and hung up softly.

Sometime after midnight, Player took the last few beers from the refrigerator and stumbled out to the tiny balcony just off his living room. He pushed a rusty charcoal grill aside and collapsed onto a lawn chair, stretching its cheap plastic webbing with his dead weight. He had not slept in three nights.

The apartment building where he lived sat on a hillside overlooking a small valley of stores and apartment complexes. From the balcony, Player could see miles of hamburger stands and gas stations stretching to the expressway beyond. He sat on the balcony and watched the lights of the city for hours. The cars thinned out slowly, until their headlights and red taillights finally vanished from the smaller streets, but the signs in front of the doughnut shops and the sodium lights over the parking lots never went out. Most of the remaining stores and gas stations closed steadily until a surreal darkness finally settled on the landscape below, and the traffic roar diminished to an undercurrent of trucks out on the expressway.

He smoked and drank beer as he thought about everything that had happened in the last two days, and he watched the grids of streetlights until they began to blur and dance sideways, until the night became a replay of confused pictures and thoughts flitting in and out of his mind. He drifted back and forth between consciousness and stupor as bizarre scenes played in his head;

scenes of Marikay on a white yacht with teak trim; Raoul and the gold chains hanging from his neck; Sharpe imploring him with a vein standing out on his forehead; Jaye on a dance floor in her black cocktail dress; broken glass crunching beneath his feet; Les screaming at him; a finger bending crazily until it snapped like a carrot; and finally a cigarette slipping from his fingers.

Oddly, he found himself walking, but his movements were slow because his legs were so strangely heavy, and his feet seemed planted to the ground and every step forward took tremendous effort.

Sand! He must be in sand for it to be so difficult to walk.

And darkness; he couldn't see where he was going so it must be nighttime. And the sound of water somewhere out there. Then, with absolute clarity he saw himself and Sharpe walking on a pale beach.

The flat whiteness of the beach gleamed supernaturally under a full moon, and off to their right, waves roared and tumbled in from the black infinity of the ocean. They scuffed through the water's edge, throwing up silver sheets of spray with every step, and against the dark ocean, they looked like ghosts radiating silver fire. Their faces were amazingly young, the way faces are remembered much later in life.

They laughed softly as they walked, friends' laughter, but a moment later Player turned and headed away from the water, up to the hard packed sand where the tide had been just a while earlier. He took off his shirt and started to jog in place, challenging Sharpe with a sideways snap of his head, and Sharpe accepted without a word, moving into position alongside him. They jogged side by side for a few yards to warm up then glanced at each other. The laughter left their faces as rivalry took over, a rivalry as strong and unspoken as their friendship, then they nodded in agreement and broke forward at the same time.

Sharpe was lean and quick and jumped ahead by sprinting hard, but after two hundred yards he couldn't hold the pace. Player was steadier and stronger and he gradually pulled even then went into the lead. Even though he was big, his thick legs were tireless and his chest always seemed to be leaning forward.

At five hundred yards, Sharpe's stride lost its rhythm and he started to fall behind while Player held his pace. At eight hundred yards, they settled into an uneven race as Player pulled well ahead, increasing his lead. Soon he was so far ahead Sharpe had no chance of winning and he barely heard the shout, turned and saw Sharpe's arm raised in surrender.

He slowed down and waited for Sharpe to catch up, then glanced at Sharpe scornfully and trotted around him backward to show off his easy win. Sharpe dropped to his knees on the sand and looked up with a sullen face.

"You won't always win," Sharpe said, between gasps.

Player laughed wildly, dancing from foot to foot, shadowboxing with speed and power to show he was still strong. He was high on victory, high because he was young and he could do anything.

"Someday you'll lose."

"Never!"

He danced to the water's edge and raised his fists skyward and he took in gulps of the salty wind, screaming in delight as the waves crashed at his legs. The ocean was dark and awesome, yet he held his ground. It coiled and unrolled in the moonlight like a living being but Player dared the raw, booming power to knock him down. After all, he was invincible. Young and strong, his fists jutting toward the stars, Player felt the being out there and he decided to challenge it. He leaned against the waves and screamed into the wind, railing at the swirling opponent he had made out there in the darkness.

"I defy you! I defy you!"

Chapter 13

It was probably the alarm that brought him out of it. Back in his bedroom, the clock radio snapped on and tinny music sounded through the apartment and out to the balcony. Then, an annoying disc jockey's voice nagged at his awareness, and the words "six fifty-five in the A.M." penetrated his dreams. Player was instantly aware of his heart. It was booming fast and hard, driving its pulse through a spot near his right temple.

He opened his eyes and the first thing he saw was a coating of dew that had beaded on the guard rail of the balcony. He stretched his stiff legs which set a pile of beer cans in motion at his feet. One of them rolled under the railing and disappeared off the balcony edge. He straightened and felt an ache in his lower back caused by hours of slouching in the plastic chair, then he rubbed a hand over his face and it occurred to him that he needed a shave badly. There was sweat on his palm; his face was slick with it, too. Why was he out here? Then he remembered the dream, and Saturday night at the bar, and a sick feeling gurgled through his abdomen.

A half-finished beer sat near the right side of the chair. He tried it and it tasted awful, but it was better than nothing so he drank a couple of swallows.

Far below his apartment, the streets were building with rush hour, and farther out, the expressway was already locked down with commuters as the interchange funneled cars to nowhere. The workers rushed off the entrance ramps and darted into tiny gaps in the stalled lines of traffic. Once in a lane, cars accelerated, then braked frantically. Jumped forward, then stopped.

It all looked senseless to Player as they inched forward, fighting for advantage.

A gray haze hung over the interchange as the first rays of the sun appeared beside a squat office building. The haze glowed meekly in the early sunlight, hanging over cars and access ramps, dulling everything in sight to a vague presence.

To Player, the landscape seemed to be a vision of hell, a concrete hell that only man could conceive and endure. He watched the commuters and thought how futile it all was, how pointless the hurry and struggle that only produced more years of the same.

He had never felt so devoid of hope in his life.

Player finished off the beer and dropped the can onto the mound of empties below his chair, then he got up and slid the screen aside and went into the living room. It was gray with morning light, and the familiar objects appeared dim and bleak; a cheap sofa, a few neglected plants. He walked across some newspapers scattered on the floor and kicked an old pizza box aside.

Crossing into his bedroom, he intended to pick up the phone, but the message light was blinking. He didn't want to hear any messages, but it occurred to him how late it must have been recorded on the machine. Maybe it was Sharpe, or even the police, but Sharpe had told him they never called; they just showed up at your door. Well, it might be an emergency.

Finally, he pushed the playback button and listened. It was Sharpe, his voice sounding urgent, leaving a warning.

"Hey, Player. Got some news for you, and it's not good. The possible charges against you just went through the roof. Les has been murdered. A cop I know called me, asking about the fight when Les fired you. Right now, I advise you to leave your apartment, avoid the cops altogether. We'll talk in the morning."

The recording tape clicked off, and he staggered a bit, sat on the bed in a daze. He tried to think, but found the process beyond his grasp.

His head whirling, Player picked up the receiver and started to dial, stopped to reconsider, then swore to himself that he would never hesitate about anything again. He quickly finished dialing Jaye's number, convinced Sharpe would be there.

She answered, said nothing after Player's voice came on the line. She passed the phone to Sharpe, and he answered it gruffly, still asleep. It took Player a moment to clear his throat and speak. He hadn't had anything to eat in days, and after so many cigarettes and beers, his voice came out sounding cracked. It was a different, harsher voice than the one he'd had just two days ago.

"Sharpe, call your office. Tell 'em you're on vacation for the next month. Tell 'em anything you want. We're going to do it."

Chapter 14

About eight, a loud knock, sounding like a clenched fist, shook the front door. Player figured it was the cops, but they probably didn't have a warrant this soon, and he wasn't going to make it easy for them. Opening the door and answering their questions was not the best thing to do. After two more rounds of it, the pounding stopped.

Still hung over, he managed to go back to sleep and stayed that way past noon, then got up, took a shower and shaved, caught a bus to a restaurant next to Lenox Square. Sharpe had nothing more to add about Les's murder, so Player sat and ate two large salads and a hamburger while Sharpe laid out his plan once more, but this time Player truly listened. When Sharpe failed to provide details, Player asked questions, and if there was no firm answer, Player made a mental note.

By the time he finished his third iced tea, Player was fairly sure he knew everything Sharpe had considered as far as the plan went, and just as he'd suspected it was awfully thin, nothing more than a vague scheme really, so he decided to leave the serious work for later. The whole thing needed to be mapped out on paper and the holes plugged with specifics, but first he had to tackle the primary flaw he saw in the idea, so when Sharpe finished talking, Player pushed his plate away and lit a cigarette.

"Sharpe, I've still got one big problem."

"What's that?"

"Jaye."

"Me?" Jaye's eyes flared with surprise that Player could consider her a problem in any way.

Player ignored her response and kept his attention on Sharpe. "I don't want her involved in this."

"I already explained why we need her. She's got access to a boat."

"That's not good enough. She doesn't understand what she's getting into and I don't want to feel responsible for her regrets later."

Jaye came halfway out of her chair. "Since when are you responsible for my decisions?" Then an idea seemed to hit her and her voice tightened even more. "But that's not what's really bothering you, is it? Your pride got wounded, that's all." She tossed her napkin at him in annoyance. "Well, tough shit. I'm not going to miss out on a million dollars because of your pride."

Player put a hand on her shoulder and gently eased her back into the chair. "My pride has nothing to do with it. Keeping us alive does."

"Oh, come on," Sharpe protested.

Player cut him off with a look, then turned his eyes on Jaye once again. She fumbled in her purse for a cigarette in an effort to control her anger.

"Your presumption is truly incredible," she said.

"Jaye."

"Somehow I thought you were better than that."

"Are you finished?"

"No. Yes. I'm finished."

"Listen, I thought this over carefully before I committed to it, and I have a clear idea what we're in for. Do you?"

She crossed her arms and pinched her lips together. "Of course, I do."

Player was silent for a moment and then said very steadily, "Do you think you can point a pistol at a man's face and pull the trigger?"

She squirmed in her seat despite her efforts to look unaffected; finally she looked away rather than answer the question.

"Of course she can't," Sharpe interjected. "None of us are killers. And it doesn't matter anyway because there's not going to be any of that movie stuff. Raoul's setting this thing up so violence won't be necessary. It's just a business deal."

"Oh?" Player turned to him. "You know that for sure?"

"Pretty sure, yeah."

"Both of you better understand right now," Player said. "This isn't a 'pretty sure' thing to do. It'll be dangerous. Otherwise, why is there so much money in it? You think you can make millions overnight by doing something that's 'safe and easy?'" He gave Sharpe a hard eye as he quoted the phrase Sharpe had used on him a few nights before in the parking lot.

"We may have to do some ugly things."

He looked at Jaye again, though not as cold as before. "Are you certain you can handle this?"

"I'm certain."

Player sat back quietly and deliberated the step he was taking with a clever but impractical lawyer and a beautiful woman he barely knew. It occurred to him that nothing about this trip was certain, nothing but his own resolve to succeed at something, anything, to salvage the remains of his self-respect.

The following week, driving down I-95 into south Georgia, Player had plenty of time to think and he went over the plan again and again in his mind, trying to determine if there were any big holes he'd missed. They'd spent days in Atlanta going over the details and assigning responsibilities, pouring over maps and filling legal pads with notes. Sharpe's dining table had turned into a war room where they argued routes and timetables, calculated tonnages and estimated fuel consumption, until finally Player had a real plan burned into his mind, one that he thought had at least some sort of chance of success.

The venture really wasn't so complex that it demanded that kind of precision, but he had insisted on it anyway. He figured if they did that kind of excess planning up front, it would save them a lot of guesswork later if they had to improvise or adjust to a problem during the real thing. He tried to build options into every stage of the job because he knew the plan would have to be flexible at certain points no matter how well they thought it through in advance. He didn't want to get halfway across the Caribbean and not have an alternative available if something went wrong.Jaye and Sharpe thought most of the detail work was unnecessary, but that was okay too, because it helped him see their shortcomings and it established the role each of them would play. They, simply left too many things to chance, so he decided he had to do a lot of thinking for them.They didn't consider things such as the stepped up Coast Guard and DEA efforts in south Florida that made it extremely risky to take a load into there now. He persuaded them that just one more day's cruise up the coast to Georgia or South Carolina greatly improved their chances of dropping the load off without being caught.

Jaye had even argued they make the run for coke instead of marijuana, that its compact size and higher profit would make the whole thing simpler, but Player pointed out that those very attributes also made coke a much hotter item to handle, made it too inviting for someone else to try to steal it from you before you could deliver it. That was why the coke trade was dominated by light aircraft pilots who made one-night runs into South America and then dropped the goods onto small islands just off the Florida coast. At least pot was a bulky item to haul, so the way Player figured it, they were less attractive as targets if they stuck to pot.

Sharpe seemed impressed with Player's reasoning and deferred to him more and more as they worked out the details until eventually Player took on the dominant role in planning the job. One day Jaye asked how Player knew so much about the drug trade when Sharpe was supposed to be the one who had inside connections and knowledge.

Simple, he told her, the newspapers had covered the south Florida drug scene for years and it was all there for anybody to read. She looked skeptical, but Sharpe spoke up and told her it was true. Player read the paper every day at the bar, cover to cover, and he remembered everything.

"I know how his mind works," Sharpe said. "He can absorb

every detail about a subject if it interests him."

She still looked skeptical.

Sharpe grinned at her. "It's a fact. One time I made a fifty dollar bet on his memory. Told some bozo at the bar that Player could recite that day's batting average of every active player in the National League, without any preparation and without making a mistake."

Player laughed, remembering the incident. "And Mitch won the fifty bucks."

"What was in it for you?" she asked.

Player merely laughed again and shrugged. But after they told Jaye that story, she didn't challenge his knowledge again, and after days of discussion, he won every point he thought important.

His biggest concern, despite the assurances Raoul had passed on to Sharpe, was their unavoidable contact with professional smugglers during the buy and the drop-off. Those were the most dangerous times they would face during the entire job, because at that moment when money and drugs changed hands, the risk of being gunned down was at its greatest. He felt sure many of those professionals wouldn't settle for anything less than all the money and all the drugs, and they wouldn't hesitate to kill for it.

He thought if they could at least control the site of the drop-off it would give them some edge when that dangerous time came, and they finally agreed on a tidal creek he remembered in south Georgia not too far from a shrimping town called Darien, about fifty miles south of Savannah.

One summer he and Marikay had explored dozens of the creeks and small rivers that wound seaward through the marshes, emptying into the Atlantic between the barrier islands lining the coast. At high tide the creeks were deep enough to take a large boat well inland, but at low tide, boats with a draft of more than a few feet could get stuck upstream and not make it back to the ocean until the tide came in again.

The creek he remembered was like that, shallow enough that the tide was a factor they could use in their favor. The creek was also secluded, miles away from any towns or tourist sites, so the boat traffic would be light. It was adjacent to a Federal wildlife refuge that protected one of the wild barrier islands from developers, so there were few residents or prying eyes to cause problems. He also remembered an old abandoned shrimp dock located somewhere on that creek that was so isolated the dirt road leading to it was half grown over. The dock would make a perfect drop site, if it was still there and unchanged.

It was his job to drive down I-16 to the coast and then south on I-95 to find the creek and make sure it was the way he remembered. Meanwhile Jaye and Sharpe had gone ahead to Ft. Lauderdale to secure the boat and meet again with Raoul about the cash to fund the buy.

He spent a day on the back roads leading out to the marshes that lay between the mainland and those barrier islands with exotic Indian names. Ossabaw. Sapelo. Wassaw. They were remote islands by choice, almost as remote as they'd been for millennia; mostly government owned, they were difficult to reach by car so the land would remain pristine. For the most part, the islands were low and sandy, covered with a jungle of vines, trees, and scrub palmettos. Once you moved up off the beach or marsh, giant Sea Oaks with huge gnarly branches and draping moss guarded the interior of the islands.

When he finally located Raye's Creek or Faye's Creek, whatever its name was, he learned that it was still suitable for the drop. He rented a motorboat for a day and scouted the surrounding marsh and found that the dock was unchanged, though more rickety than ever.

The marsh was still a flat plain of grass stretching all the way to the horizon, passable only on the meandering tidal creeks that wound darkly through the vast fields of spartina.

Later, when he again drove the surrounding area and found the barely used road that led to the dock, he decided it was definitely the place to use for the drop. With good timing and knowledge of the terrain, he thought they had a reasonable chance to get out of there with their payment. He spent two more days scouting several other tidal creeks and nearby roads until the layout was imprinted in his mind, then he turned his rented Chevy south again toward Florida on I-95.

As he crossed the state line just before Jacksonville, the bug splats grew thicker on the windshield, and he tried to clear his mind and think the whole thing through once more for weak spots. After a couple of hours, he concluded he had done everything he could do in advance. Jaye was taking care of the boat while Sharpe was making final arrangements with Raoul for the cash, and he knew he couldn't do those things himself. He admitted he had no control over some of the preparations, and he simply had to rely on his partners to do their share.

He'd decided back in Atlanta that it would be better to let Sharpe handle all the negotiations with Raoul even though he didn't like leaving it entirely in Sharpe's hands. If he became involved, the talks might get cumbersome and cause the whole deal to break down. He had to assume the deal with Raoul would go well, otherwise their financing would fall through and they would simply have to call it off due to lack of money for the buy.

As for Jaye, the boat they intended to use belonged to her family and it was up to her to borrow it from them somehow. Whatever story she decided to tell them didn't matter to him as long as it worked. They'd considered several possibilities while talking around Sharpe's dining table. She could tell them she needed a long vacation or that she'd had a bad romance and wanted to be alone. They even discussed the idea of telling her parents that Sharpe was her new husband and they wanted to use the boat for a honeymoon cruise. None of them were very good lies because ultimately her success depended on how well she could handle her family and she had to do that on her own.

That left one major problem Player couldn't control in any way and that was the buy in Colombia. That was something he couldn't plan, he couldn't scout in advance, and he couldn't prepare. It was the riskiest part of the whole venture as he saw it, yet he would have to arrange it on the spot, with language and lack of local knowledge working against him. It looked tough, perhaps the most difficult and dangerous part of the entire job, but for now there was nothing he could do about it except hope Alvarez's contact there was a good one.

Chapter 15

One of the guards at Alvarez's mansion helped Jaye out of the boat while the other grabbed the bow line and tied it to a cleat on the dock. Sharpe took care of the line at the stern as Player shut the engine down and put the key in his pocket. The older of the two guards stood back a few feet, holding his submachine gun lightly, while the other guards frisked them with a few light pats to their sides and thighs.

A flash of alarm crossed Jaye's mind because she hadn't expected this, but she managed to keep quiet. She hated guns and men who used them.

The guards escorted them across a brilliant green lawn toward the mansion, and the dogs joined them and trotted alongside, their coats glistening in the sunlight. They reached a red tiled patio that sat at one end of the house where there was a clear view of the canal in both directions.The older guard pointed to an outdoor table with a painted tile top and a yellow umbrella over it, and they went to it and sat down under the umbrella to get out of the sun. Then they waited. There was nothing to do but sit and look at each other and grow edgy while the guards stood in the shadow of the house just off the patio.

The guards got out their cigarettes and smoked, grinning at the nervous white guys while watching Jaye's legs. She knew they must be making lewd jokes about her, because she could see it in their darting eyes. She tried to keep her legs still and under the table as much as possible, but it didn't stop them from leering.

After twenty minutes, she watched as Player began to tap his feet and change position in the chair, glancing irritably at Sharpe, then at the guards. He obviously wanted to get up and move around but they all knew better than to show their unease. After a few more minutes he grimaced and rapped on the colored tiles of the table with his knuckles. Mitch tried to ignore him until finally Player cleared his throat and jabbed Sharpe with a finger.

"What do you want me to say?" Sharpe whispered. "I can't help it because they're late."

She knew Jack hated it when people made him wait. He'd told her that too many so-called businessmen at Les' Place made people sit and squirm while they arrived deliberately late for a lunch. He said they did it for effect, that somehow those guys thought it gave them an edge. Maybe it made them feel more important to control other people's time, but he said people who really counted didn't need to rely on that stuff. She had never thought much about it; to her it was simply somebody running late.

By the time Raoul and his father came out of the house, they'd been sitting there so long, she was annoyed too. Nonetheless, she hoped Player would keep his mouth shut and let Mitch handle this, because she thought Jack might say the wrong thing out of anger and blow the deal. After all, Mitch was the lawyer, and he knew better how to handle this sort of thing. All she wanted to do was get this meeting over and get out of here.

At last the father and son joined them at the table and they stood as Raoul handled a brief round of introductions. There were no handshakes or greetings. Raoul moved a chair and sat down, slightly behind his father, and when Carlos took his seat, a maid appeared.

"Drinks?" Carlos asked, revealing very white teeth.

"Whatever you're having, sir," Sharpe answered, in his best lawyer tone.

"Lemonade," Carlos said, without looking at the maid. She disappeared and Carlos turned his dark eyes on them and looked them over slowly and deliberately.

His tanned face was expressionless; his eyes black and

impenetrable behind an aquiline nose. The teeth were capped to perfection, she thought, but the silver hair seemed to be natural. His face was an unchanging facade hardened by years of giving orders and telling lies. She recognized that quality in him because she had met many men like that through her father when she was younger; she knew the signs of powerful, ruthless men. She suspected that he had worked half his life at keeping emotion from showing on his lips, or in those dark eyes, and he had succeeded. He was a man like her stepfather who rarely showed his feelings, and when he did show emotion, it would most likely be anger, the only feeling that seemed acceptable to them to express.

She knew it would be almost impossible to tell what the man was thinking, and of course his words would be a careful mixture of fact and evasion, tools used for deception rather than expression.

The maid reappeared with a pitcher of lemonade, and when she left, everyone waited for Carlos to speak. He sipped his drink and looked them over once more, his eyes finally stopping on Sharpe.

"So, you are the ones who wish to be rich."

Sharpe leaned toward him and smiled engagingly.

"Yes sir, and to that end, I've worked out the details with your son. My partners here are satisfied with the arrangements as well."

Alvarez pulled out a cigar and a guard came over and leaned in front of Sharpe to light it. Everyone stopped talking and waited for the guard to move, but the guard took his time, making a show of his big shoulder holster. Jaye couldn't avoid looking at the heavy automatic that hung just inches from her eyes and it made her shiver so she deliberately looked away. Alvarez puffed on the Havana and noted Jaye's reaction to the weapon.

When the guard left, Sharpe began again. "So, Mr. Alvarez, we are prepared to move forward as soon as possible, but Raoul insisted we meet with you before closing the contract."

Alvarez sipped on the lemonade and took his time before

answering.

"Frankly, Mr. Sharpe, I insisted on this visit. Like many fathers, I sometimes question my son's business acumen."

Raoul looked uncomfortable, stared at the sky. Here, he was the son of a domineering father, not the brassy dealer Player had met back in Atlanta.

"I do not always agree with his proposals, but my son represents this family, and when he vouches for you, you get a hearing." Carlos puffed on the cigar. "The arrangement, however, is anything but closed."

Player stiffened and glanced at Sharpe. Jaye could see that he was getting tired of this dance already and she hoped he would hold his temper. He was almost certainly wondering again if Sharpe had a deal with these guys or not.

"Despite my son's assurances, I am doubtful of your resolve and, let us say, your caliber."

Sharpe put the palms of his hands together and pointed his fingertips earnestly at Carlos. "Rest assured Mr. Alvarez, despite our newness to this sort of enterprise we are totally committed to its success. Let me put aside any doubts you have about our determination to—"

"Mr. Sharpe," Carlos interrupted, "How can I have confidence in your success? Most of my people spend years on the streets learning the indelicate ways of this business before I entrust them with an operation of this size."

Mitch went at him again with the lawyer juice. "We are very able people in our own right, Mr. Alvarez. Each of us brings certain skills to this operation that you won't necessarily find in street people."

"Understand my trepidation," Carlos said, as his mouth stretched into a faint smile for the first time. "I'm sure you are indeed talented, but this business requires skills other than persuading juries and serving drinks." He tilted his head toward Player and Jaye. "It requires much stronger resolve than that born of temporary personal dissatisfaction."

She watched the dark eyes moving behind the words, the blank smile. This man was toying with them. If he didn't intend to give them the money, why would he waste time to go through all this talk? Just to embarrass his son? No, she thought, he would simply have ordered Raoul to tell them no. If he didn't take them seriously, why meet with them at all? To drive a harder bargain? It didn't make much sense to her.

Apparently it didn't make much sense to Jack either because she saw him searching the old man's dark face for answers, leaning closer as Carlos spoke again.

"It is true that I am constantly searching for new ways to move shipments, and Raoul helps me in this, but perhaps he became overly zealous in his work." Carlos paused and pointed the cigar accusingly at Raoul. "However, we don't normally fund operations proposed by newcomers. I'm sorry if my son misled you."

Mitch started to go into his lawyer routine again, but when she heard him say, "Mr. Alvarez," yet again in that same measured, addressing-the-client tone, she could see the tension and anger building inside Jack the way it had that night with Les. She didn't know if Sharpe was blowing it or not, but Jack obviously didn't know what was going on and didn't like it. She had heard enough to suspect that Mitch's approach was playing right into Alvarez's hands in whatever it was that the old gangster was trying to do.

She looked over at Mitch as his hands made more of those fantastic political gestures, and she heard something about "assure you of our intentions" and "versatility of the team" and that was all it took for Player to erupt.

"Wait a minute," Player said. He put his fist on the table and rose from his seat. The guards mistook the move for a threat and swung their guns toward the table in one quick, almost casual motion.

Carlos seemed surprised by the tone of Player's voice, but he saw there was no need for alarm so he calmed the guards with a wave of his hand.

Player put his other fist on the table and leaned closer to Carlos. "If you want to do business, let's do it." Player used the same tone on Carlos he typically used on Sharpe, and Jaye wondered if anyone had dared speak to the old man like that in years. "But let's cut the crap, okay?"

"Please," Sharpe began.

"Shut up, Mitch."

Player kept his eyes fixed on Carlos. "I'm through playing this game. We know the risks of the job and we're willing to take the gamble. That's why we're here. You know that, too, so let's drop this 'resolve' business."

Carlos eyed him curiously, perhaps thinking how different this Anglo was from the other, so much more direct.

"Go on."

"You must need runners like us as much as we need a financier like you. Otherwise I don't think we'd be sitting here."

"Why do I need people such as you?"

"Because we're clean. Nobody's watching us because we've never been in the business, and what's more, we look clean. How many of your regular people can claim that? We offer perfect cover because we don't look like pros and we won't make the same moves as pros. Can you say that for your usual people?"

Alvarez twirled the Havana between his lips, seemed to take Player's words into consideration.

"It's true that I always need good new people."

"Then back us. If you're dissatisfied with the terms Mitch and Raoul have negotiated, then let's talk about the terms. But if it gets down to whether you can use us or not, you know the advantages as well as I do."

"But I do not know you. How can I trust you to not run away with my money?"

"Can you trust anybody on that point? Every time you make a buy that you don't handle personally, you run that risk. It's no greater or smaller with us."

Carlos stared at Player for a long time. His face was mute as he appeared to be making up his mind about this aggressive blond man.

"What you say is correct, Mr. Player. But there are still things to consider that you don't understand. My son and I must discuss this further."

"No," Player said firmly. "You know what you're going to do

right now. Tell us. Yes or no."

Player stood his ground, glaring at the wooden face, and for the first time she saw a glimmer of emotion in the dark eyes. Jack had made Alvarez angry. She knew Jack was on dangerous ground, but he seemed elated and suddenly confident. She understood that he'd made the decision to do this whole thing because he was tired of feeling controlled by outside forces, by other people, and because he wanted to accomplish something on his own. Now, at least, he was making things happen, dangerous or not.

Carlos tried to stare Player down but he refused to look away.

Sharpe tried to break the standoff by coughing loudly and then speaking to Raoul, but it had no effect.

The two adversaries continued to stare at each other in silence, and Jaye became acutely aware of the bright sunlight out on the lawn, the yellow umbrella overhead. She heard palm fronds rattle up in the trees, but Jack's eyes didn't move. Finally it was Raoul who ended the standoff when he took Sharpe's cue and started to speak for the first time, but Carlos immediately cut him off with a glance.

When Carlos turned his attention back to Player, his face was fully composed, the emotionless facade in place again.

"Well, then, here's your answer. The terms of the agreement are satisfactory, and we have a contract."

"Excellent!" Sharpe said loudly.

Alvarez ignored him and continued to address Player. "All the necessary commodities will await you at the Billfish Club on Bimini. Arrange the drop time and signals with my son at the agreed site. You've secured your vessel I assume?"

Mitch stumbled all over himself to answer, "Yes, sir. We're ready to move immediately."

Alvarez rose to leave, then paused and stared sharply at each of them one at a time to make his point.

"One final caution," he said very slowly. "When the thought occurs to you to abscond with the capital or the shipment, and trust me you will have that thought, dismiss it. The consequences of stealing from me are most severe."

Chapter 16

As they walked back across the emerald lawn toward the dock, Player felt charged with energy. He wasn't sure exactly what he'd done back there with Alvarez, but he felt sure he'd won something, because he could feel it coursing through his body, electric as a drug, a feeling of victory. Yeah, that's what it was. Victory. Maybe that was what had been missing these last few years, he thought, as they climbed into the speedboat, just some sense of winning.

He eased the boat away from the dock, reveling for a moment in that great feeling, until he heard Sharpe saying something about how his old buddy had really done the Cubans in. Yessir, old Jack had really put it to the Cuban godfather, showed the old man he couldn't screw around with Jack Player and Mitch Sharpe, that they were more than just a pair of Latino punks to push around.Player jammed the throttle forward and tore down the canal to drown out Sharpe's voice, but Sharpe kept shouting to Jaye over the sound of the engine until Player couldn't contain his anger any longer.

He cut the engine, turned and yelled at Sharpe, "Shut the hell up."

"What?"

"Just shut up."

Sharpe looked at Jaye for an answer, but she was likely confused, too.

Jaye came forward to Player and handed him a beer. "What's the matter, Jack? You really were something back there and there's nothing wrong with Mitch saying it."

Player stopped the boat in the middle of the canal and turned to Sharpe.

"You've been down here a week and you only had to do one job—work the deal out with Raoul. And that's after you claimed it was already half done back in Atlanta. Then you tell me Carlos is not a factor, just a formality. 'Everything's set,' you said. Instead, we get in there and I find out nothing's set. What have you been doing here? Eating out of Raoul's hand for a week?"

"But—"

Player threw the beer over the side in disgust. "Some dealmaker."

"The deal was set, Player. Raoul told me so."

"Raoul was nothing but a whipped puppy at his old man's feet. You couldn't figure that out after a week of meetings with him?"

Sharpe sat down heavily on the gunwale.

"Jack, it all worked out okay," Jaye said, trying to smooth things over.

"Yeah, it worked out because of that staring match I pulled with Alvarez. It's just luck he didn't shoot me on the spot. If Sharpe had done his damn job, I wouldn't have had to pull a trick like that." He glared at Sharpe and mimicked the smooth lawyer voice, "When are you going to learn to trust me, Player?"

That got Sharpe's anger up. "We had a deal, damn it. Just like I told you. The contacts. The split. Everything was set. How am I supposed to guess Carlos is going to jump into the middle of it?"

"You should have known it."

"It seemed reasonable to me that everything was cool."

"Reasonable?" Player said in amazement. "That old guy kills people, and you talk about reasonable?"

Sharpe raised his hands helplessly.

"Sharpe, you gotta realize that your lawyer jive won't work with these people. That's no good where we're going."

"Listen to the expert."

Player returned to the wheel and started the boat down the canal again without saying anything else. He realized there was no point in arguing anymore. Sharpe wasn't going to listen. From now on, Player decided he couldn't leave anything important to him. Thinking about it now, he felt sure Carlos might just as easily have blown his head off back there as let him get away with that stunt. And the thing of it was, it was an avoidable risk he'd had to take only because Sharpe hadn't done his job.

Player turned to Jaye and spoke brusquely, "I hope you did a better job with the boat than Sharpe did with Alvarez. Which way?"

"You mean you want to see the boat now?" she asked.

"No, next week," Player said, glaring at her, but he managed to control his voice and spoke calmly, "Yes, now. I'm going to make sure you two haven't screwed that up, too."

Jaye looked at Sharpe uncertainly.

"What is it?" Player said. "Is something wrong with the boat?"

She said nothing as Player shifted his gaze back and forth between the two of them.

Sharpe shrugged and pointed down the canal in the direction of the ocean. "He wants to see it now, let's go see it now."

After a twenty minute run through heavy traffic, they reached the giant marina on 17th Street, where they saw thousands of boats tied up or stored in dry dock. As Player steered into the south entrance he wondered what kind of problem he was going to find with Jaye's boat. She hadn't said a word the whole way over, yet he knew something was wrong; he could feel it. The boat must be a rust bucket, he thought, or maybe a little runabout that wouldn't be seaworthy, but something was wrong. Still, he kept his suspicions to himself as she directed him through the maze of docks and waterways that seemed to go on for miles.

It was late in the day and most of the boats were already in for the night or were just arriving from open sea, so the place had a busy feeling about it. They saw hundreds of boats lined up side by side in their slips, forming perfect rows down each side of the long docks which ran parallel to each other for hundreds of yards before ending at the huge parking lot up next to 17th Street.

They cruised past a row of sailing yachts that bobbed in the low sunlight with their masts swaying overhead like metronomes, while the tanned men who worked on the yachts were putting sails away for the night. The deck hands strained with sail covers, pulling and wrenching to stretch the nylon bags over the booms and get all the sailcloth stuffed inside. Some of the hands washed down the teak decks, while others coiled lines by looping the rope down around the elbow and then up over the palm in a big circular motion. Player nodded to the men as he went by, lifting a finger off the steering wheel. Most looked up and nodded in return.

On board the motor yachts it was different. There were fewer workers, and the owners sat out on deck with tall drinks in their hands as they watched the masts swaying gracefully against the red sky. They were usually older looking couples with deep tans. They wore white pants and didn't speak to strangers in small boats who happened to pass by.

Player was surprised by the sheer number of boats in the marina that were built for serious cruising. Out of the hundreds of boats they passed, few were less than forty feet and almost all were suitable for deep water. There were also a lot of foreign registries and unfamiliar ports stenciled on the transoms.

"Turn there," Jaye said, pointing to a waterway just ahead.

Player made the turn and steered down the line of slips to their left, and after about fifty yards, she put her hand on his shoulder and nodded toward a big sport fishing boat docked just ahead.

"That's it. Slip fifty-eight."

Player thought she must be kidding when he first saw the boat, but then he rechecked the slip number and glanced at Jaye and knew from her look that this really was it. His apprehension vanished instantly. The boat was better than he ever imagined it would be; one glance and he knew they were in business.

He estimated it was between fifty and sixty feet long, a sport fishing boat rigged for big game, with a high flying bridge and two padded fighting chairs in the cockpit. It also had a large deckhouse and enough beam to be roomy below deck. There would be plenty of space inside to carry the eight tons of weed he expected to buy in Colombia.

Player had done some rough math in his head and determined they were going to buy from four to five hundred bales, depending on the final price, and he knew a bale was about the size of a fifty pound bag of garden fertilizer. From that, he had estimated the interior space they would need and he pictured it in his mind as about the size of a medium bedroom. That was a lot of enclosed space on a boat, but this one had it, with room to spare.

He slowed the engine and turned the wheel to make a slow pass around the other side. He wanted to take a good look at the hull down around the waterline to make sure it wasn't just patched and painted to look solid. As he passed around the stern he saw black lettering on the transom that read: *FEY LADY*, FT. LAUDERDALE. One more of those curious names people give their boats, he thought.

He looked up at the fly bridge from the rear. It was well protected with a convertible cover and a wraparound windshield. That was good, because he'd be spending a lot of the next three weeks up there in the sun and weather.

His eyes traced the lines of the hull and he felt sure the boat would be tough enough for the trip. It was a rich man's fishing yacht built to hunt marlin, and that meant deep water trolling for days at a time, so the engines had to be strong. It looked to be only a year or two old, so with any luck, it had the latest electronic gear too.

"Jaye, you are wonderful," Player said. "I can't believe this boat is for real. In fact, it's so good it's great. The way you were acting, I thought something would be wrong with it." He felt elated now that a major worry was off his mind. "This boat is perfect. What kind is it?"

"A Hatteras Fifty-Eight."

"A fifty-eight footer for slip fifty-eight?"

"You got it. That's my dear old mom's idea."

He was so pleased he felt like hugging her. "It's simply great.

Think we could climb up and look it over?"

He cut the engine and turned to her, but her head was down and he couldn't see her eyes because of all that dark hair in the way.

"Jack," she stammered and then stopped.

Player glanced at Sharpe, saw the look on his face and knew something was wrong after all. He turned to Jaye again. She raised her head and he saw that her composure was gone, her face turning down and tears running down her cheeks.

"What's wrong?"

Nobody answered as the boat swayed gently beneath them.

"Well?"

Sharpe crossed his arms and mumbled before he finally answered, "It's this way, Player. We have a small complication."

"A complication?"

"Yeah." Sharpe paused again. The water lapped gently against the hull.

Player exploded, "Am I going to have to wring it out of you or what?"

"We can't use the boat."

"Oh, crap." Player looked down and kicked an empty can across the floorboard. "Not again."

"Before you go nuts, just let me explain."

"What in hell have you two been doing down here the whole week? Shacking up?" Player threw the question at Jaye, accusing her with his voice.

"That's not fair," Jaye said hotly. "It's also none of your business."

"It's my business when nothing gets done."

Sharpe stepped in, "Now wait a minute."

"No, I won't wait because I'm getting tired of these bad surprises. You've had a week down here to line up her boat. Is this it or not?"

"This is it," Jaye said. "But it's not mine." She dropped into a seat. "It's my stepfather's. He hates me and he'd never let me use it. I didn't even have the courage to ask him."

Player wheeled around to Sharpe, had to do something to keep from hitting him, so he attacked him with words instead, his voice mocking Sharpe's lawyer tone. "The deal's set, Player. The boat's set, Player. No problems, Player." He took a step toward Sharpe and yelled into his face. "You dumb ass. You brought her into this scheme because you said we could use her boat. Give me one reason to believe anything you ever say again."

"I didn't—"

"Just one reason!"

Sharpe had to scream to get a word in,"I didn't know—"

"You knew we didn't have a boat and still let me square off back there with Alvarez. You've been stalling since—"

Jaye screamed at him, "Stop it, Jack!"

She jumped up and slapped Player on the side of the head. "Stop it."

They turned and stared at her because they'd never heard her blow up before.

"It's my fault. I lied to you, Jack, and to Mitch."

"What?"

"I told Mitch all along I could get the boat without any trouble. He didn't know the truth until today, just before we went to see Alvarez. He didn't tell you because he thought you'd call the whole deal off."

Player sat down, disgusted. "Why did you lie to us?"

"Because I wanted in, dammit."

Player slumped, elbows on his knees, his anger punctured. "I don't understand."

"I thought it was the only way you'd let me in on the deal."

"But you knew we'd find out eventually, so what did it accomplish?"

"Well, I'm here, aren't I?"

"You're here, all right," Sharpe said. "We're all here, and here we're going to stay without a boat."

"We're not finished yet," Player said. "At least we've got the money."

"But no boat," Sharpe said, sounding defeated.

"We're not finished."

"Oh, yeah?" Jaye said. "How are we going to get there?" She sounded a lot like Sharpe, too much like him.

"Why did you let it go on so long?" he asked her.

"Once I lied, I just couldn't admit it. I was afraid you'd ditch me."

Player stared at her. She was adapting all too quickly, picking up the worst traits of both of them. Sharpe's lying. His own violent temper. The sarcasm of both. What could he have been thinking when he agreed to let her come along? Had he done it just because he wanted her nearby, wanted to be with her? Then again, maybe she'd already possessed a good dose of those qualities before she even met them. Maybe she'd fallen in with them because she felt comfortable with their shortcomings from the beginning.

He got a beer out of the cooler and sat down to think and they all brooded a while in silence, each waiting for the other to speak up and soothe the wounds. It went on for twenty minutes as they sat and smoked cigarettes and watched the dock lights come on around them.

Finally Player spoke, his voice back to normal, speaking without being so accusatory. "I've come too far to quit now."

"Well then, what are we going to do?" Sharpe asked.

Player turned to Jaye. "Do you really know this boat?"

"Sure. We took it to the islands a few times when I still lived with my mom."

"Do you know it inside out? How to navigate and handle it? Everything?"

"Well, I know most of it."

Player considered for a moment and decided she was telling the truth.

"But what does that have to do with anything?" she began. "We can't use it."

"Oh yes we can."

"How?"

"We're going to steal it."

Chapter 17

Player's first idea was to try pure trickery. He told them his scheme while they had drinks in the Holiday Inn lounge at midnight. He would call the marina and pose as Jaye's stepfather, then tell the guards she was coming down to the docks and that she had his permission to take the boat out, but Jaye killed the idea immediately. She said it wouldn't work because the marina required owners to sign out their boats to obtain the set of spare keys which the guards kept in the security office.

Neither Player nor Sharpe could go to the marina and fake it, because the guards checked I.D.'s and compared the sign-out to the owner's real signature on file.

Every plan they came up with as they sat around the table had a similar flaw. It either wouldn't get them past marina security or the theft might eventually lead the police to Jaye. "I'm doing this to get rich, not to become a fugitive," she said. So they had to figure out a way to do it that would not make her an obvious suspect.

Player questioned her for an hour to learn everything she could remember about the marina. Since he'd only seen parts of it from the water, he listened closely to her description of the place and finally concluded they couldn't get the boat out the direct way--by simply gliding up to it from the canal and taking off--because the guards checked every exiting boat against their tenant lists and sign-out sheets. Player also doubted many boats were stolen directly from the big marina because even if you could make it past the guards and get a boat out of there, getting away was a different matter. The Coast Guard could easily bottle you up at the mouth of the canal after a quick call from marina security, which probably explained why the boats were relatively unprotected from the water. Finally he concluded they would never be able to get the boat out during daylight hours. Somehow they'd have to steal it at night and they'd have to go in through the front door to do it, because they needed to detain the guard somehow. Once they were past him, they could get the keys from the security office before they went for the boat itself.

"Couldn't we just hot-wire the boat?" Sharpe wanted to know. "Then we wouldn't need the keys and it would be a lot easier to steal."

"Sure," Jaye replied, "But none of us know how to wire a car, much less a boat."

"And we don't have time to track down a hot-wire artist to teach us," Player said. "Besides, we'd be clumsy at it and the time it would take to do it increases our risk of being caught."Player thought about the problem most of the night since he couldn't sleep anyway, and the next day he spent several hours hanging around the marina and studying the layout of the place. He had them drop him off in the rented speedboat and he walked the docks, going from boat to boat introducing himself as a new slip-holder so he could ask questions without being suspicious.

Later on, he spent some time on a couple of boats by pitching in and helping deckhands with odd jobs while he watched the security guards make their rounds. That gave him a chance to find out that a guard walked the docks all day to keep kids and outsiders from messing with the unoccupied boats, which confirmed his thinking that it had to be a night job. He found out from the deckhands that there was only one guard on duty at night who signed people in and out through the office at the main gate, and after midnight of course, the guard slept most of the time.

That night the three of them talked it over and decided if they could somehow keep the night guard from calling the Coast Guard immediately they would probably have enough time to get out to sea. They also had to get into the office where the keys were kept, which meant they had to get the guard away from the office first thing. They kept talking about it until they thought of a way to manage the guard, but that was about as far as the plan went and they left it at that.

They agreed to do it two nights later on Tuesday when there would be less people around the marina, but Monday morning turned out to be gray and rainy, a rare summer day in south Florida. When the clouds didn't burn off by mid-afternoon, Player decided they'd better not waste their good luck. He convinced the others they should take advantage of the weather and go that night.

They sat around his room at the Holiday Inn all day and didn't say much. Jaye kept the television moving from channel to channel, soap operas to game shows and back, but no one paid much attention. She packed and repacked the one nylon weekend bag they agreed to take, but no matter how she packed it, it held only a few extra clothes for each of them, their passports and wallets.

Player had them rehearse their respective jobs several times but there really wasn't much point. They already knew what they were supposed to do and it wasn't much of a plan anyway. There hadn't been enough time to devise one that gave Player much comfort because they had to be in Bimini by Thursday at the latest. Player was forced to accept the fact that he couldn't do much to control this stage of the operation; too many things were uncertain and he had to accept the risk, like it or not. What they were doing was illegal and the act carried an inherent set of problems that couldn't be eliminated.

In his mind, he knew they were attempting a wildly dangerous feat. They'd need luck and more to pull it off, but he couldn't do anything else to improve their chances now. If they didn't try to steal the boat, their only alternative was to admit defeat and go back home to Atlanta. But Player had told himself he would never accept defeat again, so now there was nothing left to do but go forward and become a criminal.

Chapter 18

That night they paid the hotel bill in cash and killed time in a doughnut shop until two o'clock. Then they had a taxi drop them off a few blocks from the marina and they walked the rest of the way along a street that was lined with boat businesses and charter services. Everything in sight was locked shut.

When they reached the marina parking lot, they hid between parked cars near the street and watched the main building for a few minutes. It was a blue metal structure that sat up on piers. On one corner beside the entry gate, the security office had an unobstructed view of the boatyard and most of the parking lot. Dark and almost empty, the lot contained only a dozen or so cars scattered about. Everything looked pale purple beneath three florescent pole lights that hummed overhead like machines. Insects zigzagged aimlessly near the bright glass.

There was no movement going on around the building or beyond the chain link fence that separated the parking lot from the docks. Player took a good look at the fence and he knew it would be tough to climb. It ran from each side of the building and formed a giant semi-circle around the entire boatyard all the way down to the water, enclosing four acres of dry storage as well as a few smaller buildings.

Satisfied that nobody was moving around inside the fence, he tapped Jaye on the shoulder and tilted his head toward the main gate. She squeezed his hand, nodded, and moved off toward the left side of the building.

Before he left, Player turned to give Sharpe a last word of encouragement. In the pale light, shiny droplets of sweat fell from Sharpe's face and his eyes darted about unsteadily.

"Are you ready?" Player asked.

"Get out of here."

"Can you do this?"

"Go on, I said."

Player wasn't certain Sharpe could handle it alone, but there was no choice. He slapped his old friend on the back and started across the parking lot. When he reached the building he worked his way to one end of the corrugated metal wall that was blind to the guard house and turned the corner of the building to face the fence.

It was ten feet high and topped with three strands of barbed wire. Waiting would only make it worse, so he reached above his head and jumped, caught the chain link with his fingers. They started hurting instantly as the small gauge wire cut into his skin, but he pulled himself up anyway, using his toes as much as he could but the links were so small he couldn't really get his running shoes very far into them. Still, he scrambled and clawed his way upward and by the time he reached the first strand of barbed wire his fingers were bleeding around the nails. It took all his strength to haul himself up to the top and swing a foot onto the upper edge of the pipe that secured the mesh at the top, which relieved much of the pressure on his hands.

He breathed for a moment and straightened his fingers to get some of the ache out of them before he worked his other foot up, then he held on to the top strand of barbed wire and managed to get both of his feet up on the pipe. His legs quivered as he strained to keep his balance for a moment, squatting precariously on top of the mesh, hanging onto the top strand with his left hand. There was no way to get over the wire now without getting cut. He swung one leg over the top strand and felt a barb penetrate his calf, then he got the other leg up and threw the rest of his body onto the top strand. Two barbs cut into his stomach and he almost yelled out before he managed to shift his weight and get a moment of relief.

He worked his legs over to the other side of the fence and got a toe hold to free his torso from the top wire. A half minute of squirming got him completely over, but he gashed his stomach again and the strength was almost gone from his fingers. They trembled now and he couldn't hold on any longer. He started to fall and barely slowed the drop by grabbing at the chain-link with his hands. When he hit the pavement on the other side his weight came down on his left ankle and pain shot through it so intensely he was afraid he might have broken it.

He lay still for a moment to catch his breath as his legs and arms shook from the effort. His ankle hurt like hell but he was able to move it and it still worked okay, so he sat up. He looked back through the fence at the parking lot. Now that he was inside, the next step was up to Sharpe. He raised a hand and waved at the dark lot to signal Sharpe to start the diversion.

He watched as Sharpe opened the door of an old car with a frosty, salt air finish. Kneeling on the pavement behind the door, he took a roll of duct tape from his pocket and tore off a strip about a foot and a half long. He opened the door wider and took a look inside.

They had been lucky to find a car unlocked so they didn't have to break into one, then discovered they'd been lucky in two ways because the car had two of those raised buttons on the steering wheel yolk. They were positioned for the driver's thumbs to blow the horn, which made it easier. He watched Sharpe reach in and tape one of the buttons down tight against the yolk. The sound of the horn was piercing in the still night air. Sharpe locked the car and got away from it quickly.

The horn sounded too loud to Player. All they wanted to do was attract the guard, but the noise was so loud it might wake up somebody who lived nearby or even draw the police by chance. He got to his feet and found that his legs were still wobbly, but he could walk. He went over to the wall of the building, crept along it until he got to the back corner where he eased his head out carefully to look around the building.

Beyond a few piles of junk, he saw the security office sticking out from the backside of the building with three of its walls exposed to the boatyard. Each wall had a plate glass window to allow a good view of the docks. Inside the window, Player saw the guard sitting behind a desk, his chair tilted as far back as it could go. Incredibly, the man was asleep, and his head lay sideways on his shoulder.

How could anyone sleep with that horn going off? A small television set flickered on the desk a few inches from the guard's propped-up feet. But a half second later, the guard twitched. He took his feet off the desk and sat up straight, tilted his head to listen, then reached for the television and the flickering stopped. Now he heard it for sure. He got up and opened the door, stopped, then came back to put on his hat and holster. He bent over and flipped a switch, but Player couldn't see what it was.

The guard locked the door and headed for the far end of the building where Player lost sight of him almost immediately. It looked as if the guard was going around to the entry gate, so everything was working according to plan.

Now Player had to move fast.

His job was to get to the boat and have it untied and ready to shove off when Jaye and Sharpe arrived with the keys. The marina was immense and Player wasn't sure exactly how to find the boat in the darkness, but he knew the general direction. Off to his left were the docks for the big houseboats and yachts that were occupied most of the time. That area was fenced off and lay hundreds of yards from the dock he wanted to find, so he turned to his right and headed toward the water at a careful run, dodging piles of rusting engines and boatyard junk as he went.

Chapter 19

From his hiding place behind a truck, Sharpe watched every move the guard made. This is just great, he thought. How sweet. Mitchell Sharpe gets shot in the parking lot of a marina by a worn out old guard. Why didn't Player do this part of the job? This is the most dangerous thing, and he's supposed to be the brawn of the partnership.

At the main gate, the guard flicked on his flashlight and played it around the fence before he advanced, one hand at the radio on his belt. He continued forward slowly, pointing the light farther out and making wider sweeps with it on every step. To Sharpe, the fat old fart looked relieved to see the area was empty.

The guard unhooked a ring of keys from his belt and unlocked the gate; he stepped outside the fence and looked around the lot very deliberately. Taking a few steps, he swung the light back and forth across the parked cars, finally held it on an old faded car at the far end of the lot. He put another foot forward and apparently decided to check it out, but before he went any farther, he slipped the holster loop off the hammer of his revolver.

When he reached the first parked car, he played the flashlight beam across its fenders and hood.

"Nobody's going to jump me from behind," the guard said loudly. "No, sir, not if I can help it." He shined the light at every dark spot within range. "But it can damn well happen in this town if you're not careful." He rapped the flashlight sharply on a fender. "Them Haitians are everywhere now."

From his hiding place, Sharpe watched the guard work his

way across the lot and as the footsteps came closer, he felt his heart inside his chest raging louder and faster until he thought it was out of control. The old guy actually had his gun out now. Sharpe hadn't counted on that. Why had he let Player talk him into this? This is the last time, he thought, the last time I'm going carry the freight on this job. From now on, Player can do the heavy lifting. The guard was supposed to leave the gate open and come out far enough for Jaye to slip past him and get inside the yard, but now this old cop-for-hire was just twenty yards away, checking every speck of dust on every junker in the lot.

Something moved at the edge of Sharpe's field of vision and he looked sideways just in time to see Jaye dart from her hiding place behind a dumpster and run through the open gate. At least she was inside now, but Sharpe felt he was still in trouble. There hadn't been enough time for him to get closer to the gate and now he had to crawl beneath a muddy pickup to hide, afraid to move a muscle because this dumb ass would likely shoot him on sight. He could tell by the cautious way the guard moved, always pointing the light and the pistol ahead before he went forward.

Sweat ran into Sharpe's eyes and blurred his vision, but he couldn't reach his face to wipe it away. Space was too tight under the mud-caked frame to move. He couldn't even take a deep breath because his chest was wedged so tightly against the underside of the truck, his heart squeezed so much the wild beating of it seemed impossible.

Sharpe had no idea what to do. All he could think was that the plan wasn't working and he was about to get shot. There was no way he could get past the guard. No way, he thought. I'm dead. He watched the old guy move closer to the faded car and he could see the grey uniform pants and black shoes moving slowly past the tires and fender of his hiding place. The flashlight swung sideways and its beam raked the pavement near the truck. Sharpe closed his eyes and held his breath, hoping something would happen to save him.

Chapter 20

When Jaye got inside the fence, she ran around to the back of the main building to the security office to get the keys, but when she tried the knob the door was locked. She yanked on the knob several times, but it wouldn't budge, then she looked inside and saw hundreds of keys hanging from brass hooks on a large pegboard. They were labeled and ordered by slip number and name, and automatically her eyes zipped along the rows until she saw the hook labeled Slip 58 with the keys dangling there just out of reach.

She pulled on the door again but it was pointless. The lock was too strong. In frustration, she banged the window with her fist. The glass shook and made a vibrating sound, which gave her the idea to look for something to break the window. Nothing was in reach, but she saw a barrel standing against the building filled with scraps of metal, trim, and deck railing. She ran to the barrel and grabbed the first piece of metal her hand touched and carried it back to the office.

It was a heavy pipe and she swung it like a baseball bat at the glass and the window shattered easily, throwing broken glass all over the interior of the office. A burglar alarm began to shriek in high, pained notes. Jaye's heart felt as if it would pop as she reached through the broken window, unlocked the door and went into the office. After she snatched the keys off the board, she stopped and looked around the room at the broken glass, and seeing the mess, she felt some of the same release Player had told her he felt when he smashed up Les' Place. Now she understood the feeling he had described to her and she threw her hands up and started to laugh. She couldn't help herself. She knew she should be running for the boat, but she couldn't help it. She just stood there and laughed hysterically.

Chapter 21

As soon as the guard heard the window crash, he whirled back toward the building. An instant later the sound of the alarm got him moving and he started to jog for the gate. This old coot hasn't run for years, Sharpe thought. All he can think about is losing his job, so he's not looking down at where he's going, he's looking at the gate.

Sharpe didn't know what prompted him to action. He certainly didn't anticipate the opportunity, but somewhere in his brain something sent a message to his leg and out it went. His foot hooked the guard's ankle and threw the old guy forward onto the parking lot. The guard hit hard as his flashlight and revolver clattered across the pavement.

Sharpe got out from under the truck fast, and when the guard tried to get up, Sharpe's inner brain did the thinking for him. He took a couple of steps and swung at the back of the old man's neck and felt it give beneath his fist. Sharpe had not hit anyone since he was a kid, and it made his hand hurt like someone had slammed it in a door.

The guard went down and didn't move.

Hey, that was almost fun, he thought, as he tried to shake the stinging pain from his hand. Wonder if he's really hurt. He still wasn't moving. Well, tough shit. Sharpe grabbed the man's revolver and backed away, watching the motionless body for a moment, then he turned and ran for the gate. Once he got inside the fence he started toward the back of the building and was almost there when he remembered what else he was supposed to do. He stopped and pulled a combination lock from his pocket and started to go back and snap it on the gate according to the plan, but somehow he couldn't make himself turn around. Even with the guard down and unarmed, his fear wouldn't let him go back.

He threw the lock into a clump of weeds then threw the gun away too. That's evidence you don't want to be caught carrying, he told himself. Then this becomes a crime committed with a gun, which in some cases could get you more jail time than murder.

He ran around the corner of the building and saw Jaye in the security office. She was in the middle of the tiny room flipping manila file folders into the air and laughing hysterically. She had ripped the place apart, and scattered papers and keys lay all around her. She was holding a piece of pipe in her right hand, the boat keys in her left.

Sharpe was shaking so much he could hardly talk.

"Jaye!"

She took one look at him and screamed louder with laughter, but that only confused him more until she held up the set of boat keys. Something told him to run. He grabbed her by the arm and got her out of the office and they started moving toward the water, but he didn't know which way to go. He wanted to ask her where to run but he couldn't speak, and apparently she couldn't have answered in her current state anyway. So he took her by the arm and they ran out onto the docks without knowing where to go.

Chapter 22

Player was on the docks looking for the boat when he heard the window crash back at the building. He started to run since there was no need for stealth now. He knew the general direction he should take and he turned onto a big dock stretching out toward the canal. He ran about two hundred yards then stopped abruptly when he heard a sound come out of the darkness ahead. It sounded like a growl. He froze and listened then saw a Doberman move into the light about thirty feet away, its nose wrinkled back, its teeth exposed.

Where had that thing come from? He hadn't seen it when he scouted the marina the day before. Of course not, he realized; they only turn the dog out at night on the fenced-in docks where no one lives on the boats.

It didn't matter anyway. There was no time for anything to matter except escape. The dog started toward him and Player had no time to think, no time to consider anything. He saw the dog's muscles tense as it crouched to attack, so he turned around to run. He hadn't gone three steps before he heard the dog coming at him, its pads scratching on the wooden planks. It made a terrifying sound as it sprang through the air at his back, the growl changing pitch as it leaped.

Player ducked instinctively which caused the dog to fly over his head, its feet scrabbling for a hold, tearing scratches across his scalp. It glanced off his shoulder and fell onto the dock in front of him. As the big dog tumbled across the planks, Player had a moment to turn and run again, this time back toward the canal.

He'd gone maybe five yards when he heard the growl behind

him again, then a change in volume as the dog leaped once more. Player reacted on instinct, whirling and swinging all in one motion. His fist caught the Doberman in the neck and the blow hurt the dog, but it wasn't enough to take it out. Its head twisted on impact and caught Player's wrist in its teeth.

Player stumbled backward trying to yank his hand free and he felt the dog's teeth tearing against the tendons and bones in his arm. He realized the dog would kill him in a matter of minutes if he didn't shake it loose somehow. Soon it would wear him down and go for his throat. To his surprise, Player didn't feel pain because he was surging with energy and his mind had terrific clarity even though everything was happening at light speed. Somehow it occurred to him that he had only one chance. He threw himself off the dock into the water, dragging the dog in with him.

When he went under he lost all sense of direction. The water was black and he couldn't see a thing, but he knew that it might save him if he could hold his breath long enough and keep the dog down with him. The dog went crazy in the blindness underwater. As soon as it realized the world had gone wrong it released Player's wrist and fought for the surface, but Player got it by a hind leg and held on and the dog turned and bit his hand viciously, but Player grabbed another leg and pulled hard to hold the dog down. The dog tore at his hands and struggled to get free, but Player could feel it choking because it didn't know how to keep water out of its lungs and fight at the same time.

When the dog quit kicking, Player was completely disoriented. He let go and swam for what he thought was the surface, but after a few feet he ran into a dock piling and almost knocked himself senseless. He slowed down and tried to get his bearings. He wasn't thinking clearly anymore with the pressure of carbon dioxide building in his lungs. But he knew enough to follow the wooden piling with his hands so he felt his way along and thought he was going up, but his hand struck something soft and he realized it was sand. He'd gone to the bottom and that was bad because his lungs were about to give way.

He managed to get his feet underneath himself and he pushed off against the bottom. He knew the right way now and he kicked up through the blackness, but it seemed to take forever and then he felt his lungs go; the air came exploding out of his mouth and he thought he wasn't going to make it, but then his head popped out of the water and he saw lights and he could breathe again, and he felt elated.

By the time he found a ladder and climbed back onto the dock, he was feeling weak and the saltwater was stinging the gashes on his wrists and arms. He managed to stand up and stumble forward, his mind locked onto the idea of reaching the boat.

He didn't hear Jaye and Sharpe until they were almost on top of him. They came running up and Jaye threw her arms around him and Sharpe was yelling something in his ear. Player looked at Jaye and saw tears streaming down her cheeks. She looked at the blood on him and reached to touch the cuts on his arms and face. Sharpe was babbling something about having killed somebody.

Player ignored their rants and kept moving down the dock and they followed. When they got to the boat Player began to undo lines, but Jaye and Sharpe couldn't seem to do anything but talk nonsense, with Sharpe asking why the lines weren't free already and Jaye telling him to get on board.

Player realized he had to take control and he pushed Jaye up toward the control station.

"Start it, Jaye."

"But I can't--"

"Go start the engine. Now."

Sharpe wouldn't shut up, but Player shoved him onto a side deck anyway and pointed to the front of the boat.

"Go up there and get those lines off."

Sharpe did as he was told and Player turned back to undo a stern line, but there was so little strength left in his fingers he could barely handle the knot. He was still working on it when he heard a siren rising and falling in the distance. The guard must have called for help.

"Hurry, Jaye!"

"I'm trying, but I can't--"

Player looked up at the fly bridge and saw that she was shaking so badly she couldn't get the key into the ignition. He climbed up and helped her, and when they got the key in and tried it the twin engines started immediately, coughing a bit at first but quickly settling to a low rumble.

"Oh, what a boat this is," Player said thankfully. He leaned out and looked forward."Sharpe, what about those lines?"

"Wait. Yes, now they're clear."

"Now Jaye, go," Player said.

She eased the *Fey Lady* out into the channel, taking it slow because there was so little room between the slips.

"Faster," Player said. "We have to get out of here."

He looked back down the line of boats and saw a light flashing dimly on the tops of the palm trees beyond the marina. The siren added its volume to that of the burglar alarm and the car horn, and it occurred to Player that he hadn't heard all that noise for the last few minutes, but now he realized how loud it was. Everybody in the world would be after them before long.

Jaye steered the boat into a wider passageway and it was now a straight shot to the canal and then to the Atlantic. She pushed the throttle forward and the boat picked up a little speed, and then they saw a chain link gate barring their way to the canal. In all the excitement Player had forgotten it was there. He reached past Jaye and shoved the throttle as far forward as it would go and the engines roared deep inside the hull.

"Jack, don't!"

The *Fey Lady* settled deeper into the water for a moment, then the long foredeck tilted upward and the boat lunged down the passageway.

"We've got to crash it."

"Not at this speed," she screamed.

"No choice," Player shouted back.

Player kept his hand on the throttle to prevent her from easing it back and the boat was still gaining speed when it hit the gate.

They heard a metallic tearing sound and the boat shuddered slightly as the gate flew off its hinges and disappeared out in the darkness.

Sharpe climbed onto the fly bridge with them and shouted something, but the roar of the engines was so loud, Player couldn't understand what he was trying to say until he saw Sharpe pointing behind them.

Player looked back and saw the marina ablaze with lights. A tiny figure ran to the end of a dock, dropped to one knee and fired a pistol at them. One, two, three shots popped from his extended arm like a flash on a camera, but he was too far away and they didn't even bother to duck.

The boat was leaping now and their wake blasted off the walls of the canal, leaving small boats and docks bucking wildly behind them. In less than four minutes they shot out the mouth of the canal into open water and they ran at top speed toward the faint, low clouds out on the ocean.

It was such a dark night, there were very few boats out and they didn't see any lights beyond the first couple of miles. After twenty minutes of running at high speed due east, Player motioned Jaye to cut back on the throttle and turn south. They looked at each other, grinning, and for a moment the hysteria and danger back at the marina was forgotten. The wind tore at their hair and the warm sea air was a balm to their frazzled nerves. It felt wonderfully free up there on the bridge and for a while the entire episode seemed like an adventure, and they forgot who they really were and the reality of what they had done and what they were about to do.

Chapter 23

Their run due east had put them in the Gulf Stream and after they turned south it was slow going against the mighty seaborne river that rushed out of the Caribbean and tracked up the Florida peninsula. Jaye wanted to head closer to the coast so they wouldn't have to plow directly into the current, but Player told her to hold the course. If the Coast Guard was chasing them, he didn't want to take an obvious route.

Player left her alone at the wheel and went below to clean himself up. In the galley he found a first-aid kit and poured hydrogen peroxide on the bite wounds and covered them with band-aids. He wrapped gauze around his wrists to cover the worst gashes. As far as he could tell, the dog hadn't broken any bones or ripped any ligaments loose so he didn't think there was any lasting damage. He'd been lucky and he knew it, because a serious injury would have made the days ahead a lot tougher.

When he finished bandaging himself, he put the kit away and went searching for Sharpe and found him stretched across a bed with a pillow over his face. A half-empty bottle of bourbon sat on the nightstand next to the bed. Player sat down, took a small drink and spoke to the pillow covering Sharpe's face.

"I see you beat me to the bar."

Sharpe didn't answer.

"Did you really kill the guard?"

"I don't know for sure."

"What happened?"

"I hit him on the back of the neck."

"With what?"

"My fist."

Player almost laughed out loud with relief, but he managed to smother the reaction. Only Sharpe could imagine himself killing a man with a single punch. Sharpe was a lot of things, but tough wasn't one of them.

"You couldn't kill a grown man with a machete. What makes you think you could do it with your fist?"

Sharpe looked out from under the pillow. "He was an old guy."

"Why do you think he was dead?"

"He didn't get up."

"So you stunned him, knocked him out. That doesn't mean you killed him."

Sharpe took the pillow away and sat up, looking a bit relieved, but his voice still sounded worried. "If he's dead and we get caught on this boat for any reason, they'll trace it straight to us. That's manslaughter, or worse, and you'll be an accessory."

Player took another swig from the bottle on the nightstand. "I don't think you killed him. He's the only one who could've got out on the dock fast enough to take a shot at us, so don't worry about it."

"Maybe you're right," Sharpe said. "Maybe that was him who fired at us."

"Well, nobody else could've gotten inside the fence so fast. He must have had keys to some other gate, because you relocked the front one, right?"

Sharpe drew back from him and fell back on the bed and put the pillow over his eyes again. "All I know is, I did my part and I'm the one who almost got shot back there."

Player was far more concerned about the flashing lights he'd seen over the marina, because those lights meant that it was just as likely a guard from a backup unit, or even a cop, shot at them, not the night watchman.

He sat on the bed a moment longer, wondering if Sharpe really had killed the guard. He doubted it, but then he had to ask himself if that was just because he didn't want to believe it.

It occurred to him that he didn't want to accept the possibility the guard might be dead, because he didn't want to admit their adventure had already become deadly serious, perhaps even turned into murder. Stealing a boat was one thing, but murder was something else entirely, something only terrible people did, not people like himself and Sharpe and Jaye. After all, they were just out to make a buck, weren't they? It wasn't the same kind of thing those terrible people did; this was just a once-in-a-lifetime run by everyday guys who'd never had a shot at anything big. Didn't all that make it different?

Despite what he'd said to both of them at the beginning, he had never believed they would have to kill people to pull the job off, and he hoped he was right, because no matter how desperate his life had become, he hoped that he'd not fallen so far as to kill another human being over money.

He left Sharpe in the stateroom and went back up top to check on Jaye, and when he saw her standing up there on the fly bridge it was apparent the skirmish hadn't affected her as it had Sharpe, or himself, for that matter. Sharpe had turned morose, and he himself was doubting the entire job before they'd even left the Florida coast, wondering if they were doing something they'd regret forever, but Jaye seemed energized by the whole thing and more alive than ever. He could see it on her face at a glance. To him, she looked very young and vital when he saw her standing up there leaning into the wheel.

She turned and smiled at him and it was the same smile she'd used that first time he looked at her in Les' Place, and it felt wonderful to have her smiling at him that way again. Her tee shirt was popping in the wind and he watched it stand against her body, conform to her shape, then ripple and stand again.

He went to her side and they looked at each other for a moment, and he thought about that way she had of making him feel better just by giving him an affirmative smile. He didn't know how she did it, but he was glad she was doing it now.

"You were something back there," she said. "You really were. You got us out of there when I was nearly hysterical and Mitch was petrified."

He squatted out of the wind and lit a couple of Marlboros and passed one to her. Even though the fly bridge was dark, he could see the excitement still crackling in her eyes. She seemed to get a charge from the danger of what they'd done.

"What was that crazy laughing about?" he asked.

She threw her head back and her hair unfurled in the wind. "I don't know for sure. I've never felt anything like it."

"Thrilling, huh?"

"Yeah, and scary. But it felt good," she said.

"I think I know what you mean."

"It was the same way you felt when you broke Les' finger and smashed up the bar, wasn't it?"

"Yeah. But that didn't feel good for long."

She didn't seem to hear that.

"It's a feeling of total release," she said. "It's letting your emotions run wild until you don't care what happens."

Player turned away and looked across the water, wondering if she was right. Maybe it was that simple, that primitive.

"I think it's the same thing that must happen to people when they go to war," she said. "What do you think?"

"I don't know."

"You didn't go to Vietnam?"

"No, I missed it."

"Seeing the way you are sometimes, I would have thought you went to 'Nam," she said.

"Why? I seem violent?"

"Well, volatile anyway."

Player lit another cigarette. He felt heavy with self examination.

"I've always had a temper, but I hate to fight," he said. "It doesn't feel good afterward."

"I don't believe that. Temper doesn't entirely explain the anger that's inside you. I think you're seeking violence in a way."

"Maybe. No. I don't know."

"Why didn't you go to Vietnam? You're the right age."

"I joined a reserve unit instead."

"And, let me guess," she said. "That was the first time in your life you backed away from anything."

"I didn't back away," he said, resenting her remark. "It was a stupid war. Nobody in their right mind went over there unless they had to go."

"I know that," she said.

"People forget what it was like then."

"I remember. I was really young, but I remember."

"I'd do the same thing again."

"And feel the same regret all over again?" she asked. "The same guilt?"

Player leaned against the rail and was silent for a few minutes. He'd never thought of it that way before; that he was experiencing some sort of generational guilt; that no matter how sensible his decision to avoid the war had been, it nevertheless was the first of several acts of withdrawal that had made his life so directionless for the past fifteen years.

"I'm not saying you were wrong, Jack. I'd have done the same thing. No reason to get yourself killed over there."

"Maybe not going to war messed me up as much as going would have," he said. "After that, it was easy to duck tough decisions. Easy to coast along at Les' Place. Easy to sit back and do drugs to pass the time."

"You're not the only one," she said. "Those years did that to a lot of people."

"That's no excuse. I managed to screw things up all by myself."

He felt his mood falling and didn't know what to say. He sensed that she didn't like it when he fell into that brooding mood, and it was so hard to open himself up he might not get another chance to tell her how he really felt about anything.

She set the auto pilot and took the pack of Marlboros from his shirt pocket and lit another one. She leaned against the rail next to him, smoking, waiting, but when he didn't say anything, she spoke up again.

"Mitch says you were different in college."

He shrugged.

"Tell me about it," she persisted. "He said you were really something, then."

Player didn't want to talk about it, but then almost without effort, he found himself sharing his thoughts with her. "All my life I was good at everything," he said. "School. Popularity. Everything. It never occurred to me that I could fail, because it all came so easy. Then, suddenly I was out of school, a working adult, and one day my wife got tired of three room apartments and walked out. I realized I'd been pouring drinks for ten years."

"That's not so bad. You're still young."

"Not so bad?" Player was incredulous. "I could have been anything I wanted."

"But you couldn't decide what you wanted?"

"Something like that."

"And all that time, Mitch kept moving ahead."

"Yeah."

"While you stood still."

"Yeah."

"And now you've decided to do this run to make up for lost time."

"Yeah."

Something in her voice made Player turn and look at her. She threw the cigarette away and a wisp of smoke trailed from her lips. Then she reached out and put the palms of her hands on his chest.

"You can start with me," she said.

Player was surprised. He hadn't thought she would make the first move, and now that she had, he was uncomfortable with it. It wasn't that he didn't want it to happen; he did, but something in her frontal approach didn't feel right. It somehow diminished the moment. He'd had so many women give themselves easily to him over the years, he didn't want it that way anymore. For him, it reduced the experience of uncovering another person who might be important. He needed that moment of heady discovery, that sense of exhilaration, but now, she of all women was doing something that didn't suit her, or at least didn't match the way he saw her in his mind.

"No," he said, trying to step back.

"Oh, but yes." Her hands went inside his shirt and he felt her fingernails slide along his ribs, then around to the trough of muscle along his spine. Her lips were very close to him now, brushing lightly against his chest.

Player felt a tightening inside and knew then he couldn't stop what was about to happen. Maybe this wasn't perfect; the way he'd hoped it might be with her, but she was simply too desirable to resist. Even as he was still trying to say no, his face tilted down and her mouth opened automatically, and he kissed her very gently on her open lips and knew instantly he was lost in her.

She didn't try to impress him with technique or fervor; she simply yielded her body to him. He felt the length of her softness press in against him and there was such assurance behind the contact it erased his doubts. She had the unfailing confidence of beauty and it was dazzling to him. She was a woman who could have any man, but she wanted him, and she communicated that she wanted him without saying a word. Her assurance was absolute that she could have him, because she knew he wanted her and now he could have her. He'd felt that sensation only a few times in his life and only with truly beautiful women, and now that he knew she was able to give him that feeling, he was lost in her.

The salon door down in the cockpit banged and the sound tore into his thoughts like an alarm. He pushed himself away from her and tried to shake away the numbness he felt in his limbs. He stepped back and found that it was hard to do because she was boring into him with a direct look that said she didn't care if Sharpe knew or not. In fact, her look challenged him to go ahead and reveal everything to Sharpe.

Player turned to the instrument board and ran his hands through his hair, trying to clear his mind. He hoped there was no giveaway look on his face as he heard Sharpe come up the ladder. It wouldn't be good to get caught like this, looking and feeling guilty, even though he knew there was no reason he should be guilty for having feelings for her. After all, Sharpe was the one who had interfered with them just as things were starting to happen.

"Are you two having a party up here without me?" Sharpe asked, as he climbed onto the fly bridge.

"You better believe it," Jaye answered. There wasn't a trace of unsteadiness in her voice.

She did it so well, Player couldn't help but turn his head and look at her to see if the control on her face matched that in her voice. She walked straight over to Sharpe and threw her arms around his neck as if they'd been together for years. She was so cool about it, no one would've ever suspected anything.

"I tried to seduce Player while you were below," she said in a teasing voice, "But he wouldn't have anything to do with me."

"That's sweet," Sharpe said, sounding drunk and playful, the way he usually sounded at Les' Place. "That's really sweet."

"And why is that?" Jaye purred.

Sharpe laughed loudly, slapped her on the rear and then pulled her close. "It'd be a damn shame to have to fight my oldest buddy for you, now wouldn't it?"

Chapter 24

None of them slept much that night because the excitement of the escape had left them feeling wired, so they mostly hung around on the fly bridge talking aimlessly even though there were plenty of things that needed to be done. But once they sighted the lights of Bimini off to the left, Player said they should make use of their time until daybreak, so he asked Jaye to walk them over the entire boat for a training session.

She covered the decks, the machinery, even the cabins, as she told them everything she knew about the operation of the *Fey Lady*. It made her feel that she was somehow making up for her earlier lies about being able to get the boat from her family. When they worked their way back up to the fly bridge, she started to go over the instruments to show them how the electronics and automatic controls worked. Player said he was pleased that she knew the boat as well as she'd claimed, because it gave him reassurance that he'd get some relief at the wheel during the next two weeks. He had said all along that Sharpe wouldn't be much help on the boat, and so far Sharpe was proving him right.

When she showed them how the autopilot worked, Player understood it immediately, but Sharpe couldn't get it straight so she showed him again step by step, then after a third time he still didn't follow her so she decided to try something else. She turned to the Loran navigator and showed them how it worked and again saw the incomprehension on Sharpe's face. By then, they all knew he was never going to understand the instruments.

She grinned at Sharpe and asked him half-seriously, "How did you ever make it through law school?"

"He cheated," Player said, laughing.

When Sharpe glared at him, it occurred to her that Player had struck a nerve. Maybe he hadn't been kidding at all.

Sometimes she wasn't sure whether they were joking or giving each other real trouble in that sarcastic way they had. Occasionally, she'd catch a glimpse of them and know they were speaking to each other beneath the words on the surface. No one else would know what they were actually communicating with those insults and petty arguments because nothing was said outright, but she was getting to the point now where she could tell at times when they were doing it. She concluded they had learned long ago not to let people see how close they were, that their communication was that subtle. They would not want others to know that they were in many ways a mirror image of each other.

"I don't need to know this stuff anyway," Sharpe grumbled. "All you gotta do is steer the wheel like a car."

"It's okay, Mitch," she said, patting him on the back. "Jack and I will handle the boat."

"I'm just not mechanical," he said.

"Or practical," Player added, again drawing a glare from Sharpe.

Jaye continued her demonstration until she'd covered the entire instrument board, and when she was finished, she felt sure Jack could handle the boat with ease. The *Fey Lady* was just a bigger version of the boat he'd used those summers at Hilton Head, he told her. In fact, it was easier to handle because it had more electronics than the other boat had. If we don't hit rough weather, she thought, we'll be all right on this boat.

Sharpe stayed with them and listened as they discussed the problems of cruising deep water, but they were ignoring him and she noticed that he began to grow impatient.

Player noticed, too. "Why are you jumpy?" he asked Sharpe. "I haven't seen you so agitated in a long time."

Those anxious minutes back at the marina seemed to have robbed Mitch of his composure. Sharpe interrupted her thoughts to say they ought to quit talking and get on with it, because he was tired of waiting.

Jaye gave him a dubious look. "Go into Bimini at night?"

"Yes, right now."

Jaye shook her head in exasperation. "We've already been over this. South Bimini is not much more than a drug warehouse. The Bombs and Cigarettes come over from Miami every night, pick up their stuff and run it back to Key Biscayne. It'd be nuts to go in there now."

"It's Alvarez's territory," Sharpe insisted. "We'll be all right."

"We don't know whose territory it is," Player said. "We wait until daylight."

Sharpe turned away and started down the ladder but he couldn't resist getting in the last word. "Why don't you two experts make all the decisions from now on, okay?"

Jaye stayed up top with Player and they were quiet for a while as she watched him get the feel of the helm. He kept the bow pointed south into the current to hold their position, using a green beacon on shore as a fix. It wasn't easy to do because the powerful push of the Stream was relentless, a force that moved people and boats according to the whims of the ocean. No matter how much the pilot nursed the engines and the wheel to beat through the current, that force still piled up against the hull, forever pushing it sideways and back, always demonstrating where the superior power resided.

Player remained quiet and she guessed he wanted to think about Sharpe storming off or maybe about the move she'd put on him earlier. It might have been lucky that Sharpe came up and interrupted them when he did, she decided. He was in no state of mind to handle a conflict over her; that was clear. There was no telling what he would do if he got into a wrangle with Player over which one of them could rightfully claim her, a notion that made her giggle inside.

And she figured Player didn't want the distraction of her in his head, not now, no matter how nice it was. When her hands were on him, she sensed there was no room for anything else in his mind; all other thoughts went flying out along with his inhibitions and that wasn't good for his focus on the job. Had he deciphered her true intentions? Something seemed to be bothering him about that forward move of hers. She wondered if she'd overdone it. Had it been too controlled? Had it seemed real or more like transparent manipulation? She had to be careful how she handled the two of them.

"Keep an eye on that marker or the Stream will put us in Freeport by daylight," she said.

"I know how to handle a boat."

"That's obvious, Jack. But you don't know these waters, and I do."

"Meaning, I didn't grow up tooling around the islands on a yacht like you did."

"Damn it," she seethed. "Damn you. I meant no such thing. Just when things are about to start going good between us, you say something really lousy, as if you want to push me away. Have you got something against my family's money, or what? For somebody who is burning to be rich, you sure resent rich people."

"Maybe you do, too. Maybe you resent your rich family so much you used us to get back at them."

"What do you mean?"

"Isn't that why you led us to this boat?"

"No."

"To pay back your parents?"

"What's wrong with you, Jack? A while ago you were kissing me, and now this?"

"What's wrong is that I'm tired of being lied to. Tell me what your parents did to make you want to get back at them so badly."

"My family is none of your business."

He took her by the arm, squeezing until it hurt, forcing her to answer. "Tell me."

She tried to slap him, but he held on tight. She hated to be manhandled like that and hated to relent, too.

"Tell me."

She tried to shake free, but he was much too strong. "They cut me off," she said finally. "How would you feel if you'd been raised with things like this boat and then you were thrown out to wait on tables for a living?"

"I wouldn't know how that feels."

"Then I'll tell you. It stinks."

"Why did they do it?"

"Mom got a divorce from my Dad when I was seventeen and I hated her new husband. He watched me too much, you know? His eyes were on me every time I walked through the house. It got so bad I wouldn't even put on a swimsuit and go into the pool. So I kept running away to be with my Dad. The money was hers and she threatened me with it, but I still ran away. So she cut me off."

"And that's why you steered us to this boat, wasn't it? To get even."

"It was your idea to steal it, Jack."

"Sure, after you engineered it. We had a deadline to meet and no time to look for another boat. You figured one of us would suggest stealing it. You set us up to get back at them, didn't you?"

"No."

"Spoiled little rich girl strikes back," he said, taunting her and shaking her arm.

"Okay," she admitted in a high voice. "Maybe that was part of it."

"I want to know all of it."

"That is all of it."

"How can I be sure? You lied to me before."

"But I'm not lying now."

"No?"

"No!"

She struck out with her free hand and caught him on the chest. Then she hit him again and kept hitting him on the chest and shoulders and head until the strength was gone from her arms and she couldn't raise them again. Then he let her go and she fell back against the railing, the resistance gone out of her.

"What do you want from me, Jack?"

"The truth. Why are you here?"

She looked up at him expectantly, but his face was hard, doubting.

"You can't figure it out?" she asked.

He looked into her eyes and she allowed her inner self to be unveiled for an instant, to let him see the turmoil inside and the essential human need behind her face. Even though she had certainly manipulated him, there was no mistaking that look on his face when she revealed herself to him. He'd stripped away her defenses, and what did he see there, exposed at the bottom of her, she wondered?

He reached out and touched her face and wiped her tears with his fingers, then he started to stroke her hair, but abruptly something stopped him; somewhere inside, some kernel of doubt must have flared, and he withdrew his hand as if burned.

"You're Sharpe's woman, not mine."

After opening herself to him and letting him see inside her, rejection was the harshest thing he could have done, and her anger peaked again and gave her the strength to lash out at him once more. He didn't try to dodge the slap and her open hand caught him near the mouth and her nails tore the skin of his lower lip. He reached up and dabbed the drops of blood from his tongue. She drew herself up straight to salvage her pride.

"So, you say no to me, just because he made the first move. But get this, Jack, I don't belong to anybody."

She turned and went down the ladder, leaving him alone with the dark ocean.

Chapter 25

Player worked the boat against the current for a half hour, trying to sort out his thoughts, but he couldn't get any clarity of mind. He was pretty sure he was in love with her because of the weakness he felt when she touched him or even brought her body close to him, and now he thought she was in love with him too, but still he couldn't dismiss the warning feeling that came every time he started to give in to her. Maybe it was the job ahead and his subconscious was telling him to keep his thoughts clear. Maybe.

And maybe the barrier was his friendship with Sharpe.

He couldn't ignore the fact that Sharpe was sleeping with her, even though he felt sure it was just a convenient arrangement to Sharpe that didn't mean much. He'd seen Sharpe go through too many women to think anything else. In all the years he'd known the man, he could never remember him being in love. Maybe Sharpe couldn't feel love. He wasn't sure about that, but he was sure that Jaye was no different to Sharpe than any other woman had been. Sharpe would forget about her as soon as the next desirable body came along. So where did that leave Jack Player? Looking in from the outside like a fool, he supposed. Only a fool would stand by and let Sharpe toy with this woman when she might be the one woman in the world who could turn his life around, but Player knew he couldn't betray Sharpe, even if Jaye meant nothing to him. It just wasn't in Player to betray his friend.

He heard laughter down in the salon and the sound made him feel empty and alone. He decided he couldn't endure the next two weeks on this boat unless he somehow managed to calm himself down about her. He set the autopilot and went down the ladder to the cockpit, deciding it was better to face it now before things grew worse.

He opened the door to the salon and found Jaye in Sharpe's lap. They were stretched out in a deep chair, sharing a drink, and Jaye's shirt was riding up her torso. Player could see her tanned waist and the line of a rib beneath her skin. Sharpe's face was hidden in her hair, his voice purring at her ear, drawing out her laughter.

They looked up as Player stepped inside.

"I just came down for a cup of coffee."

Sharpe made one of his sly faces. "The hell you were, Player. You heard a party and you had to check it out."

Player walked past them and went down to the galley where he found a coffee maker on the counter next to the sink. Someone, presumably Jaye's mother, kept it ready to go with a filter and the grounds already in place. He punched the brew button and practically ran back up the steps to the salon.

Sharpe let out a barroom laugh and threw his hand toward Player. "Come on, Player. There's plenty of room for three."

Player forced himself to look straight at them and keep his face from showing anything. Jaye caught his eye for a fraction of a second and her look told him to go to hell in a hundred ways.

"I've got to get back up top," Player said.

"Don't be so standoffish," Jaye taunted. "Mitch will share me for a few minutes."

Sharpe howled. "Damn right, Jaye. Anything for my old buddy."

Player opened the door and saw that the swells out beyond the transom were taking on a gray definition. Despite all his effort at control, a flatness sounded in his voice and almost gave away the desolation he felt inside.

"It's getting light out here," he said. "How about one of you bringing me a cup of coffee when it's ready."

He went out the door and Sharpe called after him, his voice sounding drunk and wasted. "Sure thing, Player. Anything for my old buddy."

Chapter 26

Player felt hot and irritable as they approached the harbor entrance on South Bimini. At nine o'clock in the morning, the sun was already strong and it was so low on the water the glare was intense. He looked back toward the white hot expanse of the open sea and saw flat layers of cloud on the horizon that he knew would mushroom into giant cumulus by early afternoon.

When they were well into the harbor, Player thought they must be in the wrong place. He was expecting a colorful layout of docks like that of any south Florida yacht club, but instead of immaculate white cruisers and sailing yachts, they found a tiny harbor jammed with old sport fishing boats and dirty cargo workhorses that showed rust streaks at the seams.

"Let's see that map again," Player said.

Sharpe unfolded the chart Raoul had given him and spread it out on the instrument panel where they could look at the markings. After a couple of minutes, Player and Jaye agreed this had to be the right spot. There was nothing else that could even be called a harbor on this side of the island.

"This must be it," Player said. "These islands are too small for us to be lost."

They found a space near a diesel pumping station and Player swung the *Fey Lady* into place against a row of old tires nailed to the side of the dock. As they tied the boat down to a couple of salt-frosted cleats, they saw crates and cardboard boxes stacked all around the dock. There was so much cargo that it was hard to see over the stacks in some places. Rough-looking dockhands lolled about, smoking and jabbering at each other in their Bahamian accents. Player thought the place looked more like a third world port than a marina.

"Now you see why straight yachts don't come in here anymore," Jaye said.

"That must be the club," Sharpe said, pointing to a cluster of two story buildings that sat up off the water on a slight rise overlooking the marina. At one time, the blue painted buildings with their tin roofs might have been quaint, but now they just looked run down. Everything looked run down.

"Not much fishing out of here now," Player said.

"Whatever they do over here these days has nothing to do with fishing," Jaye said.

Player reconsidered the plan of her walking out on those docks and into town with all the hard, poor men who must be waiting out there, hoping for any opportunity to take a dollar or to hustle a stranger. He looked at her and said, "I'll go ashore instead of you."

"No, let's do it the way we decided. One of you two should stay with the boat, and they're expecting Mitch, not you."

She stepped up onto the gunwale and stretched her other foot across to the dock. Sharpe followed her and Player watched them start down the dock toward shore.

"Remember, nothing cute," he called out. "Just get the stuff and get back here."

Sharpe nodded without looking back and Jaye turned and threw up a fist, her longest finger extended skyward. He watched them all the way to the end of the dock where they turned to the right, then he lost sight of them as they passed a pair of gas pumps then saw them again as they climbed a set of concrete steps leading up from the water to the buildings overlooking the marina.

Player went below and found a cold Coke, brought it back up top and settled into a fighting chair to wait. About thirty yards away from the *Fey Lady*, a group of dockhands sitting on some crates eyed him as they smoked and talked. He tried to ignore them, but after a few minutes they were still watching, so he stood up and stared at them with equal challenge until they sneered and went back to their card game.

Chapter 27

Jaye and Sharpe walked up a broken sidewalk and reached the cluster of white roofed buildings that housed the few businesses still alive in the harbor. Fading signs for bait, charters, and boat supplies hung in the windows of the first building they saw, but the signs looked old and business seemed slow inside. The people they passed on the sidewalk either gave them a cold stare or ignored them, and after a few encounters of that type, Jaye moved a bit closer to Sharpe's side and gave him an apprehensive glance.

"I suppose we're not dressed for the occasion," she said.

They saw a sign cut in the shape of a marlin hanging over a doorway in the next building, and up close the words, Billfish Club, showed faintly in blue. They went in and found themselves in a dark bar where a few video machines whistled and dinged against the far wall. Another doorway led outside to the remains of a veranda overlooking the water, but it had been a long time since any patrons sat out there and watched boats come in with trophy catches.

The dark men playing video games glanced up at them as they crossed the room. To Jaye, the men looked bored and lazy. One of them gave her a wink and nudged his companion. She looked away from them and saw a black man sitting by himself at a table in the corner, his head bent over a newspaper. She couldn't help but notice his separation from the others. He wasn't leering at her the way the others were, and of course there was his shirt, an unforgettable brilliant yellow.

She moved a step closer to Sharpe and hooked a couple of her fingers through a belt loop on his jeans. They walked over to the bar and stood there waiting while the bartender took his time before he came over and placed his hands flat on the wooden surface in front of them. He was heavy and not inclined to excess effort, and he didn't ask what they wanted; he simply tilted his head toward them, waiting for their order.

"Alvarez sent us," Sharpe said.

The bartender seemed surprised, but he immediately straightened up and answered in a respectful voice. "Wait here."

He disappeared into a back room while Jaye fidgeted next to Sharpe. She could feel the men in the room staring at her and she wished she hadn't worn shorts that were so tight. She leaned close and whispered in Sharpe's ear, "Everybody's acting so creepy in this place, Mitch. You think they know why we're here?"

"If they do, we'll never get back to the boat with it."

The bartender reappeared quickly, walked up to them and spoke quietly. "Around back. The door's unlocked."

Sharpe nodded and they walked back across the room and went through the front door and stepped out into the morning glare. As they turned toward the back of the building, they heard a tremendous engine roar down in the marina. It was the same sound they'd heard back in Lauderdale when the Cigarette blew past them on the Intracoastal, except this time it was much louder. They went around to the side of the building and looked down at the docks and saw four large speedboats slicing through the harbor entrance. The scream of the engines was deafening and the sound brought the men out of the bar and they, too, watched as the wedge-shaped boats streaked into the marina and maneuvered into position against an empty dock where they were quickly surrounded by dockhands. The engines died abruptly and the hands swarmed over the boats before they came to a full stop.

Sharpe gave Jaye a shrug and they went around to the back of the building and found the door. After a moment, they heard the door unlock from the other side, so they pushed it open and went inside where it was dark. Sharpe found a string dangling from the ceiling, pulled it, and a naked bulb clicked on overhead. He closed the door and the bartender stood watching them, and without a word, pointed to a crate in the corner. They went over and looked inside the crate and saw three large army surplus duffel bags.

The bartender looked at Jaye's slim arms. "They're heavy," he said.

"They look it," she agreed. "You think you can handle one by yourself, Mitch?"

She said it so straight the bartender didn't get it or maybe he was too slow. Sharpe didn't laugh either as he reached for one of the bags, and she saw a few lines of annoyance appear on his forehead.

"You're getting to be as funny as Player," he said to her.

"And you, dear Mitch, are losing your cool."

Chapter 28

Player had climbed to the fly bridge when he first heard the roar, and from the high vantage point, he was able to see over the cluttered docks and watch the speed boats as they muscled their way into the marina and tied up, two sections over from the *Fey Lady*.

The speedboats were all dark colored and had that low wedge profile that supposedly made them difficult to spot at sea. The boat in the lead was painted all black except for its name, "Numero Uno," which was painted on the prow in graceful yellow script. What a flashy piece of boat, Player thought. The man at the wheel was dark and muscular, a very tough looking Latin wearing a sleeveless tee shirt. So that's Numero Uno. These guys had no subtlety at all. They flaunted everything. Money. Boats. Muscles. They loved to flash everything.

Player wondered what the Cigarettes were doing, with dockhands scurrying over them in broad daylight. He wondered if business had reached the point on Bimini where drug runners loaded and unloaded right out in the open at a public marina.

He watched the hands, trying to figure it out, when he felt the *Fey Lady* shift slightly beneath his feet. He looked around to port expecting to see Jaye and Sharpe coming aboard, but instead he saw a dockhand with his foot on the gunwale about to jump into the cockpit.

"Hold it, right there," Player said.

He went down the ladder fast, sliding between the handrails and he landed on the deck directly in front of a kid who was maybe twenty, dressed in sandals, tee shirt, and cut-off jeans.

"What do you want?" Player said.

The kid gave Player an insolent grin. "You look to me like a spy, mahn."

Player wished he had a moment to think. This kid with a two-day growth on his chin was trying to scare him, but Player didn't know why, and he wasn't sure what to do about it.

"What are you talking about?"

Instead of answering Player's question, the kid pulled up his shirt, revealing a pistol stuck in the waistband of his shorts. He put the heel of his hand on the pistol butt.

"Strangers see too much here," he said, "They disappear." He flicked a finger at Player as if he were knocking a fly away.

The threat kicked Player's body into gear. He felt the heat of anger streak up his neck and flood his face in seconds. Gun or no gun, Player's instinct was to be aggressive when he was pushed.

"Get your filthy foot off my boat."

The kid's fingers moved to the grip of the pistol as Player started to lean toward him, anger pushing his body forward at the same time his brain tried to hold it back. He glared into the dangerously young face, but his attention was fixed on the pistol hand, his senses straining to detect any quick movement down there. Player decided he was either going to have to jump this guy and risk getting shot in the struggle or he could wait and maybe get shot without having any chance, if the kid moved first. He started to tense his muscles, calculating the move forward, when a voice came from behind the kid.

"Tony!"

The dockhand didn't move and Player held himself in place.

"Tony!" The voice came from someone who was hidden behind a stack of boxes. *"Venga, aqui."*

The kid showed no response at all. He simply removed his hand from the pistol and backed away. He kept his eyes on Player until he was well out of reach, then he turned and quickly disappeared among the stacks.

Player felt a trembling in his legs and slumped into a fighting chair with sudden exhaustion. He pushed the hair back off his forehead and realized how lucky he'd been, then he swore that he wouldn't put himself in a position again of escaping on luck alone. He had to anticipate danger sooner, because luck turned sour too easily to count on it.

He got out of the chair and decided to go find Jaye and Sharpe. They could already be in trouble out there, and he knew then he should never have let them go alone. It would've been far better to leave the boat unprotected, because after all, what protection had he provided it anyway? The kid could've shot him with ease. Simple as that. As he climbed up the ladder to get the key from the control station, he saw Jaye and Sharpe just thirty yards down the dock, struggling with three huge duffle bags. Instead of pulling the key, he revved up the engines and then ran down to help them.

As soon as he reached them, Jaye and Sharpe dropped the bags on the dock and sat down on them. They were covered with sweat from the effort of carrying so much weight, and Sharpe whistled in relief as Player came to a stop.

"I never thought I'd be so glad to see a brute like you, Player. My arms are—"

"Come on," Player ordered, as he grabbed one bag and hustled them toward the boat.

Jaye protested, "Jack—"

"Hurry, dammit."

They caught the urgency in his voice and followed him to the boat, dragging the remaining duffle bags with them. Player threw one into the cockpit and jumped in after it, then he reached over to the dock for the other two, yanking them into the boat as Jaye and Sharpe jumped aboard.

"Take the wheel, Jaye," Player said. "Get us out of here now."

She ran up the ladder to the fly bridge as Player threw a duffle bag through the salon doorway.

"Let's get these out of sight, Sharpe."

They tossed the other two bags into the salon and closed the door, then they hurried fore and aft to clear the lines. When they finished, Sharpe came back to the cockpit and asked Player what was going on.

"Let's go up top. Maybe we can see something."

They climbed onto the fly bridge just as Jaye started to nose the boat around toward the ocean. They were in a narrow channel between two jutting docks and she had to work the length of the *Fey Lady* around slowly.

Player looked across the marina and saw that the Cigarettes were still there, about a hundred yards away, with dockhands passing cardboard boxes aboard each of them. A few men who looked to be standing guard formed a rough semicircle around the dark boats.

"What's up?" Jaye asked.

"I'm not sure," Player said. "But it's not good."

A few seconds later the men guarding the Cigarettes broke into a run and crossed over to a walkway that lay between the Cigarettes and the *Fey Lady*.

Sharpe was the first to spot the cause of the commotion, and he pointed out a man who was running away from the general area of the Cigarettes. The man appeared briefly and then disappeared again as he weaved his way through the crowded stacks of boxes to elude his pursuers. He ran blindly past the waiting cargo, changing direction when he caught sight of the guards, but he couldn't know what they plainly saw from their vantage point; the guards were converging on him from two sides.

"They're forcing him out toward sea," Player said.

"He doesn't have a chance," Sharpe added.

The man was much faster than the guards, but they had the advantage of numbers, and it was obvious they were turning him farther out onto the seaward side of the marina to deny him any chance of escaping by land.

Jaye maneuvered the boat through the crowded waterway and managed to pick up speed as they rounded a tip end, but she had to work the boat past one more T-shaped extension before they had a clear path out to sea.

While Jaye worked the helm, Player and Sharpe watched the chase and saw that it was getting worse for the man who was trying to escape. The guards had forced him onto an extension that ran parallel to the channel they were taking out of the marina.

The man was running out the dock alongside them at top speed, with the guards not far behind. They were close enough for Player to see pistols in their hands, and he recognized one of them as the kid who'd tried to board the *Fey Lady*.

"Hurry, Jaye," Sharpe said. "They've got guns."

She turned and took a quick look at the men running alongside, not far behind the man now. "He's got nowhere to go," she said.

The man's situation was hopeless. His pursuers were right behind him, and they would be able to shoot him easily as soon as he reached the end of the extension.

Player saw the dirty kid stop and brace his hands on top of an oil drum for a quick shot. The pistol fired, but the man ran faster from the apparent miss. The kid took up the chase again, now a few steps behind the other guards who had passed him at a run after he tried the shot.

The man was running a few steps ahead of the *Fey Lady* now, but he was almost out of dock; another twenty yards and there would be nowhere left to run. He swung his head to the right to take a quick look at them and they could see his face clearly. He wasn't afraid; he was straining and thinking, still searching for a way out. Player could see from the look on the man's face that he hadn't quit yet. Even though his situation was hopeless, he was still fighting to stay alive and that won Player's admiration instantly and completely.

Another gunshot sounded and the guards were just thirty yards behind the man.

"Jaye," Player said quickly, "Swing as close to the end of that dock as you can, without slowing down."

"What good will that do?" she asked.

"It'll give him a chance."

Sharpe became irate. "Are you crazy? We don't want to fight these guys."

"We're not going to try," Player said. "We're just giving him a chance."

"No. They'll shoot at us."

"Don't slow down, Jaye. Just swing close to the tip of the dock."

"No!" Sharpe yelled.

Jaye wasn't sure what to do. "You two decide, right now."

"Let's give him a chance," Player said.

"Why?" Sharpe demanded. "We don't even know him."

Player wouldn't give in. "I don't like the guys who are chasing him, okay?"

Sharpe threw up his hands in surrender.

Jaye steered to the left, taking them within a few feet of the boats tied up to the dock, and when they reached the end of the T-shaped extension, she swung hard left so the boat curled around the tip. They weren't going too fast, so the man would have a moment of opportunity, but he would have to be awfully good to seize it.

When the man saw what they were doing, he knew the *Fey Lady* was too far out but he had no choice but to try it. He ran off the end of the dock at full speed and made a one-legged landing on the foredeck of a small trawler, and he somehow managed to keep his balance and continued forward with another big jump onto the deckhouse of a second boat. The jumps hardly slowed him down at all as he made a final stretch across twelve feet of open water. His foot reached the gunwale of the *Fey Lady* but the boat was moving away from him and he couldn't get his balance. He teetered for a fraction of a second before he started to fall backwards into the water.

Jaye saw what was happening and she gave the wheel a quick spin to the right to throw the rear of the boat sideways. The leftward kick shifted the stern toward him and the man tumbled into the cockpit and landed hard on the deck.

It all happened so fast, no one could quite believe it. They looked down at the cockpit, where a panting, grateful man was sprawled on the floorboard. The sound of another shot snapped them back to attention, and they heard a bullet hit the hull near the stern. They ducked as Jaye shoved the throttle forward. The roar of the engines drowned out the next shots as they ran for the harbor entrance at full speed, once again elated that they'd taunted danger and slipped away untouched.

Chapter 29

Player drove the *Fey Lady* south at top speed most of the afternoon to get as far from Bimini as possible by nightfall. He and Jaye took turns at the wheel and tried to catch some sleep to make sure that at least one of them stayed awake all the time. By five o'clock Player began to feel relatively safe and decided they could go below to talk about what they should do with the stranger on board.

Player didn't know what to think of the guy who he hadn't said much, hadn't even said thanks. He just sat quietly in a fighting chair in the cockpit and watched them at work about the boat. Since they were tired and busy, they didn't make much of an effort to get to know him either. Instead, they remained wary of him and kept him at a distance until they had a chance to think and talk it over.

The guy undoubtedly wanted to get away from Bimini as much as they did, so Player didn't mind turning the wheel over to the Bahamian for a few minutes while the three of them went below to talk. After all, the guy wasn't going to head back north where those men on the Cigarette boats were trying to kill him.

They sat down around the coffee table in the salon, and for the first time, Player had a free moment to take in how luxurious the interior of the boat was. It was too bad they'd have to scuttle the *Fey Lady* at the end of the run, because it was truly a beautiful boat.

Sharpe handed him a beer as Player stretched his legs across the coffee table and took a swallow. It felt good to relax on a comfortable sofa. Player had been on his feet and going for over a day now with almost no sleep.

Sharpe sat down across from him and asked, "You sure it's okay to leave that guy up there at the wheel alone?"

"I think so."

"He's good at the wheel," Jaye said. "He knows more about boats than I do."

"I didn't mean that," Sharpe said. "I just don't like having him on board."

"Well, we couldn't let the guy get murdered," she said.

"It wasn't our problem," Sharpe replied.

"Like it or not, it is now," Player said. "We can't drop him off on an island until we get farther away from Bimini, but I wasn't planning to stop again until we reach Great Inagua."

"Yeah," Jaye agreed. "Better to keep moving. Those men with the guns might still be after us."

Sharpe looked irritated. "How far is that?"

Jaye and Player looked at each other. "Three or four days," Jaye guessed.

Sharpe got up and paced the floor for a minute, then sat back down. "I don't like it. That's too long."

"Have you got a better solution?" Player asked.

"Sure. We dump him on the next island we see."

"That's the same thing as letting him die," Jaye said. "Most of these islands don't even have water on them."

Sharpe threw up his hands. "We can't let him stay on board for three or four days. What if he's a crazy and tries to murder us to steal the boat?"

Jaye grabbed her purse and started to dig around inside it with the nervous hand movements Player had begun to recognize as a sign of anger. She grew annoyed and threw the purse on the coffee table in frustration. "Jack, can't you see I'm looking for a cig?"

Player handed her his pack of Marlboros and she fumbled one out and lit it, then sat back and her eyes narrowed at Sharpe.

"We're not leaving him to die," she said.

"Ditto," Player said.

Sharpe rubbed the back of his neck. "If you hadn't let him on board in the first place, we wouldn't have this problem."

"It's done, Mitch," Jaye said. "What's the big deal anyway? It's just a few days."

Sharpe got up and motioned for them to follow him. "Come down here and let me show you something."

He led them to the galley and had them sit at the little dining table while he closed the curtains. Then he went to the pantry and opened the door.

"While you two were up top, I got a chance to look at this." He removed one of the duffle bags from the pantry and brought it over to them. "Now, look inside it and tell me if you still want a stranger on board."

Sharpe unzipped the duffle bag and dumped it upside down on the galley table, and they fell quiet when they saw what he was talking about. Packets of hundred dollar bills spilled out of the bag and covered the tabletop. He shook the bag and more bills tumbled out, piles of them. It was more money than Player had ever seen before, ever dreamed of seeing.

"Thousands," Jaye whispered.

"Hundreds of thousands," Sharpe said.

He shook the bag again and more packets fell out. The money scattered across the table and fell into their laps and spilled onto the floor, and the smell of it filled the tiny galley. It had a rich and inky smell that subtly changed the atmosphere in the cramped space, and it filled their lungs and went to their heads, and Player knew the sight of so much cash had changed them irrevocably.

Player felt his throat tighten in spite of himself. He'd seen people go wild at the sight of money in movies, but he'd always thought that was unreal, that only an idiot would act that way. Now he knew he'd been wrong. He picked up a double handful of cash and brought it up to his face and the sight and smell of it was overpowering.

He could see they all felt the same. Their faces gleamed with the transforming power of money as they breathed in its power and caressed its thick weight. It represented so much to them, so much of what they all desired. One look and each of them knew beyond a doubt why they had joined this venture. They wouldn't have admitted it to themselves, or each other before this moment, but each of them knew now it was the money, pure and simple. The gut clinching love of money had drawn them into this strange, dangerous world of uneducated and harsh people, and all the other motives they had imagined for themselves paled in significance to it. It was all about this pile of raw, green power. Down at the core of it, they knew this was why they'd agreed to do it.

At almost the same instant, they became aware of the tense silence and looked at each other, embarrassed by the intensity of their reaction and the immediate, decisive control the money exerted on them.

Player broke the silence. "It is a tempting thought, isn't it?"

Their eyes turned to him in alarm. They understood what he meant, but fear wouldn't let them voice the thought as he had.

"Don't even consider it," Jaye said.

"Alvarez would find us," Sharpe added. "He'd kill us."

"So it occurred to you, too," Player said.

"Forget it," Sharpe said. "We'll make a lot more than this when we deliver the load."

"You're right," Player conceded.

Sharpe went to get another duffel bag out of the pantry. Player laughed softly, wondering if he might ever get the chance to see so much money at one time again.

"I've got to hand it to you," Player said. "To talk Raoul into fronting this kind of cash is amazing."

"Back in Lauderdale, all you could talk about was how I screwed everything up," Sharpe said.

"Well, you did screw things up, but this makes up for it." Player flipped a packet of bills into the air and caught it on the way down. "We would've never come close to this kind of financing if you hadn't made things happen with Raoul. How did you manage it?"

Jaye tossed a double handful of money into the air and giggled with delight as most of it fell on her head, a kid in her sandbox.

"Raoul owed me," Sharpe said. "Last year, I used a little pull to get a charge reduced. Got him probation, instead of time."

Player nodded and thought about it for a moment. He'd wondered since the beginning what sort of leverage, if any, Sharpe had used with the Cuban.

Sharpe came back to the table with a second duffle bag which was so heavy he strained to lift it onto the table. The delight evaporated from Jaye's face when she unzipped the bag and looked into it. She gestured for them to take a look inside for themselves.

Player reached into the bag and touched a hard edge of metal and knew what it was instantly. He pulled a machine pistol out of the bag and held it up to see. It was an ugly, boxy-looking gun that was small enough to be fired with one hand, but it had a long, straight clip protruding from the bottom of the hand grip that must have held several dozen rounds.

"I think they call it a Mac-10," Sharpe said.

"The drug smugglers' favorite," Player said. He removed the clip and checked the chamber, then flicked the trigger a couple of times. "It's been modified for automatic firing. See this right here?" He pointed to a piece of plastic behind the trigger mechanism. "That converts a legal semiautomatic pistol into an illegal automatic weapon. One touch on the trigger and this thing will empty the entire magazine in a couple of seconds."

"Why change it to an automatic?" Jaye asked.

Player looked at her and considered his answer for a moment, then decided it was best to tell her the plain truth.

"This gun has been modified to do one thing, to kill people with maximum speed."

"Oh," she said. She sat down at the table, her forehead looking strained. "I hope we don't really need these things."

"They're just for show," Sharpe assured her. "Raoul didn't think we'd actually have to use them."

"As he sits safely in Fort Lauderdale," Player said.

Player emptied the remainder of the duffle bag's contents

onto the table. There were several magazines and boxes of ammunition, as well as a second Mac-10, two M-16's, and two 9mm pistols. Even a couple of grenades spilled out, hitting the tabletop with a heavy clunk.

"Well, Raoul sent plenty of everything we're not going to need," Player said.

"I don't even know how to shoot a gun," Sharpe said.

"The first thing they teach you in the Army is to call it a weapon, not a gun, and you're going to learn how to fire all of them in the next few days." He picked up one of the rifles. "I fired an M-16 in the Reserves, so I already know how to use it, but we'll all need to practice with the smaller ones."

Player measured the rifle's weight, sighted down the barrel at a porthole and pulled the trigger. Immediately, he realized the mistake he'd made. To touch the trigger without checking the safety or the chamber was incredibly stupid. He was rusty, and that made him dangerous with a weapon, and if he was dangerous, it would be absolutely foolish to put an automatic weapon into the hands of his two partners. He put the rifle down respectfully and resolved to take them all through a crash course in the next few days, because none of them should handle these firearms without preparation.

As he looked at the guns and the money scattered across the galley table, Player remembered how much he'd hated everything about firearms when he was in the Army Reserve. Oh you hypocrite, he thought, you were so high-minded fifteen years ago about Vietnam, and now here you are preparing for your own little war.

And there you have it, Jackson Player, you've already cloaked this thing in the guise of necessity. If you shoot somebody, you're already saying to yourself it must be necessary. Afterwards you'll blame it on the situation or the other person and somehow justify it as self-defense, you'll justify it any way you can, even though the truth is spread out before you on the table. You're doing all of this for one thing only--not your self-esteem or your redemption--you're doing it for money. Now, after seeing all this cash, you know you'll go ahead with it even though the whole thing feels more wrong every day. Maybe Sharpe had been right all along, maybe money was the only truly important thing in life, because it certainly was the thing fueling him now. Even though he was becoming convinced he shouldn't go through with this, he would anyway, and with that certainty he knew how far he'd fallen.

He was so deep in his thoughts he didn't notice them refilling the duffle bags until Sharpe pushed his elbow aside to get at one of the machine pistols.

"Come on you two," Sharpe said lightly. "Don't take it so seriously. The guns are just insurance."

He got up slowly and helped them stuff the money back into the duffle bags.

"I hope you're right," Jaye said.

She looked over at Player with uncertainty. "I know I told you I could do it, Jack, but now, seeing these awful guns, I'm not sure I can shoot anybody even if my life is at stake."

A voice sounded from other end of the galley. "Then stay away from the drug trade, Lady."

Chapter 30

The voice came from the top of the salon steps, so unexpected it startled them. Their heads turned simultaneously, and there was the stranger, standing above them in the salon, taking in the whole scene, the money, the guns, all of it in one glance.

"What are you doing in here?" Sharpe demanded.

The Bahamian ignored the question and stood there looking them over then he took one step down to the galley and pointed at the guns on the table. "If you are afraid of guns, turn the boat around. Forget Colombia."

Colombia? Player wondered how this guy had guessed where they were going. Had Jaye or Sharpe blabbed to him? What was going on?

Apparently Sharpe didn't know either, because he tried to bluff his way out of it. "What are you talking about? We told you, we're on a fishing trip. These guns are for our protection."

"The Bahamian let out a big, mocking laugh. Even his laugh had that thick accent, half Black *patois* and half colonial British.

"You deceive no one," he said. "With no bait on board. No crew. No outriggers. You even sailing away from big game waters. How do you explain so much dollars?"

"Those dollars are none of your damn business," Sharpe said. He started toward the Bahamian threateningly, but the guy was extremely cool. Instead of backing away, he came toward Sharpe an equal distance to show he had no fear. Then he brushed past him on the bottom step and descended into the galley without invitation.

At that point, Player shifted his body to put himself between the man and the guns on the table. The stranger got the message and stopped. He respects my size more than Sharpe's tough talk, Player thought.

"So, what's it to you if we're not fishing?" Player asked him. He wanted to hear the guy out, because he wanted to know why they had been such an easy read. It hadn't occurred to him that they should make the boat look right; he'd thought there would be no need for camouflage out on the open sea.

The stranger faced Player with a serious expression. "You are amateurs. In this hard business, you will be caught or killed."

"How do you figure that?"

The man grinned slightly, shook his head. "To survive in the Bahamas, you must know drugs. It's the way of life. You learn to keep the mouth quiet and eyes open to stay alive."

Sharpe snorted. "You weren't doing such a good job of staying alive back on the docks."

"Those Colombians. They threaten everyone, in the war with the old Cuban."

The old Cuban? Jaye gave Player a quick look. He wanted to know more, too, but kept himself quiet.

"The Miami Cuban."

The man detected that he'd touched a live wire and knew when to press an advantage. "I think you must work for him. His people show at the old fishing docks some, but the Colombians run it now. They push out his people and steal his loads. More all the time."

"And this guy you're talking about, the old Cuban," Player asked, "He can't do anything about it?"

"He fight back, sometime, but the Colombians take over. He must be so old now, to hire amateur people."

"Nobody hired us," Player said.

The Bahamian studied Player's face. His look seemed to recognize that they would not be so easy to sway. "If you go to Colombia, only you three, you have bad journey. The drug trade belong to gangs now. Four, five years ago, many independents such as you. Not now."

"Tell us what you want," Player said.

The man's black watery eyes shifted from one face to the next until he had made eye contact with all three of them.

"Very dangerous these days," he said, "but if you are smart, lucky, still you can make a fortune. One run, one fortune."

His eyes came to rest on Player, as though this one among the three was the one he must convince. "You lucky for me, already. Saved my life on the docks. If I join you, I help you to be smart. And lucky."

"Join us?" Sharpe laughed, a genuine laugh from his belly.

"On your own, you will not make it. I know more than you know. To help you do this."

"And what if we don't want you to join us? Player asked him.

The man frowned. "Three of you, with guns. You could throw me into the sea, but are you killers? Let me join you and be partners."

They looked at each other, not sure what to say.

"We'll let you know," Player said. He tilted his head toward the salon doorway, motioning for the guy to leave so they could talk about it.

At least the Bahamian knew when to talk and when to shut up. He turned and took the steps in two long strides, and he was out the door in seconds.

Chapter 31

Shortly after dark, the moon came up and transformed the surrounding ocean into a postcard version of the tropics. A wedge of silver moonlight sparkled on the water, wide and diffuse nearby, then narrowing as it got farther away, finally sharpening at the point where the moon sat, dark yellow and enormous on the horizon. The moonlight was so bright they could see for miles across the shallow flats of the Great Bahama Bank, and as they watched the light tremble and re-form on the ocean's surface, they were transfixed by the beauty of it all.

Standing and watching it from the fly bridge, the stranger talked constantly even though he seemed to be a quiet man by nature . They learned his name was Benji and these waters were his home. He shared every piece of information they might want to know to convince them he was valuable.

The waters of the Great Bank were dangerous to a boat the size of the *Fey Lady*, he said, because the ocean was rarely more than ten feet deep, and in most places it barely covered the vast plain of sand bars, reefs and shallows that made up the archipelago.

Any craft that drew more than a couple of feet traveled at risk in these waters, because a ripped bottom or a broken propeller shaft might require the passengers to make a forced swim to one of the thousands of nameless islands dotting the bank, and he didn't have to tell them that making such a swim at night would be terrifying. They already knew the kind of marine life that flourished in these warm waters.

Since the surface was bright enough to see by the moon, they decided to take advantage of the high visibility and cruise with their running lights off. At a careful ten knots, Player said it was worth it, because he didn't want the *Fey Lady* to be any easier to spot than necessary. He doubted that the Colombians would chase them this far from Bimini, but he wasn't about to make it easy for them if they were out there somewhere. Player said they'd already made too many mistakes and he didn't want to make any more through carelessness, so he kept the boat moving southward as quietly and unobtrusively as he could.

Jaye watched Player handling the boat and she knew things were going right; Player had taken charge and that was what she wanted. He was sure and confident with the boat and his judgment, and she felt his steadiness could get them through this if anything could.

She also wanted to get to know the Bahamian while he was eager to talk, and she asked him why the Colombians had been chasing him that morning on the docks.

"I fell onto their pick up," he said. "On the docks at the wrong time. They think I wanted their drugs. Now they think the same of you."

"Do you think they're still searching for us?"

"Don't know. They have many eyes and ears in these waters."

"Looks clear to me," Player said. "They probably don't think we are that important."

"Maybe. Maybe, not."

Benji kept his eyes on the horizon as they talked, and Player stayed at the wheel while Jaye sat and smoked cigarettes. The night was beautiful, and she didn't want to go below where Sharpe was getting them something to eat. She knew she should go down and help, but she guessed he was drinking. He'd been gone so long, she stayed where she was.

The longer Jaye sat there, the more her eyes kept returning to Benji's shirt. It was an unforgettable shade of yellow and she thought she recognized it, but she couldn't be sure. As she stared at it for the tenth time, it occurred to her that she might have seen it when she and Sharpe were at the Billfish Club. That was it. He'd been at the table near the bar, reading a newspaper. She remembered because the man in the yellow shirt hadn't leered at her the way the other men had. In fact, he hadn't even seemed to notice them, yet now here he was on their boat. She let the thought go and looked out at the water. It didn't matter anyway. The night was too beautiful to think; better to just sit and let the warm air flow over your skin.

The ocean was calm and still sparkling with moonlight as they came up on a number of islands ahead, dark humps squatting on the horizon. Some were near and some far, but it was hard to tell because there weren't any lights on them. All uninhabited, she supposed.

Benji showed Player when to rely on the chart and when to read water on his own. Under a good moon, dangerous water could often be spotted by a subtle change in color, he said. He pointed out the difference between surface ripples that were nothing more than fish playing and others that had a trace of foam about them, caused by the chop breaking on a bar.

The depth recorder at the control station was practically useless in these waters, Benji explained. It was really only good for fishing and wasn't much help with navigation. Player experimented with it anyway, and he set the alarm function at six feet since the boat had a draft of just under five, but the bottom was so irregular it kept going off. A red light would flash and then it emitted a high squeal that drove them crazy, so finally he turned the volume down and ignored it.

Benji told him to depend on his eyes rather than the electronics, and she realized they could never have learned all of Benji's tricks on their own. Every hour he spent on the fly bridge made it more apparent how useful his experience could be to them.

Still, she wasn't about to trust him that easily. Anybody who'd seen that pile of cash on the galley table was a threat, because that kind of money could alter a person's judgment and loyalties overnight. She thought the money was so incendiary she'd hidden one of the 9mm pistols in her bunk. She had no intention of letting him lull them into false security and then cut their throats while they slept. She knew from her own reaction to that pile of money that it could inflame many people to do exactly that.

Despite her caution, she had to admit that she liked the guy and was already giving him the benefit of the doubt. A big part of it was that he showed himself to be very competent. The guy knew what he was talking about, and she secretly wished for someone to help take part of the work load. It was a relief to have somebody to talk to who could offer an informed opinion so she and Jack didn't have to think of absolutely everything. The more she considered it, the more she believed the operation was too big a job for three people anyway and had been all along. What was more, it might get tougher the farther they went and Mitch was less help all the time. She guessed that Player was nowhere near convinced to take the guy on, or to trust him at all, but she had to admit the idea was beginning to make some sense.

Chapter 32

About eleven o'clock, Sharpe interrupted her thoughts by climbing loudly to the fly bridge. He was singing and had a pile of sandwiches on a tray, but he tripped on the top rung of the ladder and scattered them across the fly bridge deck. She was surprised to see him drop to his hands and knees to pick up the sandwiches. She had yet to see him stoop to pick up anything. She took a closer look and saw that he was drunk, as she had suspected he would be.

She bent down to help, because Sharpe was too clumsy to collect the sandwiches on his own. As she gathered bread slices and meat, she wondered how much scotch he had put away. She had noticed earlier that he was edgy and spent long stretches alone down below, but she decided it was nothing more than they needed a good night's sleep. None of them were used to the tension they'd faced the last couple of days.

As Sharpe bent forward, his polo shirt rode up his back, and she saw one of the grenades bulging out the hip pocket of his jeans. She was so annoyed with his carelessness, she felt like slapping him.

"I'll take that, thank you," she said in a normal tone, as she quickly snatched the explosive from his pocket, shaking her head at him in warning. Player might go ballistic if he saw Sharpe handling a grenade in his condition. She carefully shielded it from sight as she hid the heavy but small sphere inside her own shorts.

Player and Benji ignored the dropped sandwiches, keeping their eyes on the ocean ahead, while she tried her best to disguise her own thoughts. Apparently, neither of them had noticed her shoplifting the grenade, which relieved her apprehension a bit.

When they stood up with the sandwich makings, Sharpe said he'd already had some food and offered to take the wheel while they ate. Without waiting for an answer, he stumbled to the instrument board and began to elbow Player out of the way.

"Mitch, you're drunk," Jaye said.

She reached out to settle him down, but he shook off her hand.

"Don't treat me like a kid."

"The best hand must have the wheel," Benji said. "This is dangerous water."

"Who are you to tell me anything?" Sharpe said, glaring at him, then he turned to Player. "Is he making decisions here now? I thought it was strictly you and Jaye-bird in charge."

She could see Player losing his patience fast. "Don't be a jerk," he said. "Why don't you go sleep it off?"

Sharpe was too belligerent and drunk to be deterred. He pushed Player away from the wheel and got hold of it. Player relented, apparently deciding it was better to let Sharpe have his way.

"Okay, man. It's all yours."

He signaled the others to let it go and sat down beside Jaye, calmly starting on a sandwich.

Benji kept quiet and went to the rail at the back of the fly bridge, where he lit a cigarette.

Finally, Sharpe stopped singing and everything was quiet for a few minutes. To get away from the tension, Jaye decided to go below and wash up.

"Okay, guys. I need to get—"

The sound of powerful engines firing up cut her off. More than one big boat was cranking its engine to life and the combined roar of them skated across the water like sudden thunder.

They jumped to the rail and looked in the direction of the sound. It seemed to be coming from a cluster of islands that sat a mile or two away. They stared at the dark humps on the horizon as the sound grew in volume, then a second later they saw four wedge-shaped profiles detach themselves from the silhouette of land.

She recognized the shape of the boats instantly and knew in her gut it was the men from Bimini. The Cigarettes were low and dark and moving very fast now, slanting across the horizon on a path to intercept the *Fey Lady*.

"We've had it, mahn," Benji yelled.

Sharpe reacted instinctively, spinning the wheel to the left, away from the Cigarettes. Then he tried to open the throttle, but he threw the lever in the wrong direction and the engines fell immediately.

"The other way!" Player shouted.

Sharpe jammed the throttle forward and the engines jumped, but with the wheel turned sharply to the left the boat lurched sideways, throwing them into the rail. Jaye grabbed an awning strut and hung on with both hands. Sharpe managed to straighten the boat and steered away from the pursuers, heading toward a pair of tiny islands nearby, perhaps a few hundred yards away. As Player and Benji struggled to their feet, the *Fey Lady* raced across the flats, gaining speed every second and bouncing on the chop. The pitch of the hull was so severe it knocked them back down twice. By the time Player got up and grabbed the rail, the speedboats were much closer. They kicked up huge rooster tails of spray and the combined scream of their engines was much louder than before.

Jaye looked forward and saw a pair of islands directly ahead. Suddenly the sea changed color, going from deep blue to milky green in seconds. The light on the depth recorder began to wink, and the warning signal squealed like a frightened rodent. Panic tugged at her mind.

Benji pointed urgently. "Sand!"

"Turn!" Player yelled.

Sharpe seemed unable to move.

Player jumped forward and took the wheel, looking out the side of the fly bridge. There was a patch of white underneath the surface just ahead. He yanked the wheel sideways and the *Fey*

Lady swerved violently to the left.

When Jaye felt a sharp jolt on the right side of the hull, she looked down and saw a sandbar gleaming whitely in the water. They had struck it a glancing blow, but almost as quickly as she saw it, it was gone, and the water became dark blue again.

Player pushed Sharpe aside with his hip and got both hands on the wheel. They were almost on top of the islands now and he steered for the narrow gap between them.

For all they knew, the water was only two feet deep in the gap but it was too late to go anywhere else. As Player aimed the bow at its center she took a quick look back. The Cigarettes were so near she could see dim figures in the cockpits as the dark wedges made a crisp maneuver and formed a single file behind the leading boat. The move was so practiced she had a mental flash of a fighter squadron on show.

The chase would not last long, because they couldn't possibly outrun those boats. The Cigarettes would shoot the gap right behind them, then fan out again and surround them in seconds.

As the *Fey Lady* sliced cleanly through the trough of water between the islands, she went to the rail at the rear with Benji and saw the lead boat just yards behind them. She could read the yellow letters of "Numero Uno" on the prow.

Unsure what to do, she snatched the grenade from her shorts, knew she couldn't throw it well.

Without a thought, she shoved the grenade into Benji's hand. "Here, use it!"

He didn't delay a second, priming it and cocking his arm in one fluid motion, then releasing the throw over the stern.

The instant the name of the boat registered in her mind, the Cigarette bucked upward and erupted in a giant ball of flame. She squinted against the explosion and felt a wave of heat slap her face. The black outline of the boat trembled for a second in the center of the explosion and disintegrated as the orange cloud expanded. Then the shape was lost altogether in roiling flames edged with black.

The sound hit them with a shocking pressure against the

eardrums, followed by a clap of thunder deep in the skull, then by a lesser wave of outrushing gases.

The flood of sound had not passed over them completely when another explosion grew out of the first. The second boat had been running so closely behind, it was engulfed in the explosion and its fuel tank ignited, too. The orange ball grew even larger and she felt another wave of heat, then a second blow of sound that vibrated deep in her chest.

Flaming bits of debris flew out of the orange cloud in every direction before the explosion collapsed inward and became a core of intense fire. As the blinding light condensed, the other two boats swerved to avoid the flames, but the passage was blocked and they had nowhere to go. With no time to slow down, the third boat made a violent cut to the right and went aground at fifty knots, crashing through undergrowth and tearing into a stand of palm trees. The final boat skated across a tiny beach until its prow caught a mound of sand and the rear went airborne. The sudden deceleration threw the driver out of the cockpit and his body flew through the air at terrific speed, looking inhuman as it twisted through the light of the flames.

Then everything went quiet, except for the sound of burning debris.

The small fires that dotted the beach and undergrowth soon provided the only light as the first two hulks burned through quickly, with the sea washing over them and extinguishing the flames as they went down.

Player shut off the engines and they sat a hundred yards away and watched the remains of the Cigarettes burn. Gradually the islands grew dark again and the crackling sounds died out as they sat and watched the last of the fires disappear.

Finally, Benji tried to come up with an explanation as she gave him a hard, cautionary look to say as little as possible. "Had to be a reef, tore open the fuel tank," he said.

"We draw more water than a Cigarette," Sharpe said. "Why didn't it snag us?"

"We broke the sea, over an old reef," he said. "That must be it."

Player wiped the sweat off his forehead and looked up at the bright and overly large moon. "It was luck," he said. "Pure luck that saved us."

Chapter 33

After running very slowly through the darkness for hours, without lights, they finally found a good place to hide just before dawn. They crept into a shallow cove surrounded by a flat horseshoe-shaped island, and as soon as the anchor took hold in the sandy bottom, they stumbled off to their cabins in exhaustion.

Before climbing into his bunk, Player got one of the duffle bags of cash out of the galley closet and took it into his cabin and locked the door. Sharpe and Jaye dragged the other two duffle bags into the master cabin and locked themselves inside. Then Player heard them collapse onto the queen bed without speaking.

Player put a loaded pistol beside his bed, but after a second thought, he put the gun under his pillow. After tossing on his bunk for another half hour, he finally went to sleep with his right hand gripping the butt of the automatic.

By noon, the sun heated up the cabins to an uncomfortable temperature because no one had remembered to turn on the air conditioning. Sleep became difficult and Player listened as everyone began to get up. He heard Jaye and Sharpe talking quietly on the other side of the bulkhead, and he realized this was the first time any of them had slept a few hours straight since they stole the boat. It was also the first time he'd been near Jaye and Sharpe when they were in bed together. He tried not to think about it, but he couldn't help but wonder whether they'd done anything during the night. Would it make any difference to them that he was just a few feet away in the next cabin? Would it bother her? He knew it wouldn't matter to Sharpe, and probably not to Jaye either, not after the way he'd rejected her advance the night before last on the fly bridge.

He heard Benji stirring up on the deck and wondered if the guy had slept on the sofa in the salon or if he'd stayed up top all night. Player told him he could sleep inside if he wanted, but he'd hesitated, knowing they still didn't trust him. And he was right; they didn't. That was why they'd kept the duffle bags in their cabins overnight.

Player remembered the pistol and pulled it out from under his pillow and held it up, examining the cross hatches on the grip. The pistol was heavy and functional, nothing fancy about it. He'd never slept with a gun in his hand in his entire life, but then he'd never made a grab for a million dollars before either.

He'd made up his mind during the night without even consciously weighing the facts. He was going to vote to let Benji join them. Now was the time to dump him or take him in, and Player had decided to take him in. He thought if Benji wanted to jump them and try to steal the money, he would've made his move already. Even though Player still didn't fully trust the guy, he thought they would be better off running a risk with him than to continue on their own, and since he couldn't be looking over his shoulder every minute, Player had to make himself forget his remaining doubts and assume Benji was okay. If he was wrong about the guy, he'd just have to face that when the time came.

What really clinched the decision for him was Sharpe's performance the night before.

His confidence in Sharpe weakened every day because his friend couldn't seem to stay level emotionally. Player supposed it was the dangers of the job wearing on him. He didn't think there was anything really wrong with Sharpe; he was just unsteady when things got tense. And when Player added that concern to Sharpe's other obvious shortcomings as a partner, he concluded he'd need more help to finish the job. Jaye was pretty solid, but he didn't know if just the two of them would be enough to pull it off.

Despite his decision to accept the new guy, Player knew he

wasn't judging the Bahamian logically. There was still no solid reason to trust him. Benji might yet try to kill them and take the money, or the load, but for some reason Player didn't think so. He was actually relying on his gut instinct, based on years of listening to people in the bar and weeding out every bullshitter and hustler who wandered in with a slick line; he didn't see any of that in Benji. To the contrary, he thought he detected a strain of honor in the man's unsmiling face. There was no bull about him, and he'd already earned a measure of Player's respect, because he knew how to do things that counted out here. Player needed to have someone along he could depend on if things turned bad, and his gut told him he could depend on Benji.

He heard Sharpe sneeze next door and thought of Jaye lying naked beside him. He decided to get up because he didn't want to overhear anything by accident. Why make his disappointment worse than it already was?

He got out of bed and pulled on his jeans and tee shirt, then found a Coke in the galley refrigerator. He went out to the cockpit where he discovered the sun to be blinding. Squinting, he shaded his eyes and looked around. When his pupils adjusted to the glare coming off the white hull, he saw that he had chosen a beautiful place to hide while they were groping around in the half-light of dawn.

An emerald curve of island wrapped around the boat with embracing arms, but the longer he looked, he realized it was just an illusion of security. The island was nothing more than a low ridge of land topped by palms and scrubby undergrowth. A thin, white beach clung to the ridge of vegetation and protected it from the steady stroking of waves that somehow found their way into the cove. The water that surrounded them was colored in more shades of blue than he'd ever imagined. At every depth, submerged coral and plant life altered the shade of the water so that it ranged from a dark saturated blue in some areas to a light transparent turquoise in others, with a hundred gradations in between.

He found Benji on the foredeck leaning over the prow,

brushing white paint over the registration numbers.

"That's a good idea," Player said. "Where'd you find the paint?"

"A cabinet in the engine room. It has polish for the rails, varnish, that sort of thing."

"Good," Player said, sitting down on the deck and crossing his legs. "I meant to change that registration right away."

Benji rolled his eyes up from the work and grinned. He slapped a few more strokes of paint over the numbers then wormed himself back onto the deck. He sat up and looked toward the stern.

"We also should change the name on the transom," Benji said, "But I guess you planned to do that later as well."

Player let out a little confessional laugh. "It would have occurred to me eventually." He finished off the coke and crushed the can. "But you're right. Now is better."

Benji's face was shining with sweat, and he wiped it off with his shirt sleeve then turned his serious gaze on Player. "So, what is your decision? When we anchored here this morning, I thought you would force me overboard for sure. Such an empty island is a good place to be rid of me."

Player looked at him and thought for a moment, then decided to stay with his earlier decision. He got directly to it, explaining the situation with his hands and eyes as well as his voice.

"I can't speak for the other two, but if you're willing to settle for a smaller share than we're getting, I think I can convince them to let you stay on."

"How much smaller?"

"Say, we give you one hundred thousand apiece."

Benji looked out across the cove, thinking. Player didn't know what to expect. It had to be more money than the guy could earn in ten lifetimes as a black Bahamian, but then the guy was no ordinary dock worker either.

"Why would you give me so much?" Benji asked.

"I don't want you to be tempted to try to take more. In return for that share, I expect you to give us all your effort and loyalty."

"How much more will you make?" Benji asked.

"I won't know exactly until we cut the deal in Colombia, but we hope to clear at least eight hundred thousand each."

"So, I make less than half what each of you makes."

"That's right, but you didn't help plan the job either or help us steal the boat or get the money. A lot of work is done already."

"What you say is true."

"And then again, we don't have to offer you anything."

Benji nodded, "You mean you could risk fighting me right here. See if the three of you can take me."

"Yes," Player said.

Benji wiped his forehead again and studied Player's face. "Yes, I think you would fight, and you have guns."

It was incredibly hot sitting out in the tropical sun on the white deck. It was time to settle it.

Benji said, "I think that's a fair offer, but will the drunk man agree to it?"

Chapter 34

Player squatted on the swimming platform that jutted out from the stern at the water line. Painting over the old name on the transom, he used most of a can of white paint to blot out the huge black letters. They'd have to choose a new name before leaving the cove to print in place of the old one when the white paint dried.

Sharpe and Jaye sat in the twin fighting chairs, facing him across the transom. The decision on Benji had turned into an argument as soon as Player told them about the offer he'd proposed. Sharpe wouldn't even consider it.

"I say we drop him off right here," he said flatly.

Jaye wasn't sure. The idea of extra help appealed to her, she explained, and she liked the logic of giving Benji a good payoff, so they wouldn't have to worry about him. "Mainly," she said, "I don't want to be part of leaving him here where he will die."

When Sharpe said nothing, she tapped on his arm.

"We have to agree on one thing," she said. "We do nothing to hurt the guy."

"We won't have to hurt him," Sharpe said, as if it were the most certain thing in the world.

"Oh, yeah?" Player countered. "How are we gonna get him off the boat and keep him quiet till the job's done?"

"There's got to be a way," Sharpe said.

"The only way is to leave him here or shoot him. And who's going to do that? You?"

"We wouldn't have this problem in the first place, if you hadn't let him on board."

"That's not the point. He's here. Are you going to get a gun and take care of him?

Sharpe came out of his seat, fuming. "I'm not splitting my share, dammit!"

Jaye turned to him with a glare. "Please, just shut up."

He sat back down and they all fell quiet; most likely Benji had heard them arguing.

Player got up and looked forward. Benji was painting a fake registration number on the prow; he looked busy and didn't seem to be listening. He probably knew it was smart to leave them alone for a while and let Player carry the decision if he could.

"Hell, he can't hear us," Sharpe declared.

"He will, unless you keep your voice down," Jaye said.

She lit a cigarette and Sharpe rapped the arm of the chair with his knuckles.

Sharpe seemed to be getting more and more agitated, and Player wondered why he was so adamant about not keeping Benji on board. Was it purely the money? Had he reached the point where a million or so dollars wasn't enough?

Jaye broke the silence. "I vote we keep him. I don't see any other way."

Sharpe rolled his eyes skyward.

"Listen," Player said to him. "If it's the money, Jaye and I could split his share so you don't even have to touch your cut. How about it, Jaye?"

She nodded in agreement. "Okay with me."

"What do you say?" Player asked. "We can use him, and Jaye and I will pay for it."

Sharpe was in no mood to be reasonable. "We can do the job by ourselves," he said.

That was too much for Player. He put the paint brush aside and stood up. "You mean the way you did your job last night? You took the wheel while you were stinking drunk and almost killed us. You don't know a depth finder from a porthole, yet you sit there and talk about how we can handle everything alone."

"The boats surprised me, that's all. I didn't know they were out there."

"You didn't know because you weren't thinking. What the hell's wrong with you?"

Sharpe squirmed and made some huffing noises, and Player saw that he was hiding something. He almost looked guilty and Player had never seen guilt on his face before; he wasn't a man who felt guilt, in Player's experience.

Jaye turned her head away, and then it all unfolded.

"You weren't thinking because you were sky high," Player said. "Not just drinking. You were doing coke, too, weren't you? Anything else?"

Sharpe turned to Jaye, accusing her with his look, but she protested, "I didn't tell him, Mitch."

"So that's it." Player's voice became dangerous as he started to add a few things together. "That's why you've been acting like a scared rabbit. The sneezing. The nerves. Can't keep your mind on anything. And we agreed to stay straight on this trip."

"It was only last night," Sharpe said.

"Don't lie to me!"

Player was furious and he reached out to grab a handful of Sharpe's polo shirt. His hand closed around a lump in the front pocket. He hadn't even noticed it before. He jammed his hand into the pocket and tore out a vial that was half-full of white powder.

"You've been doing it every day, every night."

Sharpe got up to stalk away, but Player threw the vial into the ocean and grabbed Sharpe by the arm.

"Is that why you need the money?"

"No!"

"Of course it is. That's the whole reason for the trip. You owe Alvarez coke money, don't you?"

Sharpe tried to break free, but Player held on and shook him roughly. "Don't you?"

"So, what?"

Sharpe managed to get his arm loose and backed out of

Player's reach. "Are you some kind of saint, Player? You've done plenty of drugs before."

"It's not the same thing and you know it."

"The hell it's not! You either do drugs or you don't. There's no in-between. We've both done enough to know that."

"I know this. Out here, you're risking our lives if your head's not straight."

Sharpe paced the cockpit, resentful and angry looking. He pointed his finger at Player. "Well, I'm tired of hearing that line. I'm tired of taking the blame for everything. And I'm still the number one partner here."

Player held his anger down and climbed over the transom. He was going to settle this now, one way or the other. "We've got to stay straight out here. You can't do any more coke."

"Don't give me any more orders."

They faced each other and Player looked him hard, right in the eye. "No more coke. Or we turn the boat around now."

Sharpe turned to Jaye for support, but she looked away.

"He's right, Mitch."

Sharpe started to argue again, but the look on Player's face stopped him. He seemed to accept that Player would call off the run if he didn't agree. After a minute of silence, Sharpe dropped his hands helplessly and went inside without another word.

Player wasn't finished. He turned on Jaye as soon as the deckhouse door closed. "You should have told me."

"He made me promise."

Player sighed. He wondered how he could get her to understand. "What's more important, Jaye? Pleasing him or telling me something that might help keep us alive?"

She crossed her arms stubbornly. "I promised."

"Can't I count on you two for anything? You've lied to me more than once. He fouls up everything he touches. I can't believe I got myself into this."

"Well, if you don't want me for a partner either, that's too bad, because you're stuck with me."

Player softened his voice. "That's not what I meant. I'm not dissatisfied with you, but you should have told me."

"He'll be okay. He feels out of place, that's all."

Player put his hands on her shoulders. "We can't worry about his feelings right now. I need to know if I can depend on you. When you hide things from me, how can I be sure whose side you're on?"

She recoiled. "Whose side? I'm on your side. And his. Both!"

"But you sleep with him."

She tried to move away, but he held on to her shoulders, forcing her to face him.

"If you sleep with him, how can you say you want me?"

She quit struggling, and he felt a shuddering down in her chest then it moved up into her shoulders. Her eyes turned glassy, then filled, and moments later her face was wet with tears. Finally she said, "Because I want you both."

He was stunned. "What?"

"You two are like brothers, or have you forgotten?"

"But—"

"You're almost two sides of the same man to me. I can't choose between you two."

"You have to choose. I won't share you with anyone."

"I can't choose," she whispered. "Don't make me."

She brushed his arms away before he could speak again, then she turned and ran into the deckhouse, perhaps to be with Sharpe, perhaps to console herself. He had no way of knowing.

Chapter 35

"To our new partner," Jaye said.

They repeated the words in unison and four bottles of beer clanked together, but there was little joy in the toast, because the confrontation between Player and Sharpe had left a bitterness that wouldn't go away soon. It was late afternoon, and Player had called them all up to the foredeck because he hoped to ease the tension and seal the new partnership with the toast, but he also wanted to make sure Sharpe understood the new arrangement was irrevocable.

"To our new partner," Player repeated.

They drank again to Benji and he smiled hugely, which was a remarkable sight. His teeth were crooked, somehow funny. They were surprised to see that his smile gave him the look of an easygoing man, and for a moment, it even made him appear defenseless. He'd probably learned long ago not to let people see that smile, because it would not be an asset on the docks of the Bahamas. A funny smile would only invite intimidation.

They raised their bottles and drank again, and after a big swallow, Player went over and smashed his bottle on the prow and they thought it was a nice touch and did the same. With the toasting done, they milled about on the foredeck, and it took Player a moment to understand why. They were waiting for him to take the lead, because the major outcome of the confrontation had been that everyone now acknowledged Player as the only one in charge.

Sharpe had even stopped complaining when he was told what to do, at least that was the way it had gone most of the day.

When they got underway and edged out to sea, Player went to the fly bridge and took the wheel and told Benji to get some rest. He steered away from the chain of small islands where they'd spent the night and kept his eyes on the sunset off to their right.

Massive clouds boiled on the horizon where the sun had disappeared, but it still hadn't set completely because it threw bold streaks of gold through the edges of the clouds and saturated the background sky with red. He decided they weren't storm clouds after all as he watched the fiery look grow dimmer, with the clouds taking on a quiet power for the night.

Jaye joined him on the fly bridge and they stood and watched the last of the color burn out of the sky. The world around them became metallic, with everything cast in silver and gray.

Player bore south and a few degrees west because he wanted to get off the Great Bank and cruise through deeper waters. He didn't plan to track the major shipping lanes because they might encounter freighters, but he was willing to skirt the lanes so he wouldn't have to sweat through another night on the shallows. Neither of them spoke for an hour as the boat plowed on against the darkening sea, and when the moon came up it was fitful, hiding behind clouds that ran skittishly on the wind, but it offered enough light to make out the horizon and an occasional cay that rose up out of the water, even though they were now far from the banks.

About nine o'clock they saw a low mass of land take shape ahead to their right and the mass was impenetrably dark, even though it should have had lights since it was so large. Player swung the bow a few degrees to port to angle away from it.

"That must be Cuba," he said.

Jaye looked at the chart. "Or this chain of islands along the northeast coast here," she said, pointing to the map. "It's too big to be anything else."

"The last thing we need is to get picked up in Cuban waters."

"Let's make sure then," she said

"Okay." He turned the wheel a few more points to the east, and in minutes the vague mass disappeared and they were alone again on the sea. "Cuba," Player muttered. "I guess that means we've kissed America goodbye."

Jaye got a cigarette from his shirt pocket and ducked behind the windshield to light it. She tossed the lighter on the console and leaned against the rail.

"That reminds me of something," she said. "A saying when I was a kid."

"What?"

"The yacht people in south Florida used to say anyone who sails beyond the keys is looking for trouble more than fun."

"Meaning, America ends at the keys?"

"Yeah, and our rules end there, too."

A couple of hours later, Player still thought about the saying. The night had turned dark and windy, and she had gone inside to get something to eat. She'd said she would come right back, but that had been at least an hour ago. He didn't really expect her to return, because it wasn't the kind of night to spend on the fly bridge without good reason, so he spent the time alone, wondering what kind of world lay to the south. He'd never been down there, but he decided she was right. No American rules would be there. It will be a Latin world instead, he thought, a world so bent by the weight of economic inequality, many had turned to drugs for survival. He remembered reading somewhere that marijuana had become Colombia's largest export, and Bolivia's was cocaine. It will be a world populated with desperate people, not desperate to get rich like himself, but desperate to survive.

When Player heard someone on the ladder, he turned and was surprised to see Benji instead of Jaye. He had expected him to sleep all night, but the Bahamian climbed onto the fly bridge carrying two mugs of coffee, with one long index finger looped through the handles of both mugs.

"Thanks," Player said, taking the coffee in his palm.

"It's nothing," Benji said, as he sat down. "You have been out here a long time. Want me to take her?"

"I'm okay. Did you just get up?"

"I could not sleep."

Player set the autopilot and stretched his arms. He took a sip of the coffee and realized Benji was right, he was getting tired.

"What's Sharpe doing?" Player asked.

"He listens to the radio." And reading Player's thoughts, he added, "No drinking or drugs. He is quiet tonight." Player nodded, but said nothing.

"Your friend," Benji began cautiously, "You have doubts about him."

It occurred to Player that Benji might be setting him up against Sharpe, trying to drive a wedge between them. Maybe he was putting too much trust in the guy too soon.

"When the real pressure's on, he'll be okay."

Benji didn't disagree. Instead he said, "Out here, friendship is a different thing."

Player looked at him, didn't see anything but real concern on his face.

"Friendship's the same everywhere, Benji."

"No, I don' think so." He paused for a moment, blowing on the hot coffee, then said, "Will he still be your friend when . . . when the woman . . . ?"

"When the woman, what?"

Benji didn't retreat as most people did when that challenging tone came into Player's voice. He put down his coffee and opened his palms to make a point. "A child could see the heat rise from her when she walks near you, but she is his woman, right?"

Player put down his mug and faced Benji. "Yeah, she's Sharpe's woman," he said, but he didn't say it in a way that admonished him to mind his own business. It was more of an admission; yes, she is Sharpe's woman, and yes, there's heat between us, and no, I don't know what to do about it.

"Okay, Jack. He's your friend and you save my life once, maybe twice already, so I follow you. But remember, out here you must think like a general."

Player understood what he meant, that he didn't want to get killed over a third man's woman. If he followed Player, he expected sensible leadership in return.

Player knew he should try to reassure him somehow. "Listen, if I don't succeed at this, I'll have to go back to a life that's got no hope."

"So, you do this thing to prove yourself?"

"Something like that."

"And what about the woman? Is she more important to you than hope? Than money or respect?"

Player found he couldn't answer the question. He knew only one thing; he had a burning need to accomplish something big, to test himself, because he was lost otherwise. He had to succeed at something, and he had chosen this run as the way to satisfy that need, and he was going to go through with it no matter what it cost him.

"Just believe this, Benji. I'm through living at the bottom of the pit. I'll do anything it takes to get the load back home."

Benji studied Player's eyes for a moment, perhaps searching for the truth, and finally he seemed satisfied. "I believe you, Jack." Benji ceremoniously offered his hand, and they shook.

Player decided to go below and get some food and rest, so he turned the wheel over to him, wondering if he'd reassured the Bahamian. Benji didn't show much either way.

Player went to the ladder, turned, and took a look back at the tall, thin figure at the wheel. Does he truly have confidence in me, Player wondered, or is he simply hoping, as I am, that something inside me will grow to the occasion?

"Sea's rising," Player called out.

Benji nodded but didn't look back.

Chapter 36

The next morning, a Thursday, Player got the canvas duffle bags out and hauled them up to the deck. It was a clear day, and the sea was calm when he took the guns out of the bags and realized how strange it felt to be handling automatic weapons out in the sunshine and fresh air. Even though he had never fired a Mac-10, it didn't take him long to figure it out, and as he familiarized himself with it and the other weapons, he talked Jaye and Sharpe through their operation as well.

Through it all, he felt as if someone other than himself was standing there on the deck, patiently demonstrating the basics of stance and loading, triggers and safeties, balance and aiming. He seemed to be hovering outside his body and watching himself as he fired the first shots off into the blue sky, because once the noise and smell of guns were set loose in the air, everything about them seemed transformed; the look on their faces, the way they spoke to each other; it was all different; even Jaye's walk changed, became more showy, so great was the power of guns.

In a matter of minutes, Sharpe obviously grew to enjoy the sensation of tearing up the water near a floating bottle, and Player watched him grin with boyish pride when the bottle exploded under a storm of automatic fire.

Jaye already knew the rudiments of shooting, but she plainly didn't like guns. She said she'd learned about them shooting skeet when she was a girl, and her familiarity proved itself useful as she brought her rifle up swiftly but smoothly, took a bead and squeezed off a steady shot. "Hate the damn things," was all she'd say about why she didn't like to shoot.

Player found himself mentally reliving the worst six months of his life, and he finally understood why training in the army had been so relentless and repetitive. He had not forgotten a single thing. Those boring days at Fort Benning that never seemed to end had achieved their purpose--he was trained for life as an infantryman. Even though he had done everything he could at the time to be uncooperative, the army had managed to shape him after all. During his training, Player had hoped for only one thing--that he would never have to put his training to use. And now, contrary to that hope, beyond even his wildest, exhaustion-induced thoughts as a reservist, here he was on a boat in the Caribbean instructing others in the machinery of killing.

It seemed dreamlike to stand there on the clean white deck under a brilliant sky and rip the air apart with the sound of gunfire, but to Player, that deafening roar had to be the harshest sound in the world, the basest form of reality they sent clattering off across the water.

After an hour and a half of practice with the M-16, Jaye and Sharpe both could hit within a foot of a bottle riding the swells fifty yards away, which made Player wish they had one less machine pistol and one more M-16 since all of them could fire the rifle fairly accurately. But the wide spray of the Mac-10's beyond fifteen feet caused him to wonder about the mix of weapons Raoul had supplied. Most of the arsenal was close range firepower, and only when he began to visualize the situations they'd be in could he see the sense of it. Long-barreled rifles were too cumbersome to swing quickly into position in tight places, and those were the times they'd most need to be ready to defend themselves.

Benji stayed on the fly bridge all morning and watched without saying much. He told Player he already knew how to shoot, but he didn't offer to help with the lesson. Instead, he simply watched and coolly appraised the company he'd joined.

By eleven it had become so hot they were ready to get out of the sun. Player decided to break in another Mac-10 before they quit for the day, so he jammed a magazine into the hand grip of one of the boxy machine pistols. Sharpe tossed a bottle into the sea as a target, and when Player braced his feet and pulled the trigger, the gun almost jumped out of his hand. The barrel was so short and the firing rate so fast it was a difficult gun to control, and the bullets traced a crazy line of splashes far beyond the target. Player tried it again; this time with a shorter burst. He lightly touched the trigger and managed to hold the spray of bullets within ten feet of the bottle, but the magazine emptied almost immediately.

"We're going to have to practice a bit more with this one," he said.

"Not now, okay?" Jaye said.

"All right, but we have to practice every morning until we get there."

"Aye, aye, sir," Sharpe said, snapping off a salute.

Player gave him a look and saw that Sharpe was just throwing out his usual sarcasm, not really trying to provoke an argument. In fact, Sharpe seemed steadier than he had all week. Maybe all he'd needed was a night without cocaine and booze.

As they put the guns away, Player still felt the vibration of the machine pistol in his fingers. Firing the guns had left him with more of that sensation of unreality, as if they weren't really doing what they were about to do, and it was the first time he'd been so detached on the entire venture.

On reflection, he decided his mind was going into a sort of battle mode. He'd heard about it while he was at Fort Benning, from guys who'd seen combat in Vietnam. They said you started on an adrenaline rush the moment you landed in country—he still remembered the term—and you stayed on it until the minute you left. They said your unconscious took over and kept you ready for combat all the time, because it was the only way the mind could withstand the stress.

Maybe that was it, Player thought, because he certainly felt different. The jackhammer roar of an M-16, and the sight of bullets stitching a pattern around a floating bottle, had a way of driving home what you were about to do. Even though he had known what they were undertaking all along, he hadn't actually thought of shooting anyone until now, with the smell of gunpowder burning his nose.

Maybe too, it was the sight of Jaye swinging the M-16 up to her hip and bracing it the way he'd shown her; maybe it was watching an almost adolescent bravado creep into the way she held her body, even though she obviously hated guns.

Guns distorted everything, he decided. Just as surely as the pile of cash on the galley table had seared their souls, guns had the power to galvanize the violence that fluttered around inside everyone, and once the commitment was made to use them, they could be as corrupting as money.

Even Sharpe had been affected; Sharpe, who was so puzzled by anything vaguely mechanical he could hardly change a tire by himself. Even he had quickly mastered the firing of an automatic rifle and reveled in the experience like a kid with his first BB gun. Sharpe had grinned at the sensation of the recoil against his hands, the explosion of a target in his sights.

It all left Player feeling uncertain and wary of the demons that the guns had set loose. He was ashamed he had been their agent, but he had known from the beginning that violence might be necessary, known the experience would change them. Originally he had even welcomed it and thought it was what he needed. Now though, he was back to the same primitive fear he'd felt in the army, fear that he might have to use a gun on someone and experience killing. At least his own death would be involuntary, and he had no choice but to bear it someday as everyone did, but the fear of causing someone else's death, that was a terror of his own making, an unknown he had elected to face.

The morning of target practice left them all jumpy, and even though they decided to relax that afternoon, there was a crackle of tension and abandonment in the air. They were almost halfway to Colombia now and getting near Great Inagua where they planned to stop, refuel, and pick up food and supplies. As the afternoon wore on they grew more restless, wanting to get there and walk around on dry land even though they were still hours away from the island.

Benji suggested they break out some tackle along the way and put on a show of being big game fishermen. According to him, Great Inagua was watched by DEA agents and the Coast Guard, because so many smugglers used it as a refueling stop. If the *Fey Lady* aroused suspicion, they'd probably be shadowed for the rest of the trip, or at least the Coast Guard would keep an eye out for them. After all, they were very far south for a pleasure boat, so they'd better look like one. Even though the ruse would slow them down, Benji said it was worth the delay. Player agreed, so they got out rods and reels, outriggers and other tackle and set up the boat as if they were trolling for game.

Chapter 37

The afternoon was hot and Player felt an odd mixture of languor and restlessness in the still air. Later that night, he would ask himself if it happened because of the curious mood of the day, or if it had been inevitable as Benji suggested. He would never know for sure. All he could say to himself was that, at least, he hadn't planned it.

Jaye was up on the fly bridge minding the wheel while the men stayed down in the cockpit. Player and Sharpe lounged in the fighting chairs, doing their best to look like rich American sport fishermen, and Benji hung around the cockpit wearing a tee shirt and greasy hat he'd found in the engine room, looking the part of a hired mate who baited hooks and gaffed big fish. They sat and drank beer as they watched the trolling lines dance from the outriggers with tension. They didn't expect to catch anything, because the hooks were only baited with food scraps from the galley, but they watched the lines anyway, hoping a freakish strike would break the boredom of the afternoon.

About four, the sun was still high and hot. Player had taken off his shirt, trying to get his skin ready for the sun farther south, but as usual he was burning more than tanning. He massaged his bare shoulders and saw that they were already turning red. It was time for more sunscreen, and shortly, time to put his shirt back on.

"Where's the lotion?" he asked.

"Try the bridge," Sharpe said.

Player grabbed his shirt and started up the ladder. When he stepped onto the fourth rung, his eyes cleared the deckhouse roof and he stopped instantly. Jaye sat in the captain's chair, looking out across the sea, oiling herself with suntan lotion. She wasn't wearing a top, and Player could see rivulets of sweat standing out on her gleaming skin. He became vaguely aware of the radio; she had a Caribbean station tuned in and it was playing reggae. A part of his mind told him to go back down the ladder quietly, but he couldn't move because he was entranced by the sight of her body.

She sat with one leg hiked up on the instrument panel, unconsciously posed for seduction. Her skin was tanned and soft, and he could see indentations in the flesh where her fingers stroked across it. He was surprised that there were no tan lines where there should have been. It spoke of a lack of inhibition that made her even more alluring. She had never looked more beautiful, more erotic, to him.

He swallowed and discovered that his mouth was dry, his throat swollen, and he knew it was time to go back down the ladder, but the movement of his head caught her eye and she looked around quickly and saw him. She made no effort to cover herself.

"Sorry, I just wanted the lotion."

"It's okay. Come on up."

Player climbed onto the bridge and took a couple of steps toward her and extended his hand, but instead of handing him the bottle, she drew it closer to her body. Player tried to look at the bottle and keep his eyes off her skin, but she had drawn his attention there and she made a slight flexing motion with her arms and shoulder blades that stretched her breasts taut.

Player raised his eyes to hers and saw that there was no reticence in them. She hadn't planned it either, it seemed to him, but now that it had happened she wasn't going to back away. He saw her lips part, and he knew that she was feeling the same pressure inside that he felt.

"Why don't you hand me the bottle?"

"Why don't you finish me first?"

He started to back away as alarms went off in his head,

clanging their note of resistance, of survival, but she stood up and presented her body to him and every inch of her was glistening with oil. Beads of sweat stood out on top of the sheen. She raised her arms to brush the hair back from her face, and the lifting brought her breasts up as her elbows fanned out, inviting him.

"You're Sharpe's woman."

"I'm yours. You told me to choose."

"Not like this."

"You made me choose."

"Not now."

She moved toward him and Player felt his will disintegrating. He had no iron in his legs to move away.

"You're Sharpe's woman," he repeated.

She stepped closer and pressed her skin against his sunburned chest.

"I'm yours," she said.

Player's control gave way and he reached out and pulled her to him, her mouth to his mouth. His mind spiraled off as they began to move against each other, their exposed skin pressing together, their fingers working from shoulders to waist and back again.

Sharpe's voice called out from the cockpit, but they only sensed it distantly. "Player, look!"

The voice should have stopped them, but they didn't care about consequences; they only cared about the moment, the pressing need of the immediate.

"I've got one!"

This time Player heard the voice clearly, but his mind was tracking down a tunnel of sensation that allowed no intrusion. He shut the voice out of his mind and felt himself sinking into a wonderful release of self-control. He wanted only to feel this moment and abandon all else, at least for this moment.

Benji's voice rose above Sharpe's excited laughter. "Steady. Steady pressure."

"Get those other lines out of the way!"

"Steady."

Player faintly heard the sounds of Sharpe struggling with the fish for several minutes before the line collapsed. Then the groans as Sharpe fell back into the fighting chair, breathless and spent.

"It's okay," Benji said. "Must have been a shark to break that line, and who wants to land a shark?"

"Player," Sharpe called out. "You missed it. I had a shark on the line down here."

Now Player listened to the voice as he and Jaye searched each other's eyes. The moment was over and they had returned to the world, but they were melded together because they knew the world would look different and sound different to them, because everything was different now.

Chapter 38

After refueling on Great Inagua, they cruised south through the Windward Passage and the next day rounded the western tip of Haiti; after that, they saw fewer and fewer boats, then no land at all for several days. Each hour they felt more alone on the open sea, and even though no one spoke about it, tension on the boat increased.

Player didn't know if the others had guessed what happened between Jaye and him, or not. Maybe that was the source of the tension, maybe it was the job ahead, but everybody grew tighter and quieter as they approached South America. Discussions grew abrupt, answers terse as code. No laughter passed between them.

The days were monotonous and the sea seemed to go on infinitely, with one swell after another stretching to the horizon. Boredom, too, contributed to the growing unease on board. They tried to pass the time usefully, but there were only so many things to do, and finally, even their firearms practice had to be called off to save ammunition.

Jaye and Player agreed to keep themselves under control until after they had done the job in Colombia, but since their first desperate clinch on the fly bridge, he went into a dark, smoldering burn when Jaye went off to the master cabin with Sharpe at night. But they both knew it was smart to act as if nothing had changed, and Jaye said she could easily hold Sharpe off for a few days. Player agreed to put the issue aside since it was more important to keep Sharpe steady than to ease his own discomfort. If they told Sharpe what was going on between them, there was no telling how he would react, and it would be foolish to make their job in Colombia even more dangerous than it was already.

After Colombia, they would have a full week of open sea when they could tell him the truth, and he would have plenty of time then to get used to the idea that he'd lost Jaye. So they decided to wait and keep their passion under control; it would be better for Sharpe to hear it later, so they went on with the game of not revealing anything, yet the unspoken tension between everyone increased anyway.

Late on Sunday, they got their first sight of Colombia. It was hazy and mountainous in the distance and they all gathered on the deck to take a look before the sun went down. They pushed straight toward land as the sun fell behind them and the sea turned to a flat gray, but up ahead, the last rays of the sun were catching the mountaintops and the jagged line of peaks were tipped with sunlight, and for a few minutes the coastline was richly beautiful.

But the illusion didn't last long.

The closer they got to the rugged outline of the coast, the more ominous the place seemed to be. As the sun fell, the darkness grew deeper and climbed up the face of the range and huge creases of purple and dark brown shadow broadened across the mountains, reaching up and obscuring them until there was nothing but a thin rim of golden light left on the highest peaks, then that too was extinguished in minutes and the mountains reverted to their dark, implacable selves.

"It's so barren," Jaye said.

Player nodded. "As if man has never set foot there before."

"Some say there is no humanity there," Benji said quietly. "They say there is nothing on the Guajira but drugs and guns."

They worked their way south along the coast through the darkness, hoping to reach Riohacha by morning. Player slept very little as he spent most of the night at the wheel talking with Benji, trying to learn all he could about how deals were cut in Colombia, but most of Benji's information was second hand since he'd never been there either. Player determined he would have to learn more on land before they made their connection.

The connection itself would probably prove difficult. For all of Sharpe's talk about Raoul setting them up with a good contact in Colombia, all the Cuban had given them was a name. In fact, Raoul hadn't even supplied the person's real name. Instead, he simply told Sharpe to look up a man known as the Governor; anyone in Riohacha could direct them to him.

Player was furious when Sharpe told him all this, furious with Sharpe for not getting more details and furious with himself for not pressing them about it while they were still in Florida, but there was nothing he could do to change things now.

The next morning when they docked in Riohacha, he became concerned they'd draw trouble quickly. Their boat caused a huge commotion on the docks because it was expensive and clean, and one look around the waterfront made it easy to understand the response. Every other boat in sight was old and rusty, and Player knew they'd have to protect the *Fey Lady* every minute they were there.

The *Fey Lady* drew so much attention, a man from the Customs Office came out on the docks and hailed them as soon as they tied up. Player went with him to the office and filled out a couple of forms and explained they were sport fishermen who'd simply stopped for a local meal and a few supplies. He told the unshaven official who questioned him that they'd be leaving tomorrow, but the official didn't believe him and threatened to jail all of them since Player couldn't produce a passport for Benji. When Player realized what the man wanted, he bribed him with a hundred dollars, then the official stamped their passports and sent Player on his way.

He went back to the *Fey Lady* and worked out a few details to have the boat refueled that afternoon, then he and Sharpe set out on foot around eleven. They were going to have to move fast and ask questions more openly than Player would've liked, but the episode with the Customs Official convinced him they must make their connection and get out of Riohacha without delay.

Sooner or later, somebody would come after them here. It might be a corrupt policeman or a local punk, but eventually somebody would come and want money or their boat, and the longer they stayed here, the greater the risk became. So, they were going to have to ask around and figure out how to find the Governor in a way that drew too much attention, but he felt they had no choice.

They walked for an hour around the harbor area trying to find someone who would talk to them. They tried a group of old men who sat on boxes smoking cigars, but the men wouldn't even look up. Then, they questioned a few dock workers who smelled like fish and engine grease, but they wouldn't talk either.

Eventually, he realized the locals were too suspicious and he probably wasn't going to get any answers without bribing someone, so they left the docks and walked inland until they found a taxi driver asleep on the back seat of his cab. The sun was high, and when they offered him a Coke they'd bought from a street vendor, he sat up and saw the five-dollar bills wrapped around the bottle, and that got his attention. The man listened to their questions then told them they were in the wrong part of town to be asking for *marimba amarilla,* or yellow marijuana. He said the place to buy drugs was the Guajiro district, but when they asked him to take them there, he refused, saying you could get shot just driving through the streets of that area.

"*Donde?*" Player asked. "*Donde es?*"

The man ignored the question and continued his explanation.

The district was named for the Guajiro Indians, the people who mostly lived there, he continued. They were originally from the peninsula beyond the mountains, but now, most of them were involved in trafficking. The driver told them it would be crazy to go in there asking questions to just anybody; they needed a contact. They stared at him, expecting a name, but he halted until Player gave him another five. Then he told them about a bar where they could find an American called Gordy who might help them. For another five he explained how to get there on foot.

Chapter 39

They set off down a narrow street paved with stones and after a few blocks saw that the taxi driver wasn't exaggerating. The Guajiro district smelled of garbage and had an air of violence about it. The streets were crowded with dark, skinny children who followed them for a few yards, tugging at their hands and shirts, asking for money. In several places, abandoned cars blocked the sidewalks, forcing them to veer into the street where they risked being hit by whining motorbikes.

By mid-afternoon, most of the streets were in shadow, but the heat was more oppressive than ever. Radiating off the crude stone buildings and the pavement of the alleyways, it baked through the soles of their shoes and up into their bones. It cooked the air itself until breathing became a conscious act.

Player's temper and patience wore more thin with each block they walked. Sharpe struggled to keep up. "God, I thought Atlanta was hot," he said.

They walked as fast as they could without appearing afraid, but it did little good. They were unwelcome aliens in their shorts and jogging shoes, and people stopped and stared at them with open hostility. At one corner, a half-dozen teenagers slouched against a rundown storefront and shouted insults at them as they passed.

"*Hola, Americanos!*"

"*Contrabandistas*, eh?"

The teenagers laughed and patted chrome pistol butts jutting from their pockets. Player and Sharpe stared straight ahead and kept walking.

"Vamanos, Americanos. We sell you drugs!"

Player wondered how long they could last on these streets without being robbed or shot. For a moment, he wished they'd brought one of the pistols with them, even though he knew a foreigner caught with a firearm could draw a long sentence in many countries. They didn't know the law about concealed handguns here, but he was beginning to think it would have been worth the risk.

They walked for twenty minutes more but couldn't find the bar, so they stopped to ask an old woman for directions. She worked a food stall, cooking something that looked like pork over a brazier. She acted as though she didn't understand English so Sharpe tried asking her in Spanish.

She glanced furtively about and shrugged.

"Donde?" he asked again, this time showing her a twenty dollar bill.

She handed him a piece of the meat skewered on a stick, then took the twenty, stuffed it down her bosom and offered no change. Her voice dropped as she gave them directions in a rush of words they barely understood, but Player caught the name of the street, and they moved off in the direction she indicated.

They found the bar ten minutes later, and as soon as they walked in the door, Player spotted the man the taxi driver had told them about. He was the only person in the room who could possibly have been American; the others eyed them with the suspicion of locals. He sat at a corner table and didn't look up when they came in, probably because the light that poured through the doorway hurt his eyes. After the door closed behind them, they saw that it was very dark in the bar, and they had to watch their step as they made their way across the room to his table. The man stared at them with a dazed look on his face and didn't say anything.

"Are you Gordy?" Player asked.

The man eyed them for a moment more, then nodded and pushed a chair out from the table with his foot. He was happy to hear American voices and ecstatic when they offered to buy him a couple of beers. The tropics had not been kind to the man known only as Gordy. He was about fifty but looked much older, his face lined and burned by the tropical sun, and his eyes had the look of a nonstop drinker. He wore khakis stained by the endless sweat of the region.

After two quick beers, he told them his story. He was a pilot, and he'd worked the drug trade years earlier when it was still profitable to fly a few bales of pot at a time into deserted airstrips of south Florida. Now, he said, all the flying was cocaine and dangerous as hell. Most of the pot was hauled by mother ships to offshore islands, then transferred to the mainland by smaller boats.

"Strictly a bulk business, now."

He seemed to miss the States and asked them about the good football teams, and he wanted to know what kind of movies were big lately. They kept buying him beers and he answered their questions for more than an hour. He didn't seem surprised that they knew his name or that they had found him. He still made connections occasionally for people he knew back home, and it sounded as if others had stumbled onto him the same way they had.

He finished his fifth beer since they'd sat down then started eyeing Sharpe's bottle a minute later. "If you ain't used to Colombian, you better not drink it," he said.

Player ordered him a fresh one and asked about prices this time of year.

Gordy said it wasn't yet the high season for harvesting up in the mountains, so they wouldn't find great product at rock bottom, but they wouldn't have to pay top dollar either. The best stuff to get right now was a type of blond plant called *Mona*. It was grown at the higher elevations by Arhuaco Indians, and it was just starting to reach the local market in decent quantities.

He paused to wipe the sweat off the back of his neck with a paper napkin, then took another long swallow. "You sure you want to know all this?" he asked.

Player nodded, so Gordy went on, telling them the going rates and the sort of discounts you could negotiate for volume. He also warned them about the most common ways to get cheated. High grade weed might be concentrated in a prominent bale for sampling, while cheaper stuff was in the rest of the bags. Plus, some sellers would try to unload a two or three year old inventory from their warehouses if they suspected you were a novice. They'd dump dried out plants on you which would bring a low price back home.

He said there never had been, and never would be, a sure way to protect yourself when you took delivery. You just had to try your own method and take your chances. Most sellers believed in repeat business and wanted to satisfy their customers to bring them back, so it usually worked out okay, but they wouldn't hesitate to shoot you if you glanced at them the wrong way.

Again, he'd finished his own beer and eyed Player's half full bottle. Player pushed it across the table and Gordy took a deep swallow from it.

"Smart," he said, nodding to Player. "This stuff's murder on your gut 'til you get used to it. Can't get really good beer down here."

He took another, smaller swallow, finally slowing down.

"After eight years, I'm used to everything in this hellhole. Course, it's better'n prison in Florida, ain't it?"

The more Gordy talked and drank, the more friendly he became with them. He began to stress how many things could go wrong, and before long, he was trying to talk them out of it.

Sharpe asked several times where they could find the man called the Governor, but Gordy wouldn't answer.

Finally, Sharpe grew exasperated with him. "You try," he said to Player.

Player ordered yet another beer and let Gordy have a few swallows from it before trying again. "We're looking for the Governor, Gordy."

The old pilot shook his head sadly. "So you want to run drugs. Be *contrabandistas*?"

Player nodded.

"How in the world did'ja get directed to the Governor?" Gordy asked. His head sank closer to the mouth of the beer bottle, where the distance required for each swallow was growing shorter. "Who'd you say sent you here?"

"Alvarez," Player answered.

Gordy looked puzzled. "The old Cuban? Don't know why he'd send you down here and tell you to see the Governor, of all people."

"No, Raoul Alvarez," Sharpe interrupted. "It was the son who sent us. Now, how about the Governor?"

Gordy seemed to shrug away a thought that was unraveling deep in his brain. "I don't want no part a gettin' you boys killed."

"Just tell us," Sharpe groaned. "We know what we're doing."

"Oh, you do, huh?" Gordy's head came up and his voice hardened, had a sudden trace in it of the man he'd once been. "Do you know the Governor'd shoot you just for them eighty-dollar tennis shoes you got on?"

He took another swallow and moved his head close, his eyes boring directly into Sharpe's.

"They's hundreds of planes crashed and burned up on that Guajira. And for every plane, they's two wrecked boats, and for every boat, they's a good ten, dead Americans. Shot. Buried. Never seen again. And every damn one of 'em thought they knew what they were doing."

He sat back and let out a long breath, and they watched him as he finished the bottle. His voice fell again to that rasp of the man he had become. "My partner and me thought we knew what we were doing, too. Thought we'd get rich. He didn't make it."

A look of resignation shadowed across his wasted face as Player put a hand on his shoulder.

"Where's the Governor, Gordy?"

Chapter 40

Small and almost unbearably hot, the room had corrugated metal walls, with a naked light bulb dangling on a cord from the ceiling. A Colombian, with flat Indian features and blue black hair, sat in one corner of the room on an old metal desk, smoking unfiltered cigarettes, looking up at them from time to time.

Player knew every detail of the guard's appearance by now, because they'd been sitting in the room for over an hour. Without saying a word, the guard had communicated that he didn't want them to talk, so they sat in silence while there was nothing else to do but watch each other. Once again, Player's eyes ran over the man's thick arms and paused at the automatic rifle resting on his lap. Next, he noted once again that the tread was disappearing on the soles of the rubber tire sandals the guard wore The feet themselves were almost black with dirt.

The room seemed as though it once must have been an office, but Player couldn't be sure. It was located in some sort of empty warehouse somewhere east of the docks, though he couldn't be sure of that either. About the only thing he knew for certain was that there had been no sounds of other people out in the warehouse since they'd been sitting here, so he knew there would be no one to hear their pleas if they were shot by this stone faced guard.

Player had come to the warehouse, along with Sharpe, after Gordy managed to arrange a meeting for them with the Governor. It took Gordy an hour on the phone, talking with various people to set it up, and with a few more calls, he even found them a taxi which would drive to this grim section of the city. After the calls and a last minute word of advice, Gordy had sagged onto the tabletop in the bar, drunk and exhausted. Player stuffed two hundred dollars in the old pilot's shirt pocket when no one was looking, and they left him there with his face sunk in his elbow.

They took a quick trip back to the boat for some negotiating cash, and Player gave instructions to Jaye and Benji for protecting the boat during the next few hours. Then the taxi carried them to the warehouse where Gordy had said the Governor would meet them, and the driver dropped them off outside. Player gave him fifty dollars and told him to come back an hour later and to return every half hour after that until they emerged from the warehouse. The driver showed a toothy, insincere smile and assured him he would return, so Player gave him another fifty dollars and nodded to indicate there would be more if the driver kept his word.

The driver pulled away, looking happy, and they went into the dark warehouse where the guard met and frisked them. Without a word, he led them into the bare metal room and they'd been sitting there ever since.

At first, Player thought the Governor was making them wait to make certain no one was following them or watching the building, but the longer they sat there, he became convinced it was a negotiating tactic. This guy was making them sit and slow-cook, so he'd have an edge when it finally came time to talk. It was the same thing Alvarez had done to them, and he became more sure of it with every passing minute.

Sharpe was so jumpy he couldn't sit still and the emotionless silence of the guard made him worse every minute, which led Player to believe the guard's manner was calculated as well, not coincidental. If the Governor resorts to this kind of crap, Player thought, how can he be much of a deal maker? Maybe the guy falls back on these tactics of irritation and intimidation, because he can't negotiate anything straight up.

Player had been formulating his own strategy all afternoon as he sat listening to Gordy describe this local drug lord. He tried to visualize the Governor's appearance and manner, imagining how the man would act in any situation, because Player intended to control the meeting and not let himself be managed. So, as he sat in the room he continued to concentrate, planning his response to predictable questions, thinking of ways to keep the Governor off balance, but Sharpe kept distracting him until finally Player wished he'd left him at the boat.

Sharpe had grown so nervous, Player thought he would get up and start pacing the room. Up until now, the guard's stoic presence kept Sharpe quiet, but Player knew it wouldn't last much longer. He was about to whisper to Sharpe to settle down when the door of the office slammed open and crashed against the metal wall. It happened so suddenly that Sharpe jumped half out of his seat.

Two bodyguards marched into the room and took positions on either side of the doorway. The Governor himself followed behind them, his boots sounding loud and confident on the cement floor. Sharpe jumped to his feet out of nervousness or habit and moved toward the Governor to shake hands. One of the guards took a step forward and tilted the barrel of his gun at Sharpe to freeze him. Suitably cowed, he sat back down on his chair.

Player crossed his arms and slouched in his own seat as the very erect figure of the Governor crossed the room without looking at them. The Colombian marched quickly to the old desk across from them and sat down behind it, with a touch of pomp. His dress and bearing were faintly military, the shirt decorated with epaulettes, and Player thought perhaps he was a former officer. He wore reflective sunglasses over a hard, bony face and a shiny metal watch gleamed on his left wrist. He looked them over with no expression, and when he finally spoke, his words were the last thing Player had expected to hear.

"How do you appreciate our scenic city?" he asked in slow, uncertain English.

Player and Sharpe gave each other a quick look. Was he making a joke?

"We like Riohacha, very much," Sharpe replied.

Player refused to let his partner get into this and ruin things, so he cut him off quickly. "This is a real garden spot," he said. "But we're not tourists, so let's get down to business."

A little twitch of irritation showed around the Governor's mouth. He shifted in his chair and leaned forward, obviously formulating some sort of response in English, some stern words to put Player in his place and curb the big American's impudence.

Player never let him get the words out. Just as a sentence started to form on the Colombian's lips, Player broke in, speaking with deliberate volume and disrespect. "I understand you can sell us a load of Gold in quantity and deliver it dockside within twenty-four hours."

"The Governor paused a moment, seemed to contemplate the directness of Player's approach before he responded. "*Si*, I can do this. How much product do you need?"

"Eight tons."

His words held the room for a moment. The promise of such a large sale to first-timers had the desired effect.

A joyless smile passed over the man's bony face. He looked doubtfully at Player then turned his eyes on Sharpe, then moved them back to Player again. He broke into an insulting laugh that echoed off the metal walls.

"That is a large cargo for new *contrabandistas*."

Player sensed the man prying for information, but it was none of the Governor's business who they might be working with on the job or why they wanted eight tons, so he remained quiet. Let him take the bait.

The Governor made a show of doing calculations in his head. "At current rates, that would price you at, oh, one million, two hundred thousand dollars."

Player got out of his chair. "Let's go, Mitch."

A bodyguard swung his submachine gun in Player's direction, but the Governor waved the bodyguard back with an impatient flick of his hand.

"Keep your seat, my friend. Keep your seat."

Player remained standing. "Then, let's sidestep all the crap, okay?"

He couldn't see the man's eyes, because they were hidden behind the mirrored lenses, but Player could easily imagine the dark slits widening slightly with surprise. About now, he thought, they're narrowing again and he feels that little knot of anger tightening in his gut. Just like Alvarez, he said to himself — the man's not used to anybody talking back to him.

The Governor nodded and gestured Player back into his seat.

"Of course, that rate is negotiable for my friends and steady customers."

Player sat down, secretly pleased and ready to listen now. He heard Sharpe next to him, exhaling in relief.

Now that Player was seated again, the Governor decided to return to his standard tack and his voice grew harsh. "But you are not my friends or steady customers. I know nothing of you."

"You don't need to know anything."

The Governor ignored Player's remark. "I am called the Governor here, because I am the law. I know who arrives, who buys what, who leaves, and who dies."

"Big deal," Player said, and immediately regretted his words. He couldn't believe he'd said something so silly, but it just popped out. A put-down line from his teenage years; the wrong thing to say altogether.

"Big deal?" Luckily, the Governor didn't understand the expression. He wore a puzzled look on his face as he groped through his English vocabulary for the phrase.

Player tried to get the exchange back on track quickly. "We can buy elsewhere. You're not the only seller in Colombia."

"You have a quick mouth," the Governor said. "And a negative mind."

Player shrugged.

Sharpe began to stammer a response, but Player turned and gave him a hard look that shut him up.

The Governor's anger showed clearly now. His lips were white and stretched tight against bad teeth. "What is to prevent me from shooting you and your partner at this moment?" He put his hands on the desk. "And believe this, my friend, I may do it only for the pleasure."

"I have something that ought to keep you from shooting us," Player said.

He held his left palm out to steady the guards as he put his other hand down the front of his jeans very slowly. He pulled out a wad of bills he had stuffed there earlier, where he hoped the money wouldn't be found, if he was frisked. He'd been right; the guard had passed his hand over Player's groin, but only lightly because he'd been searching for hard metal, not money.

Player took a rubber band off the roll and threw the cash onto the desk where the bills fell apart like bent playing cards. There were plenty of fifties and hundreds for them to see. The Governor instinctively reached for the cash, and Player could almost hear the man's anger dissipate as he raked up the money

"That's twenty thousand dollars in good-faith cash, and we've got plenty more. Now, if you want the rest of it, let's cut the crap and talk business."

The Governor fondled the bills for a moment, straightening them out and making a neat stack on the desk in front of him. His voice shifted slightly, became calculating, as greed replaced anger.

"If you have enough money to buy eight tons, you would not remove it from your boat, I think. Why can I not hold you here, have my men kill the *negro* and the girl on board and then take the money?"

Sharpe flinched, and his reaction was exactly what the Governor wanted, Player thought. He made that threat to do more than stir us up. What he really wants is confirmation that the money is on the *Fey Lady*. He thinks we're careless and stupid, and he's taking the bait.

Sharpe tried to say something, but Player cut him off again. "The money is on the boat, all right," Player said casually.

A glimmer of self-satisfaction eased across the Governor's face as he interlocked his fingers, turned his hands inside out, and stretched them till the knuckles popped. Once again, the gesture seemed to say, the effectiveness of his tactics had been proven. Well-timed threats produce quick information, and now, the moment to apply pressure.

"In that event—" the Governor began.

"In that event," Player interrupted, "We'll just leave."

Player leaned across the desk and pulled the stack of money away from the Governor's reach, then stuffed it inside his shirt. "I'm tired of your threats. We came here to do business, not to be pushed around."

The Governor snapped his fingers and the guards pointed their guns at Player's chest. Sharpe's eyes jerked wildly, and the Colombians grinned.

"Allow me to be clear," the Governor said, "I take anything I want in Riohacha, and that includes your money."

"That may be true," Player said, patting his shirt. "But if you want the rest of our money, you won't get it by killing us. The money's on the boat, all right, but it's soaking in a bait tank full of gasoline. My friends are sitting next to that tank with cigarette lighters and precise instructions."

The Governor's face started to fall, and the guards lowered their guns. As Player went on, the man's dismay increased.

"If any strangers try to board the boat, or if we're not back there, safe and pretty, in . . ."

He glanced at his watch. ". . . two hours."

He threw his hands upward. "Boom."

The Governor's manner had changed from arrogance to uncertainty in seconds. He shifted in his seat, certainly thinking hard and fast.

Player tried to guess his thoughts, but at that point he could only imagine them—the Governor was not intelligent—he was a sledge hammer, accustomed to getting his way by threats. Likely, he was wondering about his opponent's mettle; would this newcomer dare to bluff him? Like all Americans, he looked so naive.

When the Colombian broke the standoff, his tone had

changed. "Of course, I am a fair man. I could reduce the price, in the interest of business, to, oh, one hundred thirty-five per ton."

"One-twenty."

"Ah . . . perhaps one twenty then," as if he'd made a casual misstatement. "Eight tons would make four hundred bales and--"

Player held up his hand and calculated quickly. He already had the correct numbers in his head, so the totals came easily.

"Your bales don't weigh forty each. Everyone around here says they weigh thirty-five, and you sell them at thirty-seven. So four hundred bales won't do it."

"Enough!" The Governor slapped the desk with his hand to show he'd been insulted, that the American had gone too far.

Player ignored the gesture and kept talking. "I'm willing to round off one bale a ton to fifty-six. That'll total out to four hundred forty-eight bales. Since I'm rounding off the bales in your favor, I'll give you one thousand for the loading fee, not your usual five." He ticked off the numbers in his head. "That's nine hundred sixty-one thousand dollars total, and I want only prime gold leaf. Anything less, I won't accept it."

The Governor was completely calm now. Since his bluster had not worked, he seemed, at last, devoid of pretense. He sat quietly appraising Player, and for the first time, a look of grudging respect flickered on his face, until, along with respect came awareness and suspicion.

"My friend, I have had much trouble with an old Cuban in Miami. Days ago, I lost men in the Bahamas. They were pursuing what they thought was one of his boats--a large, white one with Americans and an island man on board."

He let the statement hang, an unformed question.

Player looked into the mirrored lenses covering the Governor's eyes and he saw his own reflection, saw that his face was perfectly plausible, even as he formulated an enormous lie. How quickly he'd become adept at the dark arts, how capable of deception in its many forms.

"Don't know anything about it. We're independents."

The mirrors watched him for a moment, motionless as they studied his face, searching for unconscious signs of betrayal behind the words. At last, the Governor seemed convinced and the mirrors moved. He even flashed something like a smile, a forced expression he apparently reserved for the conclusion of a deal, even an unpleasant one.

"Your cargo will arrive tomorrow at noon on the south shore of Portete Bay. Allow me to describe the location."

Chapter 41

When they stepped outside the warehouse, it was late afternoon. A rainstorm had left the streets wet and steamy, the sky a bit more clear, but the threat of another cloudburst still hovered overhead. Dirty puddles stood among the broken aggregate of the parking area, where to their surprise, the old Chevrolet taxi waited.

"I can't believe he's still here," Sharpe said.

After the encounter with the Governor, they expected the worst from every Colombian they met, assuming the driver would take the money and not come back. He opened the door for them with a grin. Player felt a bit guilty, but on the way back to the docks, their suspicions proved correct after all. A mile down the road, the driver looked at them in the rear view mirror and said he wouldn't take them the whole way unless they paid him another fifty dollars on top of the fare.

"*Merde*," Player said.

The driver looked offended and began to protest, so Player told him he'd break his cheating Colombian neck if they weren't back at the boat in five minutes.

"One day here, and I'm already sick of this stinking country."

The Colombian watched him in the rear view mirror and continued to drive, apparently deciding he'd better not try to squeeze them more. When they arrived at the docks, Player paid the driver half the fare and told him to shove the other half. The driver didn't understand, until Sharpe gave him an ugly stare and an unmistakable gesture. The driver cursed at them but drove off in a hurry nonetheless.

"He's made a week's pay off us already," Sharpe said, laughing. "The weasel."

They hurried to the boat and jumped into the cockpit where the others were waiting in the fighting chairs. Player cut off their questions with a wave of his hand and told Benji to get underway immediately.

"Word about the money will be all over the docks by daybreak," he said. "Let's get as far away from here as we can while it's dark."

As they cast off, Jaye and Benji wanted to know what happened at the meeting, but Player ignored their questions. The look on his face must have been enough to discourage them from asking again.

Sharpe disappeared inside the salon as soon as they moved away from the dock, and a few minutes later, he came back out to the cockpit with a fresh bottle of bourbon. He took a big swallow and offered it to Player. When he took it and drank a long pull, no one said anything for a while.

After they were well out past sight of land, with the *Fey Lady* riding the big swells, Player went inside to rest. From the salon, he listened to their conversation in the cockpit as Sharpe told them what happened. Benji sounded pleased when he heard how Player had handled the Colombians, but Jaye wasn't so sure, she said. That look on his face, together with the apprehension in their voices, told the full story.

Later, Player was sitting alone in the dark salon, drinking a beer. She came through the deck door and stood behind him, massaging his shoulders.

"Tell me what you're thinking, Jack."

He wanted to know about the topside, instead. "Benji's at the wheel, I guess."

"Right," she affirmed. "Where's, Mitch"

"Went to bed." He didn't offer anything else.

"Are you worried about the pick-up?"

"No," he lied.

"Do you think the Governor is going to try something?"

"No," he lied again.

She tried to ask another question, but he reached up and put a fingertip on her lips. He pulled her around and down into his lap and felt the warmth and softness of her blend into his body. He kissed her on the lips and brushed his cheek against the skin of her throat. He wanted her again, but this time there wasn't so much urgency, and he knew they shouldn't, not then and there.

Player moved her off his lap to settle himself down, but she misunderstood. "What's wrong?" she asked.

"Nothing." He kissed her lightly to reassure her. "But we can't. Not until we're heading home, after we've told Sharpe."

"I don't want to wait."

"Neither do I, but we have to."

"I'm tired of creeping around."

"It'll be over tomorrow," he said.

She must have sensed there was a deeper worry. "What is it?" she asked, stroking his face with her fingers.

"Jaye, if anything goes wrong tomorrow, I don't want you to be where . . ." He couldn't finish the thought out loud.

"Oh, Jack." She drew his head to her breast to soothe him and whispered his name again. "Nothing's going to happen to me."

"We've been so lucky, so far. Almost too lucky."

"It'll be okay."

"I don't like the way this pickup is beginning to feel."

"Hey, listen. We've come so far, I know it's going to work out. If you stay tough, you can get us through this, then everything will be perfect. Just think of it. We'll be rich and we can go anywhere, do anything."

"But without you—"

"You have me, Jack. And after tomorrow, everything will be perfect."

He started to speak again, but she covered his mouth with her own and before long the hot flood broke again. The heat poured out of them and spilled over into each other and they were overflowing with the need to feel their skin touching, and there in the dark salon, rising and falling with the swells, they succumbed to the heat and burned together.

Chapter 42

They plowed up the coast throughout the night and made Portete Bay well before noon. Player held them out at sea the rest of the day to get the boat ready before they went in for the pickup. When they finally entered the bay, daylight was fading fast, but they easily spotted a big dock on the south end. The Fey Lady approached it cautiously, while they studied the setup from a distance before continuing.

All the way in, Player stood on the fly bridge and watched the dock through a pair of binoculars. When he saw two lights blinking on its upright posts, he knew this was it. The dock was exactly the way the Governor had told them it would be, two lights at the end, one red and one blue. A quick sweep of the shoreline revealed only one other dock in that part of the bay and it wasn't as large as the one the Governor had described.

"That's got to be it," he said to Benji.

The dock was a heavy plank and piling structure that jutted about sixty or seventy yards into the bay. A few old boats were tied up to it, but nothing looked fast enough to be used as a chase boat. Player saw a number of dockhands slouching around near some crates. Mostly, they seemed to be watching the *Fey Lady*, probably wondering why she didn't come straight in. Fuel trucks and a few four-wheel drive vehicles stood nearby.

Player passed the glasses to Benji who took a moment to look over the situation.

"How many do you count?" Player asked.

"At least two dozen."

"How many are armed?"

"No way of knowing. With the crates on the dock, they could be hiding anything, but you can bet they have firepower."

"At least there are no boats."

"I do not think they would try that. They know it might scare us away if we see fast boats. Maybe they have rockets or such in the trucks, but they won't try to take us out with those early, at least not while the money is on board."

"We can't give them any opportunity to use that heavy stuff, if they have it."

Benji shrugged. "Who knows? Maybe they won't try anything."

"Maybe not, if we show them enough strength."

Player moved to the starboard rail and leaned over to check if Jaye was in position at the salon window just below him, but all he could see was the mattresses and chair cushions they had secured against the deckhouse windows as a barricade. Then he saw the barrel of an M-16 poking through an opening they'd left.

"Jaye? All ready?"

"Okay here."

Player went to the windshield and looked out at the foredeck where he saw Sharpe crouched inside the barricade they'd rigged out there, mostly using furniture from below. They'd taken a coffee table and a few end tables and lashed them to the chrome railing where it bent like a horseshoe around the prow. The tabletops formed a crude triangular wall, along with chairs and mattresses positioned inside for reinforcement.

"Sharpe?"

His head popped up over the wall and he looked at Player on the bridge, then held up his rifle and pumped it twice in the air. "Ready," he yelled.

Sharpe's voice didn't sound too solid, but at least he looked threatening out there.

Finally he turned to Benji. "How about it, partner?"

Benji checked the safety on his MAC-10 then reached out to check his spare magazines, taped to the instrument panel. The magazines were loaded with thirty-two rounds apiece. Two additional magazines sat in the Captain's chair where they would be easy to reach. Player had also positioned several spares for the nine millimeter pistols at various spots around the fly bridge, so plenty of fresh magazines would be available.

"I am ready to go," Benji said.

Player checked his own MAC-10 then stuffed a nine millimeter into his hip pocket for back up.

There was nothing else to do now but go ahead and get it done.

"Take her in."

"You got it, Player."

Benji slid the throttle forward and eased the *Fey Lady* toward the dock. A space about thirty yards long had been cleared for them along one side and they approached it very slowly, watching the loitering hands, trying to judge their intent. As Benji eased the starboard bow alongside the dock, Player saw that the Colombians showed no weapons. They stood nonchalantly, tossing away cigarettes and stretching their arms to get ready for work.

Benji held the boat in place against the dock by working the wheel back and forth and gently nudging the throttle. A couple of the hands moved into position to tie the boat down, but Player wasn't about to throw his lines out yet or let them onboard.

A lean Colombian stepped from behind a stack of crates and walked into full view. He put his fists on his hips and looked up at the fly bridge.

"You late, Anglo."

Player looked at the man and saw a grin exposing rotten teeth, saw a dirty Pirates baseball cap on his head. So this guy must be the dock boss, he thought as he grinned back, showing no more humor than the Colombian. He nodded toward the sun that was setting behind his shoulder."I picked my time," Player said.

The baseball cap bobbed twice; eyes calculating behind the grin. "The Governor said you a smart one." He glanced toward the blinding sun. "But no need for all that, Anglo." He looked at the foredeck. "No need for the guns either."

Player laughed sarcastically as he pointed out the men scattered about the dock. If they were all armed, the *Fey Lady* was terribly outgunned.

"Here's the deal, Baseball Man." Player held up a duffle bag for the Colombian to see. "You get half now."

He tossed the bag down to the Colombian, and the dock boss caught it and checked inside. In seconds, he was counting the bundles of cash.

Player held up a second identical duffle bag for the Colombian to see. "And you get the other half when we're loaded."

The Colombian's eyes lit up at the sight of the second bag.

"No more than two loaders on board at one time," Player said. "And no guns."

"But you have guns, Anglo."

"And you have plenty of men, Baseball."

The Colombian considered for a moment, then bared his rotten teeth. "How do I know the rest of the money is in that bag?"

Player grinned back at him. "How do I know you won't try to shoot me out of the water and take everything?"

"Oh, you a smart one, Anglo."

"And I want to test the leaf first."

"Is not necessary. This is beautiful product straight from the mountains, grown near the sky so it is pale like you. We call it *Cielo Azul*. Some Americanos call it *Mona* or Gold."

"We'll test it anyway. And we'll check every third bale."

The dock boss shrugged indifferently.

"Is it a deal, Baseball?"

The Colombian hugged the duffle bag to his chest and looked up at Player, this time without the grin. "Is a deal."

Chapter 43

After dark, the tide settled and the wind died down inside the enclosing arms of Portete Bay. Without a breeze coming off the ocean, the air became still and very hot and the dockhands worked slowly, but after an hour of steady loading the job was almost finished. The loaders' torsos glistened with sweat in the greenish light of camping lanterns which sat on nearby dock posts.

Darkness pressed in on the dock from all sides, and the lanterns didn't provide enough light for the entire work area, so, much of the activity went on out in the darkness beyond the range of the lights.

Burlap bags filled with marijuana were passed out of the darkness behind the crates on the dock, and the bales swung from one man to the next along a human chain until they reached the boat. There, each bale was carried up a short gangplank to the top of the gunwale and tossed down to one of the men waiting in the cockpit who took it and waited for Player's decision. If he waved the bag on, the dockhand passed it through the deckhouse door into the salon where another man took it and stacked it inside according to Jaye's instructions.

If Player said to hold a bale, the man in the cockpit had to open the bag and let Benji dig his hand into it and break off a chunk of the compressed weed for inspection. So far, Benji had given approval to every bag he checked. Player was selecting the bags at random, not every third one as he'd told the dock boss he would. He might let five go by, then signal Benji to look inside two in a row.

Player was pretty sure the dock boss must be furious by now, because the inspection was slowing down the loading much more than the heat. Now that they were almost finished, it was obvious the load hadn't been padded with poor quality or dummy bales, but he wasn't about to quit checking them. He wanted high grade product in every bag because it would make a big difference in the total payoff they got from Alvarez. Their take was going to be based on the quality and quantity of the load, minus the front money, and of course an enormous interest charge.

The dock boss hadn't lied; it was excellent product.

Benji had taken a sample from one of the bales before the loading began and brought it up to the fly bridge for Player to examine. It was very high grade for this time of year, Benji said, as he pointed out the buds oozing with the sticky resin that determined the pot's strength.

"See the color?" Benji held the sample up in front of a flashlight so Player could see the pale leaves for himself. "This is genuine gold. It will bring top dollar in the States."

"Let's be sure," Player said, handing Benji his lighter. They knew there were ways to doctor the color of plants.

Benji nodded, lit the sample and let it flare briefly, then he blew it out. A sweet, very rich smoke curled up from the smoldering weed, and they both took a hit off it, then Benji threw the sample over the side. The smoke told them all they needed to know. They had both smoked enough pot in their lives to know how potent it was from the taste and smell; and this smelled rich.

Now, standing on the fly bridge, holding the engines at idle and watching the last of the bags being loaded into the cockpit, Player still felt a slight buzz of intoxication from that tiny sample he and Benji had inhaled almost an hour ago. The stuff was incredible, he thought, a real score. They were in the money with a load of such high quality.

Player caught himself just in time. His concentration wavered as his mind started to wander and that was the last thing he needed now. If he could keep his head together for just ten more minutes, the scattered mental focus might be gone and his thoughts would be crisp again, then they could get the hell out of there.

As he collected himself he saw the prearranged signal from Benji, and he realized they didn't have ten minutes. Benji held up four fingers to indicate the number of bales that were still to be loaded while Player considered his next steps.

He looked forward to see if Sharpe was still in position, but the foredeck was so dark he couldn't see anything up there at first. Then, inside the makeshift barricade he saw a shadow, a shape darker than the surrounding darkness. The shape moved, and he recognized the profile of Sharpe's head and he knew he was still there, staying as low as possible behind the lashed-together tables and mattresses.

Player looked down at the cockpit again and saw Benji holding his machine pistol on a dockhand who was clambering out of the cockpit to get off the boat. The dockhand moved fast for a guy who'd been handling forty pound bales for an hour. Another loader emerged from the deckhouse, and the sweat on his skin gleamed in the light of the salon door. His chest was heaving, but he too climbed quickly out of the cockpit and over the side where he disappeared in the darkness.

Benji turned his eyes up to Player. That was all of it.

"What does it look like down there?" Player asked.

"Stacked to the ceiling."

Player nodded. "Tell Jaye to get in position. Then take care of the plank and lines."

"Right."

Player went to the side of the boat facing away from the dock, where he leaned out so the windshield wouldn't block his voice. He called to Sharpe on the foredeck.

"It's time, Old Buddy."

Sharpe didn't answer but Player was sure he'd heard, because his head turned toward him.

Player looked out at the shadows on the dock where a few dim figures lurked about the stacks, but the lanterns had been moved back and the dockhands were barely visible. The boss stepped into view, his upper body lit by a wedge of lantern light, his lower half hidden in shadow. He remained close to a stack of cargo.

"Okay, Anglo. That's all."

"Okay, Baseball."

"Now, the money."

Player looked down at the stern. Benji had cut the dock lines and thrown off the plank, and now crouched behind the gunwale, holding his machine pistol in both hands.

Player looked at the bow. The forward lines were still secure. Sharpe should have cut them by now.

"Damn it."

Player tried to decide what to do next, but his mind was foggy and his thoughts wouldn't connect properly. He looked out at the dock, then back to the foredeck. He had to answer the boss now.

"The money's on the way, Baseball."

Player leaned over the port rail and called out again, this time in a loud whisper. "Sharpe. Get the damn lines."

Sharpe's head peeked out from the barricade and Player could just make out the dark mustache on the white triangle of his face. Then a lantern moved on the dock and threw light across the foredeck. Player got a good look and saw absolute, stark fear on Sharpe's face. It was the same look Player had seen on him in the parking lot outside the marina.

"Sharpe!"

The white triangle of face turned toward Player's voice, but there was no recognition in it, no sign that Sharpe had heard anything.

The dock boss's voice rang out. "The money, Anglo."

Player saw that Sharpe wasn't going to budge, so he went to the back of the fly bridge and signaled Benji forward. He couldn't think of anything else to do. Benji looked up at him, and for an instant, Player saw a look of something in the dark eyes, an accusation perhaps, certainly a recognition that he was being sacrificed. They seemed to say that the Bahamian had known all along it would come to this; that eventually Sharpe would foul up and Benji would have to cover for him. The eyes held Player's for a second, saying, I have to go forward and do his job, and it's your fault.

Player had no time to respond. After the moment of eye contact, Benji immediately moved to port and stepped up on the side deck. He held a MAC-10 in one hand, his knife in the other, and as he put his foot up on the narrow deck, he slipped. To free a hand to catch himself, he dropped his knife, which clattered off the fiberglass gunwale and into the water. He cursed quietly and continued forward on the side deck.

"The money, Anglo!" the voice rang out again, this time impatient.

"It's on the way, Baseball."

"You not trying something smart, are you Anglo? Maybe another trick?"

"Hell no, Baseball."

Player watched from the dark side of the bridge as Benji reached the bow. He had to stall the Colombian somehow.

"I wouldn't cheat you, Baseball. We'll do business again."

"Oh, I know that, Anglo. I trust you." The voice paused a full second. "But where's the damn money?"

Working to clear the lines on the foredeck, Benji was having trouble because they were knotted too much. Sharpe was supposed to have made sure the Colombians secured the bow properly, but he'd let them overdo it. And now, he wouldn't get up to help clear the mess away. Player cursed under his breath, cursed himself for letting Sharpe screw up again.

"Anglo? I'm tired a waitin'."

Gambling for time, Player grabbed the duffle bag at his feet and threw it down to the dock. It was the only move he had left.

"Here, Baseball! Count it."

A small figure darted out of the shadows and grabbed the bag on the run, then ducked into the shadows again.

The dock boss' voice reached out to the place where the figure had disappeared. "Rico?"

The night was deadly quiet. Player heard a fish jump out in the bay, then the sound of Benji's panicked breathing on the foredeck. Almost as an afterthought, he heard the engines rumbling gently in the bowels of the *Fey Lady*.

The voice of the unseen Rico shattered the clarity of the moment as he answered the dock boss's question. "*Todo aqui.*"

The dock boss stepped back into the shadows. "Thanks, Anglo. A deal is a deal."

As soon as those nasal, accented words were out, the air around Player seemed to disintegrate. A watcher in a dream, he saw Benji wrestling with the last heavy dock line and he knew they could never pull away in time. He sensed it coming and the acuity of his thinking broke down as the first huge heartbeat of fear pounded in his chest.

The gunfight started with yellow flashes of light spurting out of the darkness, quick points of fire that appeared and disappeared so quickly he couldn't focus on their location. Then the sound came, so deafening there was no other sound in the world except the gunfire battering his ears.

For an instant, he expected everything to slow down, but it happened exactly the opposite. The world jumped into a disorienting speed warp, with events hurtling forward, and all he could do was fight to keep up.

Bullets smacked into the *Fey Lady* and he heard deckhouse windows shatter below. Fiberglass splinters stung his cheek, and he ducked aside just as the side panel of the windshield exploded. He went to his knees and broken bits of Plexiglas sprinkled onto the back of his neck.

There was no time to think, not even a fraction of a second to separate the sounds and confusion, to sort out what was happening. There was nothing but hundreds of things blurring into each instant of sensation that the world had suddenly become.

In an impulse to get away, Player reached for the gear lever and threw it into reverse, then hit the throttle. The engines bellowed and the *Fey Lady* lurched backward, but the dock line at the bow held, tightened, and the boat shuddered, then sprang sideways and crashed into the dock.

Player picked himself up off the deck of the fly bridge and looked out at the foredeck just in time to see Benji rise in the air and double up at the waist. His body flew backward as if someone had kicked him in the stomach. Benji landed on the barricade, collapsing the walls on top of Sharpe. Flailing wildly at the tangle of limbs, mattresses and rope, Sharpe tried to free himself, but the harder he struggled, the more the tangle closed over him.

Vaguely, Player realized Jaye was firing back at the Colombians from the salon window below. The clattering of her M-16 galvanized him and he brought up his MAC-10 and threw a short burst at the dock. The recoil of the gun sent his blood surging and he stood up and ran through the entire magazine, yelling at the Colombians in a wordless scream.

Reaching for another magazine, he saw Sharpe rise out of the mess on the foredeck and fire his M-16 wildly into the air. Sharpe swung the barrel from side to side, his mouth open, his expression crazed.

Player crouched behind the fly bridge wall while he changed magazines, then he came up firing again. He saw that the flashes were closer now, and there were more of them. Somehow he had to get the boat free. He kept firing and spun the wheel with his left hand. The stern swung away from the dock but the bow was still tethered, and once she straightened out, the dock line began to quiver. Water boiled at the stern as the engines churned in reverse and the heavy rope vibrated with tension but refused to snap. Finally, the dock post gave way with a loud crack as a section of planks and framing tore off the dock along with part of the post.

The boat jumped crazily in a backward arc because the wheel was turned steeply, and with the bow free, the entire hull swung around and the stern crashed violently into the dock, bringing the boat to a dead stop.

The collision threw Player to the deck, but he jumped up immediately and grabbed the wheel. He threw the gear forward as bullets ripped past his head and shattered another panel of the windshield. An alarm flashed through his mind. The bullets had come from a steep angle, below and behind him.

He whirled, firing down into the cockpit, where he saw two men shooting up at him, but they were having trouble aiming because the boat was spinning like a carnival ride. They tried to brace their legs and get balanced, but their bullets sprayed wildly into the air as the deck whirled sideways beneath them.

Player fired again and one of the Colombians grabbed his stomach and fell overboard, but then Player's MAC-10 clicked empty. There was no time to get another magazine, so he grabbed for the pistol he'd shoved into the back pocket of his jeans. It wasn't there. The remaining man tried to point his gun at him and somehow it steadied. Player knew he was dead and began to fold himself inward, bracing for the hot intrusion of a bullet, but incredibly he saw the Colombian lower his gun to fire at something directly in front of him.

The man was too late.

Jaye had caught him by surprise. Firing from the salon doorway just a few feet away, she couldn't miss. The man took several hits at close range that blasted him backward as the gun flew from his hand. His face contorted and his chest exploded in red. He grabbed at the dark holes flowering across his torso, then careened around and fell across a fighting chair onto the deck of the cockpit.

Player grabbed another magazine and dropped to his belly, then raised his eyes and looked around as he jammed the fresh magazine into the machine pistol. But it was over. The sound of gunfire wasn't battering his ears so loudly anymore and he realized they had spun away from the dock, deeper into the darkness. The horizon was whirling beyond the stern and he couldn't even see the dock spinning past.

He grabbed the wheel and straightened it, then shoved the throttle forward as far as it would go. He got to his feet and blinked against the wind that poured through the remains of the shattered windshield as the boat gained speed. Player looked for a break in the dark line of land that curved around them. He found it and steered for the break, then when he was sure they were heading for the mouth of the bay, he allowed himself to turn and look down at the cockpit.

Jaye hadn't moved. She was still standing with the M-16 in her hands, staring at the pile of bloody clothes on the deck. A pool of blood widened around the body and it had reached her feet and soaked her running shoes.

Player forced his eyes away and looked back at the dock, three hundred yards behind them. Tiny blips of gunfire winked at them from the dock, but the blips grew smaller and dimmer until they finally disappeared in the night.

Chapter 44

Player looked over his shoulder once again to see if a boat was on their tail, but no one was back there. He'd been running at full speed for almost a half hour and no boat had followed them so far. Still, at any moment, he expected to see a Cigarette come slicing at them out of the darkness. The Colombians had to be following, didn't they? After a gunfight like that, they wouldn't just let it go; they had to come after them for retribution if nothing else.

Despite his fear that the Colombians were chasing them, Player knew he had to slow down soon, because this pace used too much fuel and punished the engines. He'd veered toward the northeast to set an unpredictable course, and the ocean swells grew with every mile toward the open Atlantic. He had to fight to hold on to the wheel as the Hatteras bucked against the swells, but still he pushed the big Sportfisherman for every bit of speed he could get.

He had another concern, too. No one had called out to him or come up to the fly bridge since the gunfight, so he had no idea what was going on below. He didn't know who was injured, or even dead. He hadn't seen any movement on the foredeck since they left the bay.

The entire boat was dark, because he could not risk turning on outside lights, so it was possible Sharpe had carried Benji below by himself. Possible, but not likely. It was more likely they were both wounded and couldn't move. Maybe they were still out there on the heaving foredeck, just trying to hang on.

With that thought, he decided he had to take a look. He eased off the throttle and set the automatic pilot.

"Sharpe?" he yelled. "Benji?"

There was no answer.

He turned and went down the ladder fast, barely touching the rungs with his feet before landing on the cockpit deck. Jaye was still there, propped against the deckhouse wall, and he saw immediately that she was in shock, her arms crossed tightly at the waist, her eyes fixed on the bloody corpse at her feet. The body was horrible to see, horrible and irresistible at the same time. Player had to make himself look at her instead of the dead Colombian.

He called her name, but she didn't acknowledge him, and her lack of reaction gave Player a sick feeling. From the numb expression on her face, he assumed she was scarred for life by the violence of their actions. No amount of laughter, or money, or fun could ever erase the image of the dead man from her mind. Nothing could remove that ugliness from her memory, and he knew that a youthful, better part of her was lost to him forever.

He took a step closer. "Jaye, talk to me."

She still didn't respond, and he wasn't sure what to do. She needed help, but at the same time, the others might be dying.

"Sharpe?" he yelled out. "Benji?"

Still no answer. He had to try something. He went to Jaye and took her by the shoulders.

Her mouth opened and a gagging sound came out. "I blew a hole in him," she rasped.

The sound of her voice threw him into a frenzy. Even though his judgment said it was the wrong thing to do, he lashed out at her.

"What the hell did you expect?"

Mostly, he felt the need to punish himself, but he took it out on her, trying to relieve the feeling of self-disgust that boiled inside when he glanced at the dead Colombian. He grabbed her by the shoulders and shook her violently, trying to erase the stained look from her face, knowing his own had to look much the same way.

220 • David Darracott

"What did you think?" he hissed. "That killing would be easy?"

She sobbed and he pushed her aside, because he felt like crying, too. If he watched her break down, he might do the same, and he knew he couldn't. Not now. Somebody had to hold this together and it had to be him. After all, he was tough, wasn't he? Wasn't he too tough to break down?

He bent over and lifted the Colombian by the armpits, but the dead weight was hard to move, so he had to hug the body close to handle it. The man's blood saturated his clothes in seconds and he felt the stickiness of it against his skin. The corpse smelled horrible and a coppery taste built in his stomach, rising to the back of his mouth, but he fought off the urge to vomit as he hugged the body, struggling to lift it to the gunwale.

He managed to get the body over the side and had to lean against the red-stained fiberglass of the gunwale for a few seconds. A feeling of extreme weakness in his legs made him falter, and he wasn't sure he could walk. When he turned back to Jaye, she was looking at him, at his bloody clothes and skin, her face bitter with revulsion.

"Now you know," he said. "People don't die clean and quiet. It's filthy business."

"And we're filthy, too," she said.

He wiped his hands on his shirt, but it was too soaked to do any good. The copper taste rose to his mouth again, his throat burning, and he thought he was going to be sick but fought it off.

"I have to check on Benji," he said.

He straightened up and moved toward the side deck.

She made a whimpering sound, and he stopped and looked back at her. She was shuddering. He went to her and caressed her quickly, then separated and took a step back, but she grabbed a handful of his shirt to keep him from going, so he took her by the hand and led her forward with him.

In the weak starlight on the foredeck, they found Benji lying in a pile of shattered wood and torn mattresses that had been the barricade. He was absolutely motionless, a damaged part thrown among other damaged parts on the deck. Sharpe was apparently unhurt, but in some sort of shock-induced trance, sitting off to one side and staring at the darkness.

After Player cleared the wreckage and checked Benji's heart and breathing, his hopes jumped. The man was still alive. But Jaye opened his blood-stained shirt, and they saw that his stomach was a mess, ripped open with jagged holes that bled freely.

Player forced a machine pistol from his stiff fingers and picked him up, then carried him below as he would a child, with one arm under his knees and the other under his arms. Benji was unconscious, but starting to groan by the time Player got him to a cabin.

All the mattresses on the boat had been ruined in the gun battle, but Jaye found a clean sheet and spread it across a set of box springs. Player stretched the wounded man out on the flat whiteness of the sheet, then they got the first-aid kit and cleaned his wounds and bandaged them, but that was all they could do.

Benji was beyond help.

For the rest of the night, they alternated between the fly bridge and tending the wounded man. For a long time, Player stayed at the wheel while Jaye sat beside the Bahamian. They both learned that a strong, young man doesn't die the way it happens in movies. There was no quick plunge into peacefulness.

Benji held on to life with a ruined body that didn't know it should quit. The stubborn parts of him that were still working seemed to ignore the parts that weren't, so he stayed alive hour after hour. Even when it seemed Benji wouldn't last another minute, his lungs kept snatching one short breath after another in the heavy atmosphere of the cabin. Somehow he stayed alive that way throughout the night.

Player didn't leave the wheel often, which worked out okay because he found himself unable to think clearly, much less sleep. Sometime around dawn Jaye brought him a cup of coffee which he managed to get down, but it burned like acid in his stomach, so he didn't ask for anything else. She told him Benji was about the same, while Sharpe was actually a lot better. She had put a few drinks in him and he'd gone to sleep a couple of hours earlier.

The condition of their partners seemed to have pulled her out of the shock she'd experienced right after the gun battle, Player noticed, but like himself, a bottomless gloom had settled on her in place of shock. They hardly spoke or exchanged glances as the hours wore on. Instead they moved about like assembly line workers, managing to do the things that had to be done, but the whole time acting as if they wished to be somewhere else, anywhere else, but on this boat with its bloody decks and the smell of death hanging over them.

At full daylight, Player put them all to work cleaning away damage, so the boat wouldn't be such an eye-catcher. If the Coast Guard or another drug runner saw them shot up as they were, they might have a chase or another fight on their hands. So, they cleared away the wreckage and broken glass from the window frames and re-hung curtains so the missing panels wouldn't be so obvious, then they patched and painted bullet holes. Sharpe unscrewed the damaged trim pieces and molding and threw them overboard.

Player helped, but mainly stayed on the fly bridge and kept his eyes on the horizon. He still thought there was a chance the Colombians might run them down, but each hour now, the odds improved that they wouldn't be caught from behind. Maybe they'd lost the Colombians in the darkness last night or maybe they weren't being chased at all. He wondered why, but couldn't come up with a good answer. Perhaps there was no answer.

About noon, Jaye went below to check on Benji again. She came back up a few minutes later and climbed the ladder to the fly bridge.

"He's awake. He wants to talk to you."

Player turned the wheel over to her and went below. Benji was still losing blood, more slowly now, but still losing it. Surely, he just didn't have that much to lose anymore. It was difficult to believe that anybody who had bled so much managed to stay alive. The bed was soaked through and the sheets caked with it--blood that had turned brown and crusty overnight.

He sat down on the edge of the bed and lifted a corner of the bandage to look at Benji's stomach, saw blood still coagulating around the bullet holes. Replacing the bandage, he put his hand on Benji's forehead. It was hot, plus his breathing sounded clogged. None of that could be good.

Benji opened his eyes and the weakness in them was startling. The man had been physically tireless only two days ago, and it dismayed Player to see him this way. The eyelids threatened to close again, so Player put a hand on his forearm to keep him awake.

"How you doin', partner?"

Player tried to look at him with a straight face.

"Feeling unlucky."

"Ah, luck hasn't deserted us yet. I've got us on a course to Jamaica."

"You wastin' your time. I am bleeding to death."

"No way, man."

Benji actually managed a grim laugh. "I will not make it to Jamaica. You know that."

"We can't go back to Colombia."

"I know. Jamaica's the only choice."

Benji stared at him sadly and Player shook his head. "I'm sorry, Benji."

The dying man raised a finger to stop him. "Don't. You handled it okay, Player. The shame is you did it all for nothing."

Player didn't understand. "Nothing?" He shook his head in confusion.

"You think Alvarez let you take his money away with nobody to watch it?"

Player's head came up quickly. "Alvarez?" He'd never said they were making the run for the Cuban.

"Alvarez always has back-up. You be smart enough to know that."

Player ran his fingers through his hair, stood up and took a couple of steps absently. Then it dawned on him. He sat back down and looked at Benji's eyes, stunned. "You're Alvarez's man?"

Benji smiled up at him. "I knew it was a fool's run, but he had me. Forced me to go and watch you."

Player's head whirled. "He planted you here to protect his investment? To make sure we didn't run?"

Benji nodded and closed his eyes.

"But what about Bimini? The chase on the docks?"

"They were after me, for real. Only, I had to run to your boat at the right moment to make it look good. But later, when you offered the money to me, I joined you. Nobody never offered me such a thing before."

"Why are you telling me this now?"

Benji tried to take a deep breath, but he coughed deeply instead, and that seemed to really hurt him. Blood gurgled out of his mouth and it seemed that he might die right then, but the coughing stopped, and Benji opened his eyes again and looked up. "Doesn't matter for me now, but it does for you. When you like somebody, you are blind. You don't see them clear."

"What do you mean? See what?"

Player didn't get any more answers, because Benji was finished talking. The wounded man slipped into unconsciousness, and Player would have thought he was gone except for the rattling sound that continued to rise and fall deep in his chest. Player got up and left him there, convinced those were the man's last words, but not at all sure what he had been trying to say.

Chapter 45

Later that afternoon the sky turned gray, with low clouds that ran just overhead, and the sea grew higher than it'd been on the entire journey. There seemed to be nothing in the world but the gunmetal sky and the tumbling horizon as it broke and reformed continuously around the *Fey Lady*. The boat rolled down one gray trough after another only to face more swells ahead. There was always another swell, and the afternoon wore on slowly as they pitched up, then down, always surrounded by mounds of water that beat against them so relentlessly any progress through the gray world seemed impossible.

Player should have been preparing for a storm, but the thought barely registered in his brain. He was too sick with himself to think about the weather or anything other than the wheezing man who lay below on a set of box springs, with the last drops of his life leaking through a stained yellow shirt. Player felt everything that had gone wrong was his fault, because he'd agreed to make the run in the first place. The whole thing would never have happened if he had not gone along with it, then Benji wouldn't be dying, and Jaye wouldn't be stained by violence. If he hadn't let himself fall into Sharpe's scheme, this sickness wouldn't be eating at his insides now, because no matter how he looked at it, the truth was that he had allowed greed to take control of him just as surely as it had Sharpe. Greed was the engine that had powered all of it, and to satisfy that greed he had committed murder of the worst sort. It wasn't self-defense; it was murder, because he'd killed for no reason other than money. And because of him, another man was dying at that moment down below.

As Player thought this through, he became aware of the darkness gathering around the boat, and he leaned forward to switch on the running lights. He reached across the control panel and noticed his own face looking back at him from a chrome fitting that surrounded one of the instruments. Because the fitting was curved, it distorted his features in a way that made the center of his face extremely large, with a gigantic nose and eyes, and around the outer edge his chin, ears and hairline were abnormally small, round and distant. Behind the enormous head, his body was reduced to a tiny mass dangling against the dark sky, and most startling of all, the entire grotesque being was covered with splotches of red blood. The face, the tee shirt, the shorts, even the miniscule legs were smeared with a red stain that reached all the way down to his discolored running shoes.

He looked at the image for several long seconds and found that the distortion was all too revealing. He took his eyes off the chrome and looked down at himself. There were reddish brown pinpoints of bloodstain deep in the pores of his skin and curved lines of the same color had dried beneath his fingernails. Even his shirt and shorts were stiff with dried blood.

He set the auto pilot and went below to the engine room where he got a bucket he'd seen earlier. The bucket had twenty feet of rope tied to the handle and it had a scrub brush and powdered cleanser inside. He took the bucket out to the cockpit and got down on his knees and went to work. Spray broke over the sides and seawater had already rinsed most of the blood out through the scuppers, but there were still traces of the Colombian's death showing on the deck, so Player scrubbed until he had erased every hairline of stain from the pebbled fiberglass.

Next, he went to the foredeck where Benji had been shot. To remove more bloodstains from the white surface, he shook cleanser out onto the deck then worked the stiff brush in circles. He wrapped the end of the rope around one hand and dropped the bucket into the sea several times and hauled it up and tossed fresh seawater across the deck to rinse away what had been done.

When he finished with the deck, Player took off his clothes and threw them into the ocean and watched them sink beneath the foaming wake of the boat. Then he turned the brush on himself. The blood stains were stubborn at first, but he scrubbed until his skin turned raw, taking off the outer layers and exposing new growth underneath.

During the process of washing himself, a sound started to come out of Player's mouth. His mind was numb, and he might have been emitting the sound for a long time before he became aware of it. He might not have noticed at all, except his eyes started to blur and he realized there were tears in them. Then he identified the sound as something like wailing and realized he was making the sound. Part of him understood why he was making it, and that kept a different part of him from stopping it, and all the pain of years came flowing out of his mouth and dissipated in the windy emptiness around him.

He scrubbed his body a long time, and when he felt that he had shed the stained skin, he dropped the bucket into the ocean and hauled up a clean draft of seawater and poured it over his head. The water was cool on his raw skin and he ran his hands over the stinging surface of himself and felt the wind tearing the past away. He returned the bucket to the ocean again and again and used the seawater to wash away the old and expose the new.

The wind was howling now, but Player hardly noticed. Swells broke against the handrails, and he no longer needed the bucket to feel the wash of the ocean as spray came slinging off the prow and broke over him in driving sheets. He stood on the deck, letting the water beat his body as the clouds built to a peak, until with a deafening slam of wind and spray all about, the sky opened up and delivered fresh rain to the gray world.

Chapter 46

After the rain stopped, the sea calmed again. Across the flat water, the last light of day was barely visible on the horizon and the fading colors promised a dark night ahead.

Jaye held the salon door open while the two men carried Benji's body out to the cockpit. Wrapped in clean, white bed sheets, the body looked alien, the true man concealed from them to the end. They moved to the transom where they lifted the body over the rail and let it slide into the sea. With a splash it was gone, instantly erased by the wake of the *Fey Lady*.

The next day, no one said much of anything. They all succumbed to a listless detachment, avoiding any discussion of Benji or the gunfight. Player did not know what Sharpe was doing, and he did not ask when Jaye came up to the fly bridge in mid-afternoon to relieve him. He turned the wheel over to her without a word and went down to the cockpit and spent several hours sitting in a fighting chair, thinking as he stared at the regenerating ocean beyond the stern.

He remembered very little of what had happened to him out on the deck the day before, but he felt changed in a way that was difficult to pinpoint. The thing he did remember clearly was the feeling of Benji's corpse leaving his hands at sunset, and the memory wasn't pleasant. He had a recurring picture in his mind of Benji's body drifting down through the green water and coming to rest upside down somewhere at the bottom of the ocean.

He also remembered what Benji had told him before he died, about being blind. He sifted and re-sifted the words, trying to sort out the meaning behind them, and finally, he took the words as a warning. He knew then what he had to do. Everything had gone so wrong, so far out of control. He'd killed people. Benji was dead, and Jaye was different, and none of it felt the same anymore. He could not undo the things that had gone wrong, but he could at least try to get out of this without further degradation.

He swiveled the chair around to face the salon. The door was open and he saw Sharpe standing inside the deckhouse where the bales of marijuana were stacked to the ceiling, a narrow walkway down the center. He'd hardly spoken to Sharpe since the gunfight, mainly because he was afraid of what might be said, and he wanted to avoid a confrontation, at least until he was sure in his mind that it was the right time to talk.

He watched his old friend lean close to a bale and take a deep breath of the aroma in the enclosed salon. Sharpe opened the burlap folds at the end of a bale and broke off a chunk of the compressed weed, which he kneaded between his palms until it broke apart. Then he held the buds up to his nose and smelled them with a look of satisfaction on his face.

What was it about Sharpe that drugs held him so closely? He'd always loved drugs. Talked about them, used them, cherished them. For Player, using drugs had mainly been a matter of going along with other people, but it wasn't that way for Sharpe. He sought drugs because he loved them. Always had. And now, it seemed that he couldn't get enough of the smell, the color and richness of the marijuana crammed into the salon. Perhaps it was the quality of the plants, perhaps it was the thought of the money the load would bring, or perhaps it was purely the forbidden nature of the drug, of any drug, that appealed to Sharpe. Maybe it had been that way all along, maybe it was the sheer danger, the destructiveness of drugs that had always been the attraction for him. Player decided he'd never know, and now he didn't care.

He tilted the chair back and shifted his eyes up to the fly bridge where Jaye's head and shoulders were just visible over the deckhouse roof. She was standing next to the captain's chair, giving the boat minimal attention while she smoked a joint.

Player watched her take a hit and he saw tiredness in the motion. Maybe, like him, she felt a deep down disgust with everything. Her face was tight with strain, and he considered how the last two days had hardened her. He suspected the process was irreversible. He would never be able to alter what had happened to her, but he hoped it hadn't permanently ruined things between the two of them. Surely there was a place for them somewhere, a refuge where their feelings mattered more than anything, where they still had a future.

Violence couldn't take everything away, could it?

It was getting dark. Player climbed to the fly bridge to take the wheel, so she could go below to rest. He approached her from behind and put his hands on her shoulders and she looked up and smiled, but when he tried to caress her, she refused him. Her face seemed to say she was too tired, too emotionally depleted to care about anything anymore.

"Not feeling any better?" he asked.

She waved the joint at him in answer. "I'm okay as long as I have this."

She got to her feet and slowly made her way down the ladder. Player told her to get some sleep, but he said it mainly to keep from telling her what he was really thinking, that the pot might help now, but she still had to wake up tomorrow and nothing would be different.

If he knew anything at this point, it was that covering emotional destitution with drugs changed nothing. The mistakes, the problems, were still there in the morning, still unresolved. Everything is still there, he thought, and you have to wake up to it, and even when you obscure the misery and try to numb it away, it's still there. Even when you keep on numbing it, it's still there, until finally the numbing won't work anymore and you don't want to wake up to it at all, and then you might as well be dead.

Chapter 47

Player looked at his watch by the light of the instrument panel, and he was surprised to see that he'd been at the wheel over five hours. He'd been so absorbed in his thoughts, he hardly noticed the time. It was almost midnight and he needed food. The sensation of hunger pleased him, because it was the first time he'd felt a trace of normality in two days.

He set the auto pilot and climbed down the ladder, then went into the salon where he squeezed his way between the burlap bales that jammed the room. The aroma of marijuana was pungent in the tight passageway. He reached the galley and opened the door to the refrigerator, but as he bent to look inside, he heard an unfamiliar sound around the corner. He stopped and listened for a moment, trying to identify it, but the sound stopped and all he heard was the gentle rumble of the engines below.

The sound started again and he leaned around the corner, looking down the short companionway. The door to the forward stateroom was not latched. It swung free with the motion of the boat, and each time it opened an inch or so, then closed, its hinges made a creaking sound.

As he turned back to the refrigerator, the boat went over a swell and pitched forward. He lost his balance and almost fell into the companionway. As he caught himself, the unlatched door swung wide open.

Inside the stateroom, a band of moonlight fell across the bed from a porthole and made the room bright enough to see Jaye's naked body working up and down in the silver glow. Her breasts swayed gently over Sharpe, her arms extended to brace herself against the bulkhead. With her head thrown back and profiled in the moonlight, he saw that supreme moment as her mouth opened and her throat arched outward in pleasure.

Player turned and ran up the steps to the salon, dodging between the bales, until he burst into the fresh air outside. He sucked in the clean smell of the ocean, trying to rid his head of the sweet residue of marijuana and the images of Jaye naked in the moonlight.

Player spent the rest of the night at the wheel trying to make sense of the thoughts and emotions pumping through him, but he kept returning to the same question--why had she gone back to Sharpe's bed? Was it the psychological trauma of the gunfight? A desire to control both of them? Or simple lust?

By morning, he'd decided it was time to talk.

Jaye came up about ten to relieve him. He avoided her eyes and didn't respond when she nudged his arm. As soon as she took the wheel, he went down the ladder to the cockpit where Sharpe sat, slouching in one of the fighting chairs. Player sat down in the second chair and studied him for a moment, without saying anything.

Sharpe had brought a pair of binoculars on deck, which they used to scan the horizon. As Player sat and watched him swing the glasses back and forth, something clicked in his mind. He felt layers of friendship, memories, and years of self-deception fall away, and he saw the man he thought he knew erode before his eyes. Seeing Sharpe clearly for the first time in his life, he could only ask himself how it had taken so long to come to his senses. Stripped of charm and guile out in the bright sunlight, Sharpe was merely a weak, unshaven man riddled with weaknesses.

"Sharpe, I've been thinking."

"Well then, miracles really do happen in this world."

Player ignored the crack and tried to go on, but Sharpe interrupted him. "I wonder if that's the same plane I saw yesterday." He focused the glasses on a distant point, tilted them slightly. "You don't suppose that's a Coast Guard plane, do you?"

Player ignored the misdirection again. Maybe Sharpe felt the tension building, sensed what was coming, and he was trying to fend it off.

"Huh, Player?" Sharpe tried to pass the glasses to him, but he refused them. "What do you think?" He prodded Player's arm with the binoculars, but Player didn't react.

"It was something Benji said that got me thinking."

"What's that?"

"How are you so sure Raoul will play straight with us, when we get back to Georgia with the load?"

Sharpe's eyes narrowed. "Second guessing the plan, huh?"

"Answer the question."

"I told you, Raoul owes me."

"And you two made a deal."

"That's right."Sharpe put the glasses down and looked about the cockpit.

Player thought Sharpe was avoiding his gaze, yet there was an almost pathetic look on the man's face, and Player couldn't help himself; he decided to give it one more chance. Out of their old camaraderie, their years of friendship, he felt impelled to give Sharpe one last chance. After all, he didn't want everything destroyed, everything in his whole life turned over at once.

"Mitch, let's forget Alvarez. Let's find another buyer and run with the money."

He studied Sharpe's face, hoping his old friend would say the right words and fix everything, make things right again, because he truly wanted to forgive him. That way, at least a few things could stay the way they had been before. If Sharpe would just say the word, he'd forgive everything.

But Sharpe stayed quiet.

"Listen, Mitch. With a few million to cover our tracks, we could shake Alvarez. He's getting old, losing his grip. We could go to Europe and live high, for the rest of our lives."

Sharpe remained silent, head down, looking at the deck.

"Let's don't go to Raye's Creek, Mitch. We don't need Alvarez anymore."

Finally, Sharpe turned and met his eyes, and when Player saw the set look on his face, he knew there was no turning back. Sharpe was gone.

"We can't do that, old buddy."

"Because you and Raoul made a deal."

"That's right."

Resigned now, he knew Sharpe wasn't going to set things right, so he pressed ahead. He wanted it all in the open.

"Tell me, why would Raoul send us to the Governor to make the buy? According to Gordy, his old man's at war with that bunch."

Sharpe shrugged. "Better price, I guess."

"Doesn't make sense. Carlos wouldn't let him do that."

Sharpe shrugged again, trying to look casual, but his shoulders looked tight.

"Let's suppose," Player went on, "Raoul has the gall to cross his father. Suppose he's chafing under Carlos's thumb just enough to cut a deal with you on the side, and not let his old man in on it. Or at least, it's a different deal from the one Carlos thinks was made."

Sharpe's face started to crumble as Player pushed ahead, his voice more certain with every step.

"Suppose Raoul sent us right into the Governor's lap to stir things up, so they'd hear about it back in Miami. Then he could tell Carlos the Colombians got us. Shot us at sea or something. Then, if we make it, he collects the load from us and sells it behind Carlos's back. He's cut the family out and doesn't have to split the profit with anybody but us."

"You've been doing some real heavy thinking."

"I figured something else out, too." Player's voice turned bitter.

"Yeah?"

"Your deal didn't just cut out Carlos, did it?"

Sharpe attempted to say something, but his voice wavered, then cracked, and he couldn't speak.

"Your deal cut me out, too. Didn't it, old buddy?"

Player had never known Sharpe to use violence, so he wasn't expecting it when it came, and there was no warning at all. Sharpe just reached over to the gunwale next to his chair, casually as if he was getting a drink or a smoke, and grabbed the gaff that was stored underneath, five feet of wooden pole with a sharp, metal hook on the end. He came around quickly and swung the gaff at Player's head, but Player ducked and deflected the blow with his forearm, and the hook imbedded in the padding of the chair.

Triggered by the attack, Player went after him like a madman. He was swinging at Sharpe's head even before they crashed out of the chairs onto the deck. With his advantage of strength and size, Player quickly got over him, and he swung with short punches that tore flesh every time they landed on his face.

"Betrayed me!" Player shouted. "You betrayed me!"

He kept throwing punches even after Sharpe was unable to fight back. He drove his heavy fists into Sharpe's face over and over, felt teeth and bone giving way to the impact, yelling with outrage on every swing.

"Betrayed me, for money!"

Player beat him without mercy, and he never heard Jaye screaming at him from above. All he heard was the roar of violence in his head.

Finally, a pistol shot made him stop and rise up.

His scalp froze as the pistol boomed again and the nine millimeter jerked upward in Jaye's right hand. She stood above them on the fly bridge, bracing her firing hand on the chrome railing. She lowered the gun barrel and pointed it at Player's chest.

"That's enough!"

She motioned Player to back off, and he got up and staggered a couple of steps away. His legs were trembling so much, he could barely stand. He looked at her in disbelief, then sat heavily on the gunwale.

"So, you too, huh?" Player said to her.

Sharpe managed to sit up and lifted his shirt tail, used it to stanch the bleeding from his nose and mouth. "Yes, her too, you dumbass." The insult bubbled redly from Sharpe's mouth. He could barely move his lips, but the desire to hurt Player was stronger than the pain of talking.

Player glared at her, his eyes accusing, until she averted her face. "Why?" he asked. "Why lure me into this, just to cut me out and kill me in the end?"

She refused to meet his gaze.

Player turned to Sharpe in bewilderment. There was nothing left in him now but confusion and vacancy.

"Why?" he said. "Why did you have to use me this way?"

Somehow, Player's demand to know the truth cut through the heat of the moment and caught Sharpe unguarded. The scowl on Sharpe's face eased and a look of self-contempt showed for a moment, washing the hate away.

His voice turned quiet. "I just couldn't pull it off without you," Sharpe admitted. "I couldn't make the run by myself."

Player laughed bitterly. "You weak bastard. You had Les killed, too. Didn't you?"

"That was Raoul."

"You're all bastards. Manipulated me all the way from Atlanta to South America, just because you didn't have the guts to do it by yourself."

"We're not kids anymore!" Sharpe yelled, indignant again. "Of course I made a deal with Raoul. This load means millions. You think I'm going to split that kind of money with you? Or his old man? Hell, I wouldn't split it with Raoul, if I didn't need him to sell the stuff."

Confessing what he had done seemed to renew Sharpe's anger as he snatched up the binoculars and threw them at Player, but he was shaking with outrage, and his throw went wide. They bounced off Player's arm and fell to the deck. The bad throw angered him even more, so he picked up the gaff and threw it at Player, too.

"The hell with that 'old buddy' shit."

Player jumped and got his hands on Sharpe's throat, slammed

him against the deckhouse wall, then pounded his head against the fiberglass until Jaye fired another shot. This time the bullet hit the deck near Player's feet.

Player let him go, and went limp helplessly, devastated that she would shoot at him. He didn't question if she had actually wanted to hit him, because it didn't matter. The act of threatening him with a shot was enough. She came down the ladder with the pistol trained on his chest, but there was no need. The warning shot had taken all the fight out of him.

He staggered backward and collapsed heavily into a fighting chair, his strength gone.

"Go ahead and shoot," he said. "You've as good as killed me already."

Chapter 48

The sound of the twin diesels was like the throb of a sore tooth, an ache inside his head that only extraction would relieve. Despite the noisy tremor of the engines, he heard the door lock open with a mechanical snap. He looked up quickly, craving to see if it was day or night outside, because that was the only way to determine how long he'd been tied to the huge engine mounts. He wasn't sure of the time exactly, but thought it was four days. Long enough to lose track of time and feel like a prisoner for the first time in his life. Long enough to realize his fear of jail had come true after all. Long enough to think about the mistakes he'd made.

The door opened with a clang and a blinding rectangle of light widened above him. So, the sun was high out there. Sweet daylight. A wave of salty air swirled through the engine room, and for a moment, it felt wonderful to have the stink of burning fuel washed from his nose, but the smell of clean air filled him with longing for the outdoors, and despair quickly followed.

A second later, a tall silhouette filled the glare of the doorway. The silhouette bent down and put a plate of chili on the floor, pushed it forward with his foot, close enough, but not too close.

He tried to ignore the plate to demonstrate how well he was holding up, but he couldn't help himself. He couldn't remember the last time he ate, and he grabbed for the food that sat just within reach of his tethered hands.

But the rope on his wrists was tied so tightly, his numb fingers could barely hold the plate. He got a bite up to his mouth, and despite spilling a few gobs on the floor, he managed to swallow enough to realize how hungry he was—hungrier than he'd ever been before.

The silhouette slid a plastic jug of water across to him and gloated, watching as he fumbled with the cap and sloshed water into his mouth carelessly, wasting some on his chest.

"You look disgusting," Sharpe said.

"Let's tie you down here for a few days, and we'll see how pretty you look."

"Oh, come on. It can't be that bad."

"You'd be begging by now."

"Temper, temper. Just stay cool another day or so, and we'll let you go."

"Yeah, sure you will."

Owner drank half the water and tried not to spill any more. He would be thirsty again soon, and they hadn't brought him water often, so he needed to make it last.

As his eyes adjusted to the daylight glare, he saw a pistol stuck in the front of the silhouette's shorts, but there was no way to get to it. The tether on his wrists allowed him to reach only so far in any direction.

The silhouette stifled a laugh. "Everything's been going great since we demoted you."

"You'll never find it."

"Oh, I can find the place."

"But you haven't yet, have you? That's why you're keeping me alive, right? Insurance, to guide you in there."

The silhouette looked down at him with contempt, an expression that became ever more malignant as a sneer formed on the shadowy face.

The silhouette laughed. "I always knew you'd wind up on your knees somewhere. At last, a loser."

To that, he had no answer.

Chapter 49

At the control console on the fly bridge, Jaye spread out the charts for the Georgia coast and tried again to decide which inlet was the one Player had described. She knew it was somewhere between Darien and Savannah, but there were so many small features on the map and not all of them were labeled by name. She hadn't been able to find any inlet that was fed by a waterway called Raye's Creek. She wondered if that was the locals' name for it; maybe it was called something else on the official charts; maybe it didn't even have an official name.

Sharpe kept looking over her shoulder impatiently, which made the search more difficult. "Well, where?" he said, for the third time in a minute.

"There are hundreds of creeks running through the marshes here," she answered. "They all look alike. Jack has been to the place, but I haven't."

"Well, he won't help us now, so you've got to find it on your own."

"Give me a little time, okay?"

Sharpe reached across her and took one of the charts to look for himself, but she snatched it back in annoyance, knowing he had no idea how to read it.

"You're not helping by distracting me, Mitch."

"Then get it done," he said. "We have a deadline."

"I'm not sure I can find it at all."

"You'd better find it, or I'll have to make Player tell us."

She froze in alarm. "You promised you wouldn't hurt him."

"I'll do whatever it takes to deliver this load on time."

Something in his voice caused a wave of uncertainty to pass through her, a fear that she'd already contemplated several times. Would he betray her as readily as he'd betrayed his oldest friend? Was she losing her hold on him already? She'd gone along with him so far for the money, but she just couldn't let him hurt Player.

"You ought to see him tied up in that engine room," Sharpe laughed. "He doesn't look so tough now."

She closed her eyes and struggled with the thought of him as a prisoner down there, but damn it, she was trying to keep him alive. He must have suffered, because Sharpe had tied him to some big part of an engine and there was no way to sleep with all the heat and noise and smell in that small room. To make it worse, Sharpe would barely feed him because he wanted him to stay weak. She would have taken him more food and water, but Sharpe wouldn't allow her to go in there at all. At this point, she suspected he was capable of doing anything so she didn't argue with him about it. After the fight with Player, he had been in a non-stop manic state, acting as if he could conquer the world.

"You also made a deal with me," she said. "You promised you wouldn't hurt him. If you do hurt him, I won't help you."

Sharpe smiled, not taking her seriously. "Just find the creek, Jaye-bird."

Chapter 50

Late that day, through the July haze, the coast of Georgia sat gray-green in the distance, a low profile of land that disappeared slowly beneath the red weight of the setting sun. The land grew flatter and hazier across the water, as the sun melted into the horizon.

Sharpe knew the coast wouldn't appear as a defined outline again until the sun was totally down, when the landmass would reveal itself in silhouette against the evening sky. That would be the best time to go in.

He leaned back in the captain's chair and smoked a cigarette as he watched the sunset, feeling almost giddy, excited as a kid by his prospects ahead. As a fledgling drug-runner, he could hardly believe his good luck since he took over from Player. Other than shrimpers, he hadn't seen a single boat since they passed a Japanese freighter down near Jacksonville, then everything went exactly right for him to find the drop site.

All the way north, he had been running about thirty miles off the coast to stay just out of sight of land, then in late afternoon, exactly as Player had said would happen, he saw the smokestacks of the big paper mills near Brunswick. Then he knew he was less than twenty miles from his left turn toward the coast.

An hour later, he had brought the big white sportfisherman around in a slow sweep to the west to face the sun, then he ran straight in until he sighted land and stopped the engines. Now he sat waiting, eleven miles out, holding his position until the tide came up and the creek would be high enough to carry the *Fey Lady* inland.

Like a fool, Player had held nothing back over the last two weeks, and eventually Jaye found the correct spot on a chart. Sharpe tilted his head from side to side, thinking about it. What kind of chump gives up his aces for no good reason? A smart man would've held his knowledge about the drop site in reserve, in case he needed it later for bargaining power. But not Player. Not shrewd enough. Too trusting. It would feel cool to be rid of him; he was tired of Player always making him look bad. Maybe the big goon had been their problem all along, because ever since he locked him in the engine room, everything had gone perfectly. In fact, this was turning out to be so easy, he might talk with Raoul about doing it one more time. Now that he knew how, he felt sure he could make another run by himself, and the money was too good not to try it again. Why settle for rich when you could be twice as rich?

The sun bled slowly into the Georgia marsh while Sharpe's mind continued to spin through a wonderland of calculations. He did the math over and over, trying to project how much he could make off his next run to Colombia. If he added some coke into the formula, it was staggering. It was so much money, he'd be crazy not to do it again.

Chapter 51

Tied to the mounts in the engine room, Player's prone body rocked gently with the Fey Lady. He knew they were at rest, drifting offshore, waiting for the tide. The engines had dropped an hour earlier, and for the first time in days, there was enough quiet inside the engine room that he was able to think. Escape seemed impossible at this point. He was unable to work the knots loose on his wrists; he'd even tried to burn the rope in two with his Zippo. They'd somehow overlooked it in his hip pocket, but the flame burned his skin more than the rope. So he was stuck. No escape and little hope, with time running out. The wait meant Sharpe had found the creek, and they would go in soon to make the rendezvous. When they did, Player felt certain he wouldn't live long.

If the thought of his own death in a matter of hours wasn't bad enough, he was tortured further by the sound of Jaye's voice outside the engine room door. He tried to block out the sound, but her words kept penetrating his brain with insistence.

"Jack, please listen."

He could picture it all so easily; Sharpe luring her into his scheme with promises of a bigger cut, persuading her that nobody would be hurt. And of course she would believe him. She would actually trust Sharpe not to kill him. He was convinced the only reason he was alive now was to guarantee her cooperation, because Sharpe knew as soon as he killed Player he'd have a hard time handling her.

Sure, during the fight she'd betrayed him easily enough and pointed the gun at him, but she didn't have cold blooded murder in mind. Sharpe knew it and he knew it. At the time, Player hadn't thought of it, but when she pointed the gun at him, he could've just walked up to her and taken it away, because she would never have pulled the trigger.

Her voice was urgent as she whispered, "I did it to save your life, Jack. Both your lives. You'd have killed each other."

It was too crazy to believe, he thought. You couldn't invent such a scenario, but he suspected she was probably telling the truth now. She'd pulled the gun to keep one of them from getting killed all right, but the problem was that she pulled it on him, not Sharpe. She shot at him—not Sharpe—because she'd already sold him out, already made a deal to cut him out of the money. That was the problem. So now, here he was, tied to an engine mount, his arms and legs screaming from the lack of blood circulation, and there she was on the other side of the door, trying to persuade him that she hadn't sold him out, not really. But it wouldn't work, because the fact was she'd pointed the gun at him, not Sharpe. It didn't matter if she did it to save somebody's life. She'd pointed it at him. Too crazy to even think about.

"Please, just speak to me."

Her voice was a continuous plaint that ate into his mind and made his head hurt worse. Even now, with everything almost over, she added to his hurts, so he tried to shut his mind to the sound, but it continued, still more insistent.

"Please believe me. Please, speak to me!"

He couldn't stand it any longer. The hurt part of him had to answer. "You used me all along."

"No!" Her voice jumped at the sound of his response. "It was planned, but not that way. We planned to use you, but not the lovemaking. Us. That wasn't planned. I never intended to use you that way."

"You pulled the gun on me, not him. I'm the one who's locked up."

He heard her move against the door, could sense her body leaning on it. Her voice pleaded through the weight of the barrier. "If I hadn't helped him lock you up, he'd have killed you. He's gone crazy."

Player felt a weary disappointment with her. Her explanation didn't answer anything. She had betrayed him for Sharpe—and the money—and yet here she was, crying for his understanding, trying to explain it all away. Why even make the effort?

"If he's crazy, why didn't you lock him up instead of me?"

"Jack, I didn't think. I couldn't think. It seemed the best way to save you at the time."

He groaned, half-laughing, half-crying. "Yeah, and I suppose you had to screw him one more time. Just to save me, of course."

"I had to do it. I had no choice."

"Why in hell should I believe anything you say?"

He imagined her effort wilting on the other side of the door, sensed the energy leaving her. "Because of us, you and me. I want to be with you, not him."

Even through his bitterness, the words struck home. For some reason unknown to him, she was still trying to use him, still lying to him, yet the words resounded and he couldn't help but feel an echo inside. Even after everything she had done, it was thrilling to hear her say those words, but he didn't believe her anymore, and he refused to let her know how much those words meant to him, even when he thought they were false. So, he didn't say anything in return.

After his silence, she spoke again, this time without a trace of hope or any attempt to convince him. Instead, from the sound of her voice, she spoke from simple conviction. "And I think you still love me."

Chapter 52

A few minutes after nine, the tide started in and Jaye pointed the *Fey Lady* toward the dark tabletop of land sitting to the west. As They moved toward it the horizon didn't look so flat anymore. A jagged outline of trees materialized then a gap appeared in the irregular surface silhouetted against the sky. As they drew closer, the gap grew larger, then revealed itself as a sizable inlet, which they entered along with the returning ocean.

The inlet funneled them into a waterway that made a sweeping curve around and then behind a barrier island on their right. The island was completely dark and she guessed it was a wildlife refuge, but she couldn't be sure, because it was too small to show up on her charts. As they passed it, she saw it was actually nothing more than a string of dunes and a few windblown trees facing away from the sea. To their left, the landmass on the other side of the inlet was farther away and it might have been an island too, or perhaps a tongue of mainland, but it was dark and also fell out of sight after a few minutes.

The waterway bent inland and narrowed to a creek as soon as it penetrated the marsh behind the island, then it attached itself to a firm looking treeline that formed the left bank. The *Fey Lady* made its way up the creek very slowly, winding deeper into the darkness of the marsh where there was no sign of humanity anywhere. She saw no lights, markers, or docks, not even any signs of old campsites along the banks. It was as if civilization had never penetrated this deep into the tangled marsh. The water of the creek was black as oil, and their surroundings became so dark they were able to see only dim shapes, and she had to imagine much of the terrain lying farther away.

After a few hundred yards, the spindly pines lining the left bank thinned out, and off to their right, the trees disappeared altogether, giving them an unobstructed view for the first time since the inlet. Flat marsh extended for miles to the north, its spartina grass growing uniformly as a wheat field, broken only by veins of tidal creeks running randomly through it.

They progressed upstream at idle speed, with minimal lights, their pace slower than walking, because the creek meandered unpredictably. Jaye could barely make out the creek's banks in the darkness as the hull brushed against its muddy sides on the tight turns. She felt the keel thump against the bottom more than once.

She knew this was a place to travel cautiously, so she ignored Sharpe's exhortations to speed up. He was impatient as a teenager, and just as she'd thought he would, he showed little sense about taking such a large boat up a narrow creek with hardly any lights. She refused to listen to him and concentrated on her job at the wheel.

Perhaps shrimpers had used the creek at one time, she thought, but they knew the waters, and probably the creek had been easier to travel in the past. Since then, the creek had likely changed course and become too difficult to navigate, and that's why the shrimpers had abandoned it. There was no traffic on the creek now, she was sure of that. She hadn't even seen a discarded beer can or a plastic milk jug floating in the water.

Twenty minutes later, the marsh fell away and huge trees rose up on both banks; very old oaks with gnarled branches reached out and covered the creek with a canopy of green. Spanish moss hung from the branches and whispered across the canvas roof of the fly bridge as the boat passed beneath. The woods felt very closed in and primordial, a home for predators.

Eventually the creek turned left and widened again. Jaye felt a brief acceleration of her heart when she saw a faint, green smudge of light ahead. But the glow disappeared until they rounded another bend, then she saw it clearly a hundred yards away; two camping lanterns perched on the end of a dock.

"That's the signal," Sharpe hissed.

They drew closer and saw a clearing behind the dock where a few vans were parked. Then more lanterns appeared, along with a dozen or so long-haired loaders who milled around, looking casual as they finished their smokes. Just another night drop for them, she thought, but for Sharpe it must have been a supreme moment as he seemed almost ceremonious. He signaled the dock with a flashlight, then waited for the proper response, before flashing the final message that told them the boat was coming in.

They crawled forward the last hundred yards, and she could make out the weathered planks on the dock and some old style troughs used for sluicing shrimp into cleaning bins.

They were so close to the end, she knew she didn't have much time left. She had to slip below before it was too late, but her heart felt as if it was about to explode, and it took all her will to get moving.

"Mitch, I've got to go to the head."

He gave her a sideways glance of incredulity.

"The payoff of a lifetime's waiting on that dock, and you're going to the john?"

"What can I say? I have to go."

Sharpe took the wheel with a grand flourish. "Okay, I'll take it across the finish line by myself."

Chapter 53

Player sat up as best he could when he heard the key in the door. He expected to be killed at any moment and he wanted to see it coming; he didn't want to be shot lying down, cowering like an animal. He figured this was it, because he guessed Sharpe would do it before docking, while Jaye was up at the wheel. That way there would be no witnesses and nobody would be around to stop him.

The walls of the engine room would probably muffle the shot, so it wouldn't even be heard. Alvarez would not know or care if his body was still on board, and Sharpe could easily claim that Player had been killed at sea. Jaye would be the only person who knew for certain that Sharpe was the murderer, which didn't bode well for her future either.

When the door swung open and Jaye, not Sharpe, stepped into the engine room, Player felt tremendous relief, if not elation. She didn't have a gun which meant he had at least a bit longer to live. He felt the first stirrings of hope he'd had in days, as she hurried to him with a paring knife and started to cut him free. She sawed at the heavy ropes, but the knife was dull

"Are we at the dock yet?"

"Almost, but you still have time to hide out. When Mitch has the money and they're gone, you can jump him."

The rope was almost severed now, and Player helped her by twisting his wrists and working the rope with his hands until the last strands snapped.

"I thought I'd lost you," he said.

"Oh, I couldn't let him--"

She didn't complete the thought, and instead threw her arms around his neck, sobbing and kissing his face.

Player took the knife from her and began to cut the rope off his feet. When he was done, he tried to stand but his legs were so wobbly she had to help him up. After a few seconds, he was able to bear his full weight and move around.

"I unlocked the fore hatch," she said. "You can make your way to the forward cabin and hide and Mitch won't know you're free. When they're gone, I'll send him up there and you can take him then."

He was able to walk about after a few moments of testing his strength and massaging his thighs. His legs seemed okay, or they would be, as soon as the feeling returned to them completely.

"Here," she said.

Player turned to her. She handed him a pistol that had been concealed under her shirt.

"You'll need this."

Player took the gun and looked at it, felt the terrible weight in his hand again. That heavy power convinced him. He hadn't been sure until that moment, but now he was. In truth, he had never been more sure of himself. He tossed the gun aside and started for the door.

"Come on," he said. "We're going now."

"Going where?"

"Away. Off this boat. Anywhere."

Jaye took his arm and pulled him around. "We can't leave yet. I've got to get back up to the bridge or Mitch'll suspect something. Besides, the money is waiting out there on the dock."

Player looked at her eyes. "We don't need the money."

He hadn't known he was going to say it, hadn't even been aware of thinking it really, but once the words were out he knew with certainty how he felt about the cash. He didn't care about the money anymore. He really didn't. All he wanted was to live.

She could not grasp what he was saying. "Don't need the money?"

"I want to feel clean again."

"I do too, but the money is right out there."

"Forget it, Jaye."

"What—"

Player turned back to the door. "The money's bloody. All it'll do is get us killed."

He cracked the door and saw dark water behind the stern, some trees, and then a glimpse of marsh beyond. "Come on," he said. "We can slip over the transom now, if we hurry."

The words were barely out of his mouth when the boat shuddered as the hull bumped against the dock. Lantern light fell across the cockpit. They'd have to try the front. He closed the door and went to the fore hatch at the front end of the engine room. He heard voices topside as he began unfastening the hatch, so he tried to work as quietly as he could.

When he almost had the hatch open, he turned to get her attention. "Come on," he said.

Then he saw a peculiar, forlorn look on her face. She was watching him unhinge the fittings, and he saw on her face the realization that he was leaving, that he was going to leave the money behind.

"After all we've been through, you're going to just walk away from it." She shook her head in amazement. "A man has to be crazy or soft to do that."

Her words bothered him, then her face hardened and he understood. Before he could stop her, she turned and ran outside.

Chapter 54

By the time Jaye made it up the ladder to the fly bridge, The *Fey Lady* came to a full stop, and she got to Sharpe's side just as he cut the engines. He wore the look of a triumphant actor, soaking up applause at the end of a performance, then he turned and grinned at her, the excitement showing on his face. She moved closer, and he put an arm around her waist and led her to the port side of the fly bridge.

They leaned against the railing, straining to see past the lanterns on the dock. Then Raoul appeared, mostly obscured by darkness, his swarthy face barely visible in the broken light.

"Raoul, my man!" Sharpe rose up on his toes and waved a greeting at the dark figure. "We made it!"

"Mitch, my man," Raoul called back, and started toward the boat. "Great to see you! But where's your compadre?"

Jaye grasped Sharpe's arm above the elbow and dug her nails into the skin.

"Mitch, no" she demanded.

Sharpe glanced at her with a flash of irritation, but his look changed when he saw the expression on her face, saw that she was determined to save Player. To please her perhaps, or out of amusement, he smiled and his look eased.

"Player didn't make it," Sharpe called out. "We lost him in Colombia."

Raoul nodded and walked closer to the boat, looking sure and relaxed. He passed through the beam of a flashlight and Jaye noticed that he was dressed in a white coat and white shoes. The sides of his coat fanned out as he walked and underneath it a sky-blue shirt was unbuttoned to the sternum.

"Too bad about Player," Raoul said. He let out a conspiratorial laugh and smiled up at them. "Right, partner?"

Sharpe returned the laugh. "You bet, partner."

Jaye could see Raoul's face clearly now. He had walked to the edge of the dock and was close enough that she could see his smile, but something seemed wrong. The smile wasn't really a smile at all. She intended to mention it, but another figure moved out of the darkness and distracted her thoughts. The shadowy figure stepped alongside Raoul and handed him something, perhaps a stick, then he moved into view and Jaye saw a gleam of silver hair above a tanned, cold face.

It was Carlos. Of course.

In the split second she saw the old man, she knew they were going to die. She stood paralyzed as Carlos turned to his son and issued an order with a snap of his head.

Grim and obedient, Raoul raised an automatic rifle, and before she could utter a sound, the barrel flared with light. The unreal concussion of gunfire tore the night apart.

Bullets ripped across Sharpe's chest in a tight line and slammed him to the other side of the fly bridge in less than a second. She was terror stricken when she saw the gun spitting flames at her, and she threw up her hands to protect her face. Her mouth opened in a scream, but before any sound could come out, the bullets hit her and knocked her hands aside like bits of paper. The impact kicked her backward, and she went over the guardrail and fell into the creek with a splash.

Chapter 55

When Player heard the gunshots, he nearly panicked. He couldn't be sure what had happened, but he knew Jaye was in danger out there and he had to get to her somehow. He didn't care that she'd run back to Sharpe for the money. He only wanted to save her and get them both away from the murder and greed engendered by this boatload of drugs.

Fear gave him urgency as he muscled his way past a stack of bales blocking the forward hatch, then he broke into the companionway and ran to the forward stateroom. He intended to throw back the hatch cover in the ceiling that opened up to the foredeck, but he stopped himself, thinking he might get his head shot off up there. Instead, he went to the port window, but he couldn't see very much until he craned his head and pushed his face up to a crack in the curtains. There, he managed to see a dock and part of a clearing where Carlos Alvarez was arguing with his son. As Carlos berated him, Raoul lowered a rifle and shuffled his feet.

A restless silence hummed over the scene now that the gunfire had stopped. After it had been unleashed, violence held in the air like a bad smell, and the silence itself seemed to vibrate with tension. Even the loaders appeared agitated. With the smoke of gunfire hanging over everything, they stood uneasily, rocking from foot to foot.

Player slid the tiny window open and watched as Carlos scolded his son with absolute contempt.

"—an expensive lesson," the old man shouted.

Carlos turned toward the clearing, his voice rising over the stillness. "Now, clean up the mess you've made."

Player watched the old gangster turn away and take a couple of steps toward a cluster of vans parked in the clearing. A few loaders shied away as the old man walked past them, none of them wanting to be near his wrath. They went back to their work, listless with the fear of him.

Abruptly, the sound of gunfire popped again, and everyone snapped to life.

Bullets whizzed into the clearing, scattering the workers. No one seemed to know what was happening or where the gunfire was coming from. Some of the men ran in circles, while others jumped under bushes. The loud clattering of automatic rifle fire seemed to come out of the surrounding darkness without a specific source. Shots ripped through the lighted area around the dock and a few struck home. Player saw a couple of loaders go down, clutching themselves where they had been hit.

Inside the boat, the noise level quickly rose as the gunfire grew heavier outside, with more automatic weapons opening up and bullets tearing through the clearing.

Then the source of the attack became apparent as several loaders turned to shoot downstream. Player heard the high-pitched scream of engines and ran to the salon to see out the back of the boat. He saw four, maybe five, Cigarettes coming out of the darkness. Two boats broke ahead of the others and sprinted up the creek, passing the *Fey Lady* and the dock at high speed, while spraying everything with bullets.

He crouched behind the bales, because a split second later the starboard side of the boat was drilled with automatic fire from the Cigarettes. The bullets sounded like hail against the metal skin of the hull, and some found their way through gaps in the bales and zipped past him to the other side of the salon. He had a clear view of the dock area through a port window and saw leaves shredding off bushes and puncture holes stitching the sides of the vans. He heard bullets cutting the air apart with their high speed whine as still more gunfire poured into the clearing.

Raoul raised his rifle to get off a couple of bursts at the

attackers, but when a few bullets gouged the planks near his feet, he dropped the gun and ran. He broke across the clearing, where Carlos was running a few yards ahead of him. A dark splotch appeared on the old man's back and he stumbled, going to his knees. Raoul stopped at his father's side to help, then thought twice and left the old man to die in a clump of palmettos.

Raoul made it to a van at the edge of the woods, but just as he got hold of the door handle, a line of bullet holes zigzagged down the side of the van, crossing his body at the waist. He collapsed and hung by his fingers, caught in the door handle.

More of the loaders had come up with weapons and fired back, but the speedboats seemed to be staying well away from the dock, using the darkness for cover. The battle appeared uneven to Player, with the loaders outnumbered and disorganized, and he realized he had to escape now while the fight was at full pitch. He ran back to the forward cabin and threw open the overhead hatch, easing his head up through the opening, but almost immediately he dropped back inside. The gunfire was too heavy to take a good look up there.

"Jaye!" he yelled out.

He cocked his head and listened for an answer but couldn't hear anything over the noise. Maybe his voice wouldn't even carry over it.

He decided he had to risk the hatch again and poked his head up through the opening then screamed Jaye's name. With bullets whizzing everywhere, he still heard no response from her and had to jerk his head back inside.

He couldn't stay on the boat any longer.

They were fighting for possession of the load, and he had to get off the *Fey Lady* now while he had the chance. He would have to find Jaye after he got outside. He reached up and pulled himself through the hatch as fast as he could and flattened out on the foredeck. Once his legs were through the opening, he slithered to the dark side of the deck, away from the lighted dock. Slipping under the guardrail, he let himself fall off the edge of the boat.

He dropped into the black water, then came up slowly and

allowed his eyes to clear the surface. When he got oriented, he swam away from the boat to get away from the lights. He looked at the bridge but didn't see any sign of her up there. Had she left the boat before the fighting broke out? Maybe she had jumped overboard at the first sound of shots.

He looked toward land and saw men sprawled out, a few shot and bleeding, and he spotted bodies near the vans in the clearing. From the look of it, those who'd tried to get away were gunned down as soon as they went for the vehicles.

The fight was still going strong and he saw two loaders firing down the creek, shooting at muzzle flashes which were about a hundred yards downstream. Then shots came from behind him and he whirled around and discovered that he was in a particularly bad spot. A second group of attackers was standing off upstream, firing from there to pin the dock in crossfire. He started swimming to his left to get out of their line of fire. If he didn't retreat from this area soon, he'd get shot.

But first, where was Jaye?

He strained to see through the smoke and darkness but couldn't make much out, so he headed toward the stern to get a different line of sight on the clearing. He swam with a quiet breast stroke down the length of the boat, keeping his head low in the water. Just below the salon windows, his hand brushed something a few inches below the surface. He felt cloth, grabbed it and pulled up.

It was her.

He held onto her tee shirt and lifted her head out of the water with his other hand. There was blood on the shirt and on her face, and at first, he thought she was dead. A cold twinge ran along his spine until he brushed the hair out of her face and saw that she was still breathing. Actually she was coughing up water, so she couldn't have been under long when he found her.

He held her head up by a fistful of hair and started swimming toward the far side of the creek, where it was dark. It seemed as though he was swimming toward the marsh, but it was hard to be sure because it was so dark over there, but darkness meant safety, so he kept kicking in that direction.

He hadn't gone ten feet before he saw another body floating in the black water off to the side. He angled toward it, and seconds later, he turned the body over and saw that it was Sharpe. He grabbed a handful of Sharpe's hair and attempted to tow him along with Jaye to the far bank, instantly realized that wouldn't work, until one foot struck bottom.

He was breathing hard and his legs were tired by the time he reached the other side, where he found the muddy bank beneath his feet. He was grateful the creek wasn't so wide at that point, because it had been difficult towing two bodies without the use of his arms. He hauled them up onto the bank and collapsed in the mud alongside Jaye.

He held her as she groaned and coughed more water out of her nose and mouth. When he had regained enough energy to sit up, he took a good look and almost cried when he saw what was left of her hands. Her right hand was mostly gone and her left was mangled so badly she was missing two fingers.

He tore his shirt into strips and wrapped them around the bloody stumps then tied tourniquets on each arm to stop the bleeding. He remembered what those bleeding wounds had done to Benji. At least there didn't seem to be any major bullet holes in her abdomen.

He turned to Sharpe and saw immediately there was nothing he could do. Sharpe had a streak of bullet holes across his chest and there was no question he was dead. Player began to straighten the clenched arms and legs, and then stopped himself, surprised to find that he was treating Sharpe's body with respect.

This was the man who'd betrayed him, who'd planned to kill him, so how could he feel sadness for him now? Maybe it was the fixed expression on Sharpe's face, a faint look that somehow seemed regretful. Had remorse been his last thought?

Looking at the dead body, Player could not help but think of him as his old friend, not the man he'd been the last two weeks. He wiped the wet, dark hair away from Sharpe's forehead and thought how easily this could have been him, how close he had come to being the same distorted version of himself as Sharpe. And he couldn't escape the feeling that a dark part of his inner self had died there as well, in the blackness of the creek.

Somehow, Sharpe had been the other side of him, the reverse side he could not be on his own, as he knew he had been the better side to his dead friend. They had been useful selves to each other, had needed the opposing side the other provided, but now all that was gone, erased by inevitability. He let go, and the body slipped from his fingers and settled gently into the mud.

Someone screamed in pain on the far side of the creek, and he looked up and became aware of his situation again. The gunfight was waning and there was no time to waste; they had to escape while they could. He pulled Jaye up the muddy bank and managed to drag her into some thick vines where she couldn't be seen so easily from the creek. He stood up cautiously and looked out over the top of the dense vegetation and saw miles of head-high grass, spartina, stretching to a treeline on the distant side of the marsh.

He had lost a shoe in the muck at the edge of the creek, and he was forced to go back down the bank to get it. One quick look had told him he couldn't make it across that marsh without shoes. He slid down to the water's edge and retrieved his shoe from the mud. As he pulled it back on, he heard the high-pitched revving of a Cigarette off to his left. He looked up and saw a low, wedge shape materialize out of the darkness. It seemed as if the boat was coming straight toward him, so he jumped back into the palmettos and squirmed up the bank.

When he got to the top, he turned and saw the boat hadn't been coming after him at all. It veered away and knifed past the dock in a fast maneuver against the loaders who were still fighting. It was a needless attack. All the Cigarettes had to do was sit back in the darkness and keep shooting. Eventually they'd drive Alvarez's loaders away from the *Fey Lady*, but the men on the Cigarette had become impatient. Or perhaps they wanted to do it for excitement, wanting to sweep past the dock in a fast arc as they fired on the remaining men from a changing angle, to wipe them out in one quick move.

The boat was twenty yards from the dock when he caught a glimpse of the man at the wheel, and he clearly saw a baseball cap on his head. But it wasn't an ordinary cap; it was the peculiar flat-top type the Pirates had worn a few years earlier, the kind of cap the dock boss had worn in Colombia.

Player squinted to get a better look at the man next to the dock boss. He caught a glint of light on a pair of reflective sunglasses and made out a uniform shirt, with epaulettes. It was the Governor. Player could hardly believe those two would track them all the way to Georgia, but he was certain it was them.

That could mean only one thing—the Governor had let the *Fey Lady* escape from Colombia so they would lead him to Alvarez. After the fight at Portete Bay, the Governor had followed them across the Caribbean to finish his trouble with Alvarez permanently. That was why he hadn't run them down at sea. He'd been following them the whole time instead. There was no other way it made sense.

Player knew at that moment what fools they'd been to think they could deal with these professional criminals. To these men, they'd been nothing but poker chips to waste on a bad hand. They'd never stood a chance of pulling the run off successfully, not on their own.

The Cigarette completed its pass and swung around in a tight arc upstream and roared toward the dock again. Thirty yards from the *Fey Lady*, the baseball cap flew off the head of the driver and his upper body snapped backward as if caught on a clothesline. The Governor grabbed for the wheel, but he was too late. The Cigarette ran uncontrolled for a brief stretch then crashed into the bow of the *Fey Lady*.

The speedboat seemed to rupture inside. As the hull crumpled, it punched a sizable hole into the waterline of the *Fey Lady*. Amid the mess of torn metal and shattered fiberglass, Player saw liquid spurting from the mangled wreckage of the two boats, liquid with an oil-based sheen to it that gleamed on the water.

Fuel. From the Cigarette, of course. He watched as it held on the surface of the water and spread outward in an iridescent layer.

His luck had changed. The Zippo was still in his back pocket. Windproof, but not waterproof. The flint would be wet, but he tried it anyway. He spun the strike wheel with his thumb, and a tiny spark appeared, then died. He tried it again, and Good God Almighty, it caught with a low blue flame.

He threw the lighter toward the purplish slick and the fuel ignited with a roar. A fraction of a second later, an explosion came from inside the twisted hull, and threw burning, high octane fuel onto the *Fey Lady's* deckhouse, showering the dock and surrounding woods with flaming debris.

By the time Player pulled Jaye away from the creek bank and hid in the marsh grass, both boats and the entire dock were whistling and crackling with flames. The intense orange heat felt its way over the surface of the *Fey Lady* and quickly found the tons of dried marijuana inside. The bales caught on fire and began to roar like pulpwood, and within minutes, the flames rose higher than the surrounding trees.

The fire could be seen for twenty miles around. Soon, someone would spot the rosy glow in the sky, and police would come to investigate. The smugglers who survived the explosion began to flee into the woods. The remaining boats sped back downstream, seeking the safety of the open Atlantic. After all, the reason for fighting was over. The immensely profitable load of Colombian Gold burned its way skyward, and its potent fumes dissipated on the breeze as if none of it had ever existed, as if the whole venture had been nothing but a bad dream.

Chapter 56

Player stopped for a moment, braced his feet and shifted Jaye higher on his shoulders, then set out through the grass once again. At first he'd had trouble keeping her on his back because she was so limp, but after the first couple of hours, he settled on carrying her across his shoulders with one of her arms and one leg held in front of him. That position kept her in place better than any way he'd tried, but still, it wasn't good enough. The ground was rough and he was covered with sweat, and whenever he stumbled, she slipped off, so he had to keep stopping to get a good grip on her again before he could continue.

The tide was partially in and the marsh was knee-deep in brackish water, so Player had to slog through dark muck with every step; about every quarter hour, the muck would catch one of his shoes and pull it off his foot with a sucking sound. He struggled to keep Jaye balanced on his back as he worked the muddy shoe back on his foot, then he could continue before it happened all over again.

His one free arm kept the spartina off their faces for the most part, but each blade of the grass had a razor edge which cut his arms every time he brushed a bunch of it aside. The grass was an inch or two higher than his head and every blade was the same height, so the only way he could see where he was going was to step up onto an old log or a hump when he came across one. That allowed him to look out over the plain of grass and keep his direction fairly straight.

Altogether, it made slow going. It took him almost three hours to travel the first mile, and when he looked back and saw how little progress he'd made, it occurred to him that he might not be strong enough to make it across the marsh. But after a while the tide started to recede, and he didn't stumble as often, and he began to make better time.

He crossed a couple of small creeks along the way without any trouble, but when he came to one that was about ten yards wide, he knew it was too deep and he was too exhausted to make it across. He would drown if he tried it, so he turned to his left and followed the creek bank, hoping it led the right way. Fortunately, the creek began to bend toward the far side of the marsh where he was headed, so he stayed with it. After a while, he found he could see better traveling alongside the creek, and every now and then he got a good look ahead at the treeline, and he guessed it was at least two more miles to the woods.

A half hour after he started following the creek, his back began to bend forward beneath Jaye's weight and he accepted this was going to test his strength like nothing he'd ever done before. He'd been going for days on very little food and sleep and he was feeling seriously weak. He stopped, looked around, and saw they were still a lot closer to where they had started from than where they were going, yet already he was doubling over. Again, it occurred to him he might not make it, but he pushed the thought away, knowing it was self-defeating.

The grass sliced his skin almost every time a blade touched him, and since he'd ripped his shirt apart earlier to bandage Jaye's hands, he was taking a lot of small cuts. But they didn't bleed much, and after a while, he decided they weren't so bad because the cuts became a way of measuring his exhaustion. The less he felt them, the more drained he knew he was, which meant he had to dig deeper into his will to keep going.

The sight of the treeline also helped. He could see it occasionally when the creek bent the right way, and each time he saw the distant canopy, it encouraged him because he believed he could make it if he could just get to the trees. There the ground would be firm. Once he got to the woods, this grass and mud wouldn't drag him down, and he could knock out the miles as if they were nothing.

At some point, the trees ahead started to look slightly green rather than black and he thought the sun might be coming up, but then he saw a silvery streak on the water, and he realized it was the moon. He stopped and looked back. The moon was rising behind him and he saw the enormous expanse of grass standing motionless in the pale light. Here and there, he saw a ribbon of silver where the moon reflected off the creeks. Far in the distance he saw a red glow, a dome of light against a backdrop of dark trees, and he realized those trees were farther away than the ones he was moving toward. He could tell because they made a flatter line on the horizon, flatter and darker, except for that curious red spot.

Slowly, his exhausted mind made the connection and he remembered the red spot was caused by the burning boats. Then he recalled the gun battle, and the explosion, and Sharpe lying dead on the creek bank. Already, the *Fey Lady* and the trip to Colombia, and all that violence seemed like a different world, far away, an entire life away, something that had happened to someone else.

He staggered on for two more hours, and when he reached the woods, he was nearly blind with sweat and exhaustion. He desperately wanted to sit down but something deep in his mind told him he wouldn't get up again if he did, so he stood for a few minutes, leaning against a tree and collecting himself, and it occurred to him he should loosen Jaye's tourniquets. If they were left on for too long, she might lose her arms, so he loosened the tourniquets and told himself to check them later. Her head hung against his right triceps and he could feel her breath on his bare skin; occasionally he felt her chest expanding and contracting next to his shoulder, so her breathing was strong even though her body was limp. He was confident she was going to make it, but he had to keep moving.

He left the marsh behind and stumbled off through the scrub pines and palmettos, with his back bent almost parallel to the ground. He kept his bearings by the moon, without even thinking about it. Since he had seen the moon over the marsh, he knew which way was west, and that was all he needed to know, because the interstate lay to the west and that was the way out. If he didn't get to I-95 by daylight, Jaye might lose her arms, and he'd surely be caught, and that knowledge drove him on, because now the thought of keeping them both alive and free was the goal that drove him forward more than any other.

Perhaps, unconsciously he had planned this escape weeks ago when he scouted the area, but he couldn't remember clearly. Maybe even then an unacknowledged plan had formed down in his deepest mind as a contingency, if things went wrong. So as he stumbled on, he knew what to do without thinking, always heading west, with the awareness it was his only chance. If he could just keep moving west, he would leave everything bad behind, his whole previous life behind.

But later, somewhere in that stretch of pine woods, with the moonlight shadowing softly through the needles to the ground, he believed he could not make it. He was on all fours, at times barely moving through the undergrowth, brushing silently along, feeling the dew on his face and the palmettos pricking his skin. He heard night birds calling in the stillness, and he was filled with the deep aroma of the pines, and at some point he felt as if he was hovering over his own body and watching himself crawl through the undergrowth, and as he watched, part of him realized that he had done this intentionally, had reduced himself to this state so he could look down with infinite coldness and reject everything he saw, in order to begin again.

Just after a gray shapelessness formed between the trees, he stopped at a construction wire fence that blocked his way, running straight and true, north to south. He reached up and touched one of the perfect, chemically treated posts, noticed the stretched tension of the wire. He thumped it with his finger and the wire sang with tightness. He found an opening in the palmettos and pushed the fronds aside. There, ahead, he saw the concrete surface of the interstate gleaming in the moonlight.

He managed somehow to climb over the fence and keep Jaye

on his back, but it took the last of his strength, and he fell when he came down on the other side. His legs were so wobbly he sat for several minutes, holding on to the wire until he recovered enough to crawl the last few yards. He made it through the remaining undergrowth then across a grassy area, and just before he reached the paved shoulder, he collapsed.

He lay on his belly in the grass for a long time before he tried to reach behind his head for Jaye, but still he couldn't get his hand off the ground. Twenty minutes later, a pair of headlights got him up. Far down the road, the lights didn't seem to be moving at first, but they grew every minute he watched, flattening the white concrete before them, until they became blindingly large and merged together. Player rolled over and got to his knees and crawled out onto the shoulder and threw up a hand.

The headlights slowed down and swerved away cautiously then they came back and inched closer and finally stopped beside him. Player looked behind the headlights and saw a flatbed truck, loaded with watermelons. A farmer in overalls threw open the passenger door and looked out at Player, kneeling on the pavement.

"Son, you don't look so good."

Player glanced down at himself and saw how messed up he appeared, and he realized it was miraculous the farmer had stopped at all. His arms and chest were covered with cuts and gray mud that had dried and caked over every inch of him from the waist down. He brushed at his muddy jeans a couple of times with his hands, but when he saw what a mindless gesture it was, he stopped and looked at the farmer helplessly, then simply threw out his hands in supplication.

The farmer seemed mystified by Player, and he didn't say anything more until he saw Jaye lying in the grass beside the pavement. With that, he gave Player a more critical look.

"She hurt bad?"

Player turned and looked at her. He couldn't deny it any longer.

"She's dead."

The farmer leaned out of the truck and raised his head to get a better look, then shook his chin philosophically and eyed Player again.

"You in some kind of trouble, son?"

"Not anymore."

The farmer seemed unsure. Player suddenly felt desperate; afraid the farmer would pull away and leave him there. He reached out and put his hands on the running board of the truck.

"I'll pay you for your help, Mister. I don't have any money right now, but I'll pay you back some way."

The farmer looked thoughtful for a moment, then reached down and offered his leathery hand to Player. "You don't need no money, son. Help's free."

The farmer pulled Player into the cab and settled him onto the bench seat. He got out and went around the truck and gathered up Jaye's body, put it in the back with the watermelons and covered it with a piece of canvas.

They pulled away and headed north on the interstate into the first light of day, and soon, Player saw the morning sun rise over the pine trees.

About The Author

David Darracott is the author of Wasted and other fiction available at amazon.com. He holds a Masters degree in English and is the recipient of writing awards for fiction and nonfiction, including a Hambidge Fellowship in 2009-2010. A graduate of Emory University, he lives in north Atlanta.

Visit his web site at www.David-Darracott.com

LIGHTNING
ROD
BOOKS

15786284R00164

Made in the USA
Middletown, DE
24 November 2014